H.N. WAKE

HIDDEN IN THE SILENCE

Vinci Books

vinci-books.com

Published by Vinci Books Ltd in 2025

1

Copyright © H.N. Wake 2020

The author has asserted their moral right to be identified as the author of this work in accordance with the Copyright, Designs and Patents Act 1988. This work is a work of fiction. Names, characters, places and incidents are the product of the author's imagination or are used fictitiously. Any resemblance to actual persons, living or dead, places and incidents is entirely coincidental.

All rights reserved. No part of this publication may be copied, reproduced, distributed, stored in any retrieval system, or transmitted in any form or by any means, including photocopying, recording, or other electronic or mechanical methods, nor used as a source for any form of machine learning including AI datasets, without the prior written permission of the publisher.

The publisher and the author have made every effort to obtain permissions for any third party material used in this book and to comply with copyright law. Any queries in this respect should be brought to the attention of the publisher and any omissions will be corrected in future editions.

A CIP catalogue record for this book is available from the British Library.

Paperback ISBN: 9781036704841

The EU GPSR authorised representative is Logos Europe, 9 rue Nicolas Poussion, 17000 La Rochelle, France contact@logoseurope.eu

By H.N. Wake

FBI Agent Domini Walker

Sound of a Furious Sky
Hidden in the Silence
Secrets of the Angels
Echoes of Thunder

Prologue

Through the phone line, a piercing hiss crackled like an evil laugh. Vivienne Preston jerked the phone from her ear, but curiosity won out and she pressed it back. The hiss gave way to the background din of a large room – the hum of a fan, a honk of a taxi, and distant street traffic.

The caller's screech was high-pitched and panicked. "What…What do you want?"

Was that Ben? Who was he shouting at?

"What…What do you want?"

It *was* Ben and there was terror in his voice. Someone was in the room with him.

Viv froze in the middle of her red living room carpet.

Through the line, steel pots clanged, shoes scraped wood floor, and glass shattered. Was Ben running through his kitchen, knocking things over? Was he on speaker phone?

She pressed her hand over her mouth and shut her eyes to concentrate.

Feet slapped against the floor and Ben squealed, "Get out now! I'll call the cops!"

How could he call the cops if the line was open? Oh God. Should she hang up and call the cops?

A door slammed. Was that his bedroom door?

His shriek was muffled behind the door. "I'm calling the cops! Just get out! I'm calling the cops!"

Viv held her breath.

Bang, bang.

Viv startled, sucked in air.

A muffled thud.

In her living room, the clock ticked.

Silence.

She grabbed earphones off the coffee table, inserted them, and placed the call on hold. She gingerly opened a new line and pressed speed dial for Beecher Walker, afraid to lose the connection to Ben.

Beecher answered in two rings. "Hey, Viv."

Her voice cracked. "Beecher! I need help! There's an intruder at my friend's apartment. Ben Kirschner, 47 Henry Street, Chinatown. I can't use the phone. You need to call the cops!"

"What? Yes, I'm on it."

God bless Beecher. By the front door, she grabbed keys from the shelf, rushed into the hallway, slammed the door, and spun the key in the lock. "And call your sister!"

She paused to carefully close the call to Beecher and press open the line to Ben.

On the other end, there was only the silence.

Chapter One

Tuesday

It was the type of tepid, between-seasons day that lulled you into an easy complacency that everything in life would eventually turn out fine. The leaves on the trees in the Upper West Side neighborhood were still green, but the air had a hint of chill and the sky was gray. From the driver's seat of the antique red Lancia Fulvia Coupé, FBI Special Agent Domini Walker watched the front door of an apartment building on 83rd and Columbus while sipping the morning's second coffee. The Upper West Side's calm morning sounds were a balm before a storm, a rare respite between hectic investigations.

Of course, it was October. The last week of October, to be exact. Next weekend, the streets by the finish line of the New York City Marathon would be temporarily blockaded. The neighborhood would be crowded with vigilant NYPD foot patrols, beaming families, and exhausted runners draped in tin foil blankets. Cheery pop music would be echoing off the buildings. Along Central Park West, rows of television trucks would be blasting human interest stories from the world's greatest city.

Dom took another hit of caffeine as, from behind, a school bus rumbled close and its bright yellow expanded across the rearview mirror.

Through the brass door of the building, a middle-aged Latina woman with a gentle face emerged. She was dressed in pressed nursing blues, a blue cardigan, and white sneakers. Behind her, a young black girl with a big grin led a squat Corgi by a brightly printed leash. The girl wore a pink sweatshirt with a sparkling rainbow unicorn that matched the multicolor glitter of a new backpack and sneakers.

Dom lowered the coffee.

Darlin was a survivor—not a victim—of an earlier investigation. Over the last few months, Dom had urged the city's social worker to wait for a best-in-class foster situation. Finally, Francesca Gomez, a single woman with a solid nursing career and an interest in long-term adoption, had entered the system. After a round of interviews, the social worker had approved the assignment.

Darlin giggled as the Corgi snuffled for rodents.

The school bus squealed to a stop near the corner and bright red lights began blinking. Through the open windows, the squeals of children sounded like seagulls bickering over a crab.

Not for the first time in recent months, Dom wondered about children and their place in her life. She wasn't like many other 35-year-olds. Sure, she liked kids. They were cute and honest and innocent and cuddly. She liked their energy and general happiness. She liked the idea of being a good mom, one who listened and sympathized, who later in life was more a friend than a parent. But she wasn't craving to settle down or pump out puppies. She just didn't have that overriding urge that others blathered about.

She took another sip. Maybe in a few years with the onset of the forties, she would change her mind. She knew forty was the age when fear shot through so many women's dreams, the reproductive plumbing started shutting down, and the pickings for a partner slimmed dramatically. She certainly understood the ruthlessness of time. But for now, she was nowhere near panicked.

At the curb, Francesca Gomez leaned down, whispered in Darlin's ear, and gave the girl a hug. Darlin handed back the dog leash and gave Francesca a high five.

Dom leaned against the leather seat and took a deep breath. She imagined Darlin blossoming into her new world – excelling in literature, getting homemade cookies after school, joining the high school marching band, falling in love – and leaving all the scars of tragedy in the past.

The Lancia smelled of oil. Somewhere, her father, Stewart Walker, watched as Darlin hopped up into the raucous bus. His memory whispered to her, *You did that, my Dom.*

The bus belched as it cornered onto Columbus.

Dom sipped the last of the coffee. Her lifestyle – burying into investigations, chasing bad guys, sleeping a few hours – wouldn't be fair to a kid. Or a partner. Who wanted to live with looming danger in their life? Maybe women like her didn't need it all.

On the seat next to her, the phone vibrated and her brother's name blinked on the screen.

She answered before the second vibration. "Beech, what's up?"

"Vivienne Preston needs your help."

Chapter Two

The gated entrance of Ben Kirschner's utilitarian apartment building was sandwiched between a Chinese hardware store and a dumpling shop on Henry Street in Chinatown. Standing at the gate, Viv counted eight flights up and scanned windows. Maybe she could see him. In her ear, the phone line was still open, but there was only silence.

It had been six years ago that she and Ben had met during their junior year at NYU's Arthur L. Carter Journalism Institute. In shared classes, he'd been that odd quirky guy with twitching fingers and darting eyes who always seemed as if he'd had too many Red Bulls. A big head of curly red hair, pale skin, and a beak nose belied a mental acuity that matched his nervous tension. His hand always shot up first in class.

She and Ben had been assigned to a research group as part of the Journalism Ethics and First Amendment Law class and she had disliked him immediately. He was stubborn and arrogant. But over coffees, diet Cokes, library research, and late-night test prep, their fiery debates had forged a comradery that led to a respectful friendship. Unlike many she knew, Ben had never shied away from digging into intellectual discussions of racism or sexism because she was a black woman. Ben truly did not see her as different from himself. It was remarkable and refreshing.

Her phone vibrated. Beecher had texted. *"Cops on way. So is Dom."*

The apartment building door opened as a young Asian man in a white sweater and blue jeans pushed out into the morning sun. Viv leaped forward, grabbed the door, and raced past his shocked face. She darted through the lobby to the elevator bank, cornered into an elevator car, and smashed the eighth-floor button.

During graduation, Viv had been proud that Ben was awarded top honors. He'd worked harder and longer than anyone she knew. He was recruited to Business News, started work the day after graduation, and had a stellar, rising career as a top-notch journalist. Every few weeks, they debated modern ethics and journalistic research methods over beers in bars near Thompson Square Park.

When the elevator doors opened on the eighth floor, she flew down the dim hall, her feet muffled on the worn carpet, and skidded to a stop in front of his apartment door. The door was slightly ajar.

Her heart raced. "Ben?" she yelled. "Ben?"

There was only the hushed silence of an empty apartment.

She pushed the door open and peeked inside. Early morning sun cast a yellow glow across the living room. "Ben? Ben?"

The last time she'd been here four years ago had been awkward. He'd been sitting in the armchair, she in the couch. She was telling him about a mutual female friend who had gone on a hot and heavy date. "She made the walk of shame like a boss in a black dress and slutty heels on a commuter train from suburban New Jersey surrounded by blue banker suits."

Ben watched her closely. "Did she end up seeing him again?"

Viv said, "Oh, God, no. It was a straight-up, old-fashioned one-night stand."

Something about his look pinched her chest.

He stammered, "Viv, I like you."

She knew. Of course, she knew. She'd known it for a long time. She just didn't return the sentiment.

She nodded slowly.

He waited.

She gave him a pained, twisted smile.

He had glanced away. "OK. Well, at least that's done now."

In the light of the morning sun, she yelled. "Ben? Ben?"

She stepped through to the kitchen. Pots were scattered on the floor and a bottle of wine had been smashed across the tile, leaving a river of red.

She pushed her hand to her lips, turned, and strode down the dark hallway.

The bedroom door was closed.

Her heart rate spiked.

Oh my God, oh my God.

She slowly turned the knob, pushed against the door, and whispered, "Ben? Ben?"

From inside the room, a body was leaning against the door. A still body.

She pushed hard, heard the rustle of clothing against wood, and peered around the door.

Ben Kirschner was prone on his side, his legs splayed sideways. A pool of urine had crept out from his pants.

Oh God, Oh God.

She pushed into the room, knelt by his head, and jammed her fingers against his neck. The skin was warm, but there was no thump of blood moving underneath. Nothing. She leaned her ear to his mouth. Nothing.

Bile pushed against the bottom of her throat.

Ben Kirschner was dead.

She stood, careened down the dark hall, and lurched out of the apartment.

The wail of approaching sirens echoed down the dim hallway.

She doubled over and vomited across the worn carpet.

Chapter Three

Dom squeezed the sports car between two graffitied box trucks on Henry Street in Chinatown. Red Chinese lettering monopolized ratty awnings and flags fluttered above rows of small stores. Far overhead, brightly colored signs fought for space amidst iron fire escapes. Traffic had stalled behind three NYPD cruisers—their blue and whites blinking—and an ambulance whose doors were open.

Below a restaurant window hawking orange-glazed ducks like cadaverous tributes over a steaming cauldron, Vivienne Preston sat on the curb, her face cradled in both palms.

Dom had met Viv nineteen years ago. 11-year-old Beecher was supposed to have waited for her on the school steps, but when Dom had arrived, he'd been nowhere. Within minutes, her annoyance turned to panic. Since the death of their father a year earlier, she was terrified something would happen to Beecher. She moved quickly around the side of the brick school toward the playground. If he wasn't there, she'd next check the candy counter of the local bodega. As she stepped on the sweeping track field, she heard his screech from behind a set of low bleachers across the soccer field. Dropping her book bag, she took off at a sprint across the dry grass, silent and fast. Cornering the bleachers, she braked to a stop in the shadows. Ten feet ahead, Beecher lay on the grass with a tall, thick boy with menacing a fist at his face. By his side, a skinny kid with huge eyes hopped back and forth on worn sneakers.

The bully straightened as a young black girl barreled around the far end of the bleachers, skidded to a standstill, and jammed fists against a chubby waist. "Russell Grant, you get away from him!" From a messy ponytail, wisps of hair vibrated around a round face.

The muscle-bound mountain with a double chin laughed. "Who's gonna make me?" He spat on Beecher. "Loser. Not even your own daddy wanted to stick around for you."

Russell Grant pulled his foot back, lining up for a kick.

The plump little dynamo jolted forward, finger jamming at his face. "Get away from him!"

As Russell Grant hesitated, Dom dove for the raised foot, clasped it, and yanked. Russell Grant teetered, fell, and landed on his chest with a thud. Dom bound onto his back and shoved a knee against the small of his skull. Russell Grant's right arm shot out and pounded the dry dirt.

In a flash, the jittery skinny kid bolted and disappeared around the bleachers.

The plump girl stepped forward unafraid.

Pounding dirt, Russell Grant spit. "Help! Help!"

Dom pressed on her knee and said softly in his ear, "You touch my brother again, I'll finish this. Got it?"

The pounding stopped.

The girl crossed her arms with a satisfied look.

Beecher held his breath.

Dom released her knee and stood.

Russell Grant gasped for breath.

The girl wagged her finger. "Russell Grant, you're just a big crying baby. That's all you'll ever be. Stay in your lane, crybaby, and stop trying to be a tough guy."

Stay in your lane. Quite an adult putdown for a kid.

Beecher rolled on his side and stood.

Dom had crooked her head and the three left Russell Grant on the ground, rounded the bleachers, and stepped into the sunlight.

Outside the apartment in Chinatown, Dom sat gently on the curb. "Hey, Viv."

Viv squinted against the flashing cop lights and shuddered. She was 5'4" with shoulder-length hair, a slender face, and huge brown eyes. She had grown from that brave Energizer Bunny into a funny, strong woman with a solid career in journalism that kept her very savvy about New York City politics. Dom knew from Beecher that Viv dated on and off but wasn't currently in a serious relationship. Today, she had on a white sweatshirt over black sweatpants, gold earrings, and chain necklace with a small diamond pendant that had been a college graduation present from her parents.

Viv grasped Dom's forearm; her intelligent eyes were red and watery. She swallowed.

"I'm here," Dom soothed. After that schoolyard incident, Viv and Beecher had become lifelong friends. Like siblings, they'd snuck underage into R-rated movies in middle school, struggled over trigonometry in high school, and lamented college entrance exams. They'd laughed a lot.

Viv's pupils were dilated and tears glistened her cheeks. "Thanks for coming, Dom."

"Of course. You know I'd do anything for you."

Viv nodded numbly.

They stared together as the crowd of onlookers grew. It wasn't often that such a large number of uniformed officers stomped through a residential building on this street.

Viv held up her right hand. It trembled in midair. "When does that stop?"

"Oh, I dunno. It will come and go for a bit. Maybe twenty-four hours?"

Viv dropped the hand to her lap.

"You want to tell me what happened?"

Viv cleared her throat, stammering for words. "I found him. I touched him… He was dead already." She explained the phone call, the panicked taxi ride over, the discovery. "A friend from college. Another journo. We've been friends for, like, six years. His name's Ben Kirschner. Ben writes for Business News. Super accomplished. Very different from BuzzFeed, where I am." The tears streamed down her face and she bit her lower lip.

Dom nodded slowly. Let victims talk at their own pace. Trauma was hard enough.

Viv dropped her face into both hands and began rocking. "Oh my God, maybe I should have done something differently. What if I had said something to him while he was on the phone?"

"Listen to me. Don't question yourself. This is all about the man who came into Ben's apartment."

Viv rubbed her palms against her eyes.

"Beecher said something about the Amazon Alexa; it was on…when the disturbance happened. That he'd called you using Alexa."

Viv looked up and nodded.

"Did you hear the intruder?"

"No. I never heard his voice."

"OK. I'll have a friend in our forensics department get in touch. She'll get your permission for us to talk to Amazon; maybe we can get an audio of the call."

"You can do that?"

"That Alexa is a strange beast – lots of weird rules around the data it collects. But we can certainly try."

"Oh God." Viv sniffed hard against dripping snot.

An officer in patrol blues, hands holding his belt buckle, passed on the sidewalk. "Ok, folks, move along."

Dom flashed her FBI badge.

His eyebrows rose, but he moved down the street.

Viv turned to Dom. "What now?"

"This is an NYPD case. NYPD will determine the cause of death."

Viv gaped. "Wait, what do you mean? He was killed. Someone was chasing him around his apartment and killed him!"

It was never that easy. "Well, let's see."

"What do you mean?"

"No case is ever that black and white. There are always nuances. What we do know is that someone was in the apartment because you heard it. The next thing we know, you found Ben in his bedroom." Dom rubbed her mouth. "Viv, A may not lead to B. The intruder may have left. Before Ben died."

"No way, Dom! No way."

The intricacies of casework were not always easy for civilians to understand. "Look, they'll get forensics up there for prints. If it looks intentional—"

"A homicide, you mean."

Viv had always been overflowing with determination. A spark plug with grit. When she got an idea in her craw, it stuck. When she'd been twelve, Viv sat in front of the grocery store for a month and sold three thousand boxes of Girl Scout cookies—a troop record. In high school, she and Beecher sat around a card table in the living room through two sleepless nights studying for Model UN trials.

Dom said, "Yes, if it looks like a homicide, then they'll assign a detective who will open a homicide investigation. But let's see how this plays out."

Viv turned to her, eyes narrowing. Her fists were clenched. "Look, I know what I heard. Someone killed Ben. I've done a lot of research on the NYPD and written quite a few pieces about them. A lot of the time they aren't any good at their jobs."

Uh-oh. "That's not always the case." Dom knew many hard-working NYPD, especially the detectives. But she also knew the force wasn't homogenous. There were good guys and gals, as well as bad.

Viv glanced around to ensure they wouldn't be overheard. "Even the good ones don't always have the resources to do a thorough job. In the five cases I covered systematically, they didn't even try, Dom. Bottom line: I don't trust the NYPD."

Uh-oh. Spark plug with spunk is back. "Let's wait to see how this pans out."

"Dom, what if NYPD doesn't take this seriously?"

"I can't lie to you. It's possible. But before we rush into anything, let's see how this plays out."

Viv leaned near. Her voice was thick with pain. "Dom. He called me. I was his first choice in an emergency."

Dom nodded.

Viv jutted her jaw. "I'm gonna help the investigation. I'm gonna dig into this."

A civilian spark plug with a terrible idea. "Not a good idea, Viv. At all."

"If I find anything, any clues, can I call you?"

"Listen to me. Let's see what the professionals find out."

"I'm a professional, too, Dom. I'm a professional snoop. So, if I find anything, can I call you?"

A civilian bull with a shit bad idea in a China shop. "Viv, I need you to not get involved in this."

"If I find something, you'll help? Can I call you?"

"I'm a fed. If this turns into a homicide, it'll be a local case. Not my jurisdiction. I can't work this case, Viv."

Viv lowered her voice. "Dom, I need to do this. I need to help find out what happened to Ben. I'm gonna dig. I'm gonna do this."

A bull careening around a China shop smashing plates. If anything happened to Viv, Dom would never forgive herself. Loyalty was everything. "Yeah, I'm getting that feeling."

The lights on the cruisers switched off.

Viv's eyes implored her.

Dom opened the imaginary door to the China shop and held up both hands to calm the bull. "Ok, let's do it this way. We sniff around. If this turns into a homicide and we find anything that has to do with motive, we can hand our findings over to the NYPD."

"OK."

"But I've got two conditions."

Viv waited.

"We do this quietly. We don't tell anyone what we're doing."

"Deal."

"If you find anything, you channel it through me. I'm trained for this shit."

"Deal."

Dom scanned the street scene. The crowd was dispersing. "You talk to your parents?"

Mary and Al Preston were good people. Very good people. Mary was a nurse and Alfred was a corporate lawyer in midtown. They had worked hard to make a better life for their daughter. Viv had learned determination firsthand.

"Yes. They're gonna meet me at my apartment."

Dom grasped her wrist. "Ok, I'll call you later."

"What are you going to do?"

"Start sniffing around."

Chapter Four

The dim hallway of Ben Kirschner's building was lined with faded 1970s graphic wallpaper, was carpeted in grimy gray, and held a lingering scent of garlic. In front of Ben Kirschner's apartment, a uniformed NYPD patrol officer stood sentry, his arms crossed over his chest.

Dom flashed her badge and held out her hand. "You got gloves and booties?"

He fished in his pocket and handed her latex gloves and blue booties.

"Thanks."

Working with NYPD sometimes got tricky. FBI only engaged on those cases that may involve or butt up against a federal crime. Until that was determined, FBI took a back seat. In some cases, NYPD detectives played in the sandbox nicely with others. Sometimes not. She snapped the gloves on. This may be the one-and-only access she got to the crime scene.

The apartment door opened and an EMT emerged, pulling a gurney with a white, shrouded body.

She stepped back to let them pass. Life gets lost quick. She and Beech knew that well.

She slipped the booties over her shoes and pushed into the apartment.

A dirty coffee mug had been set on a shelf by the door, as if Ben had left it before leaving for work. In a tidy small living room, a brown leather couch faced a wall of shelves. On a coffee table, a silver laptop was cracked slightly open next to a spiral notebook. An expensive pen was on the floor by the table. A neat pile of newspapers sat in the corner. There was no television. There was also no female presence. At all. He was either gay or single. She texted Viv. *"Was Ben seeing anyone? Straight or gay?"*

She stepped to the bookshelf. The top row was weighed down by textbooks on journalism and human rights. In framed photos of him smiling beside friends, Ben Kirschner had clear intelligent eyes, a soft chin, and curly red hair. In a tweed blazer over khakis, he looked the typical young journalist. A photo of Viv and Ben at graduation, both in cap and gowns, was near the back of the shelf. All the photos looked like college era, the smiles young and light, before career and stress had moved in. Before life had gotten weighty.

For Dom and Beecher, the hardships of life had arrived far earlier than college.

To the left of Ben's front door, a common New York City intercom system had three buttons: *Talk*, *Listen*, and *Door*. She peered through an eyehole. It was crusty, but there was a decent wide-angle view of the hallway. She wondered if Ben had looked through the peephole.

Her phone pinged with a note from Viv. *"He was straight. Last girlfriend was someone named Melanie. I'll find her details."*

Around the corner, in the galley kitchen, an NYPD

detective in a plaid blazer was leaning over a smashed wine bottle in a pool of red. He wasn't wearing gloves or booties. Clearly, he was not concerned about evidence. Maybe Viv was a smarter civilian than Dom had given her credit for.

She coughed gently.

He glanced up, and thin lips tightened. He scowled under thinning hair greased over a bald spot.

She flashed her badge. "Domini Walker, FBI Special Agent."

He stood, straightened to his full height, and placed both hands on hips. "Huh. That was fast. Forensics isn't even here yet. Detective Traister. Glenn Traister." He gave Dom a quick once-over, then his eyes dropped for a slow roll up her body, pausing at her breasts.

It happened. A lot. Not all these guys were sure what to make of women in law enforcement. It no longer bothered her. She waited for his eyes to reach hers, then she gave him a neutral look – no reason to get his hackles up.

He crossed his arms over his chest. "Seriously, how'd you get here so fast?"

If his body language was any indication, he was definitely not going to play nice in the sandbox. That was five cues of resistance in less than a minute. "I heard it through the radio." When it involved family, the lies came easy.

"Huh, what's the interest?"

Time for some deflecting. "You from 7th Precinct?"

"Yup."

She leaned around to get a good look at the smashed wine bottle. "What are you thinking?"

He shrugged. "We've got a friend, a gal, who claims the vic called her and she heard the whole thing go down over the phone. She thinks there was some kind of intruder." He nodded toward Alexa standing on the far counter. "The scene jives with her testimony."

"She heard the intruder?" No reason to reveal her own findings this early.

"Nah, she didn't say that. Just that the vic was yelling."

Dom nodded toward the living room. "You think the vic opened the door to the intruder?"

"Can't tell. Nothing busted on the door, so, yeah, he probably unlocked it."

"Like he knew the guy?"

He shrugged. "Pizza delivery, maybe?"

"So, he runs through the kitchen, knocks over the wine..."

Traister nodded down the hallway. "Slams the door to the bedroom, leans back against the door. We've got his body down against the door. Maybe he hit his head? Maybe he passed out from fear? Maybe something lodged in his throat? We don't know at what point he actually bought it."

"No injuries?"

"Not that I could see. I'm not making a call yet."

"You gonna try to get the audio recording?"

"Maybe."

"Why *maybe*?"

He cocked his head, as if to say, *Watch your step.* "May or may not be admissible."

"Either way, it gives you details."

He shrugged it off.

His delay didn't matter. Dom had already put in the request to the FBI Forensics office to ask for the recording.

She nodded to the bedroom door. "Mind if I take a look?" While you could get an initial read of a victim's personality by the contents of a living room, real insight often came from the bedroom.

"Sure," he said reluctantly.

The bedroom was large by New York standards and similarly tidy. A tightly made queen bed sat under a large window. There were no curtains because the view was of a brick wall five feet away. On the bedside table were three books: *A History of the Civil War and Journalism*, *The Fall of Banking: The 2008 Financial Crisis*, and *Secrets of Diversity in the Board Room*. There was no untidy laundry on the floor; it was all contained in a laundry basket in the closet. Hangers were neatly organized. On the back wall, hanging against raw brick, was a poster-sized photo of the Brooklyn Bridge – uneventful and impersonal in black and white. Ben Kirschner had not been a sentimental person.

She stepped to a small desk. A second laptop was plugged into a large silver screen with a keyboard and mouse. A mug was stuffed with a fistful of pens and a rack was crammed with manila folders like thick bread slices in a toaster. She flipped through the handwritten labels along the edges. *SEC. Human Resources. Follow the $. Senior level. Taxes.* She ran her finger across the desk – it was dust-free.

Overhead, lined neatly on a single shelf, were twenty leather-bound books. She slipped one out from the middle of the row and opened to the first page. *Jan 2018-Mar 2018*. Inside were handwritten shorthand notes. These must be his notebooks. She reached for the last book, slid it out, and opened it. It was dated three months ago. She stared at the shelf: it was impressive that he kept them so organized, but the current notebook was missing.

She replaced the two notebooks, crossed to the bedside table, and opened the drawer. It was filled with receipts, an unopened box of condoms, three highlighter pens, a flashlight, and a small can of mace. No notebook.

She stilled and let the feel of the room settle around her.

Ben Kirschner was all business, tidy, industrious, and intelligent. From what Viv had said, he was quite ambitious. The lack of personal photos or mementos in the bedroom spoke of a potentially inexpressive, emotionally distant personality. Maybe even lonely.

Who among us isn't truly lonely?

Detective Traister barked something to the officer outside the apartment.

She stared down the bedroom hallway. Detective Traister had the potential to be a problem. His theory, that this could have been an innocent delivery gone wrong, was wrong. The intruder had pushed into the apartment, chased Ben around the kitchen, and followed him down the hallway. There was one heck of a motive to drive all those actions. Further, the perp had taken a lot of risks. There were video cameras all over this neighborhood, there were likely to be witnesses, and if Ben Kirschner had survived, he would have been a fact witness. There was one hell of a motive for the perp to take all those risks.

This intrusion had been planned.

She'd let Traister run out his theory. It would keep him out of her way.

She glanced at the bookshelf. What had Ben Kirschner been working that had gotten him in trouble? And where was his most recent notebook?

Chapter Five

Viv Preston shut the door to her apartment and raised her hands. The trembling had stopped. Disparate thoughts slogged through the oatmeal inside her brain and objects in the living room felt foreign. By the couch, a pillow lay askew on the floor. Why was the pillow on the floor? She couldn't remember knocking it off. Had someone come into her apartment? No, of course not. She was imagining things. She must have pushed the pillow to the floor as she'd shot from the couch during Ben's phone call.

Oh God, Ben. The skin on his neck under her fingertips had been warm, but the lack of a heartbeat had been deafening. *Oh God, Ben. What happened?*

Had she read those books in the bookshelf? She concentrated on one title but couldn't recall the topic. Had the red in the rug always been so dark, like the color of blood? Had she taken those photos on the windowsill? Seriously, when had that pillow fallen?

Suddenly, her legs felt numb. She sank to the floor and closed her eyes. Memories of Ben flashed across the insides of her lids. They were sitting on a bench in Washington Square Park. It was the spring of senior year. The sun had been out, the park had been flooded with students, and they'd bumped into each other between classes. They had decided to kill a few minutes together.

In cheap glasses with dark plastic frames, he had looked like a cross between a high school debate captain and a creepy biology teacher. He outlined his ambitions – to be top of their graduating class, to get a job at a top New York publication, to investigate and write long-form exposés of financial scandals, and to win the New York Press Club's Gold Keyboard as his first award. He would uncover fraud, expose criminals, and save old grandmas' pensions. Like a financial Woodward and Bernstein. Only he'd be a lone Bernstein, he said as he pushed the glasses up his nose. She had never met anyone so full of bravado and arrogance, but also so authentically committed to a higher calling. In that spring sunshine, she'd completely believed he would achieve his dreams.

The memory pushed through sticky morass. She opened her eyes and concentrated on the slowness of her brain, the numbness in her legs, and the tingling in her fingertips. Dom had mentioned trauma. These must be the symptoms of trauma. *I am experiencing trauma because Ben is dead.*

She stared at a photo of Ben and herself from graduation, their black caps slanted jauntily, a purple NYU flag as a backdrop. Journalists. That was what they had studied, that was what they were now. That's what Ben *was*.

After graduation, they had met up for a happy hour beer in the old bar off Union Square with ancient wooden tables and terrible country music. Ben had landed his job at Business News the same time Viv had been hired by Buzz-

Feed. He'd shown up in a horrid yellow-striped shirt his mother had bought.

In a hushed whisper, he'd explained a promising new lead. A Fortune 500 pharmaceutical company was covering up a tainted pain reliever. At least three doctors were willing to talk to him off record. He had tracked down four patients, all of whom were willing to be part of any public accounting.

She had leaned back with a sly grin. "I think you have something."

"Do you really?"

"Of course. I think you should definitely pursue it."

"My editor says I don't have enough to go on."

"Is your editor any good?"

"It's Business News. She's good."

"She?"

"Yup. It's not all men at the top, Viv."

Viv shrugged. "What did she specifically say?"

He finger-quoted. "Drop it. You don't have it without the doctors."

"Uh-huh. I guess that's that." She observed him over her beer foam with a wry smile.

He vigorously shook his head. "Of course, I'm not gonna drop it."

She set the glass down with a big smile. "I should think not."

He looked around as if expecting eavesdroppers. "I'm gonna work on it at home, off-hours. When I've got enough, I'm gonna hand it in."

"Could she fire you for insubordination?"

He stared at her. "She won't 'cause it's gonna win my first award."

And it had. His investigative reporting on the pharmaceutical company had gotten him into the finalists for the Online Journalism Award in Explanatory Reporting that year.

Her fingers rubbed the fiber of the blood-red carpet. Journalists were perpetually curious investigators. They were researchers who dug into dilemmas. The numbness had receded from her legs. That was who Ben was. A top-notch investigator.

She looked around the room. This is my apartment. This is my home. This is where I was before I got the call from Ben and heard him die. I am experiencing trauma. But I will not let it take over. I get up after a hit, that's what I do. For right now, I will get up off this carpet, I will get into my bed, and I will let this trauma work its way out of my system.

On heavy legs, she walked into the bedroom, gently sat down on the bed, and let her head roll down, chin to chest. *Ben, wherever you are, please don't be sad.*

She fell into the pillow, tears streaming.

After I sleep this off, she thought, I will get up out of bed, make a cup of full-gore coffee, and figure out what happened to Ben. Because that's what journalists do. Because I am also a top-notch investigator.

Her eyes fluttered.

Ben would have done it for me.

Chapter Six

The streets of Chinatown smelled of cooking oil, unusual fruit, and two-day-old garbage waiting for pickup. Cars moved slowly and there were few pedestrians. The NYPD cruisers and the ambulance were long gone. Only a single blue NYPD sedan was double-parked in front of the building, which meant Traister had not assigned foot patrol to canvas the area.

Dom pulled out her phone and snapped six photos up and down the street: restaurants, two hardware stores, a pharmacy, and a MoneyGram outlet. At least three buildings appeared to be cheap hotels.

She crossed the street and pushed through the door of the MoneyGram. A young Asian woman with bubblegum pink lips and a pink hoodie watched her entrance.

Dom flashed her badge. "FBI."

She raised her eyebrows and her pink lips opened round. "Oh, what happened?"

These young people were so fearless. "There's been a death. What's your name?"

"April. Did it happen in that apartment building?"

Dom nodded.

"You for real?" April's eyes widened.

"Any chance you have security cameras?"

"We totally do." She walked out from behind the desk to lock the front door, then motioned Dom to follow. "Come on back."

A short dark hallway smelled of cleaning products. April unlocked a gray door and led her into a small, closet-sized room where a tiny desk sat under two shelves. On each shelf was a small television screen. The lower screen displayed the inside of the shop and the upper screen covered the exterior. The exterior was a wide-angle view of the street that included the entrance gate to Ben Kirschner's apartment building.

Dom pointed to the top screen. "I need that one."

April sat down at the desk, punched on the keyboard, and brought up the feed on the screen. "The recording goes back like seventy-two hours or something."

Dom leaned in, smelled April's oversweet floral perfume. "Let's go back twelve hours."

April worked the mouse, clicking and rewinding before sitting back and letting the video scroll in fast forward.

The dawn lightened the street scene. Trucks passed. An older Chinese man walked a crickety dog past the apartment building. A delivery guy on an electric bike zoomed by. A mother with a young student in school uniform exited the grilled gate, immediately followed by a teenager. The sun lightened. A thin man wearing a baseball hat and dark sunglasses walked slowly toward the building. He glanced up and down the street once and took a position to the right of the gate.

Dom said softly, "Can you slow the video?"

April clicked the mouse. On the screen, the counter slowed.

The thin man in the baseball hat stood by the gate, his gaze focused on the inside entrance.

April asked, "Is that your guy?"

Not so many people wait by an entrance. "Maybe."

Through the interior of the lobby, there was movement as a middle-aged resident emerged and pushed through the gate. Baseball guy stuck his foot out to hold the gate open and slipped inside. It was a deft move.

Yup, that's my guy.

April whispered. "Oh my God."

The ticker on the video counter clicked over.

Twenty long minutes later, baseball guy emerged from the gate and strode westbound on Henry Street. The lid of his hat was pulled down over his face. *Is this guy skilled at avoiding cameras?* He was out in the open in the full light of day with a raft of security cameras on the street. If he was her guy, he was taking a lot of risks.

On the screen, his shadow passed out of sight of the camera.

April glanced at her. "Did *that* guy murder someone?"

Good question. "Not sure." Dom handed April a card. "Here, can you send that to my email?"

"Sure." April saved the feed, attached it to an email, and typed in Dom's address.

Dom's phone pinged. "Thanks for your help."

April blinked rapidly. "He's not coming back, is he? I mean, I'm safe here, right?"

"He won't be back." Dom smiled sadly. "I'm pretty sure he got what he came for."

Ten storefronts west of Ben Kirschner's building, Dom spotted a security camera with the angle she needed—looking east up Henry Street. It was located high in the corner window of a dumpling shop.

She pushed into the sweet smell of boiling rice and hot soy sauce. A couple at a small laminate table slurped from bowls and the high-pitched singsong of a Chinese opera blasted from two speakers. Behind a glass counter, an old Chinese woman with a white chef scarf over a wrinkled face waved her in.

Dom flashed her badge and pointed to the camera in the window. "I need to see some video."

The old woman glared.

Dom waited her out. She knew how this would end. It takes a few minutes, but most folks end up helping because very few people deny the FBI.

The old lady yelled something in Chinese over her shoulder and a young Asian man with spikey hair, four earrings in each ear, and a smeared apron stepped through the kitchen door. He wiped the back of his hand across his brow. "Yes?"

Dom nodded to the street. "I need to see some footage you've got on the outside security camera. From daybreak today."

He led her through the tiny, steamed kitchen where a white-haired guy with pockmarked skin was hammering a huge butcher knife on a cutting board. Racks of cans, spices, and sauces lined a back hallway. Inside a closet, a two-screen system was similar to the MoneyGram store.

He pulled up a video on one of the screens. "This is the front feed," he said and rewound the video to 5 A.M.

In the gray before sunrise, a black Audi SUV parked in

front of the dumpling shop. The car's interior lights blinked as the back door opened and baseball guy emerged.

Baseball guy had a driver. A chill swept up Dom's spine. They were in professional territory now.

Baseball guy moved up Henry Street toward Ben's apartment and stood outside.

Dom watched as he once again stuck out his foot and slipped into the building. Twenty minutes later, he emerged.

Dom held her breath.

He moved quickly down Henry toward the screen.

Dom leaned in.

He kept his head turned down with the hat's brim slanted to the ground. He moved swiftly to the back door of the SUV and slipped inside. The video never captured his face. *Yup, this guy knows what he's doing.*

The SUV pulled from the curb and video feed captured the license plate. *Gotcha.*

She pulled out her card. "Can you send the video to my email?"

Outside, the sky was gray, looming close like a canopy. She stared at the spot where the SUV had been parked. Something was very hinky about the baseball hat guy. He had a driver and acted professional enough to cover his face and slip unobserved into a building. But he had done it all out in the open in daylight on a street with obvious security cameras. Had he not expected anyone coming after him? Maybe he hadn't intended to kill Ben Kirschner?

A puddle of thick mud covered the curb. She moved slowly, carefully, to avoid the mud and knelt. There was a clean footprint in the muck. She pulled out her camera and snapped ten photos from different angles. Later, she would confirm against the dumpling shop's video if baseball guy had stepped here from the SUV.

The noise on Henry Street had spiked: horns honked, loose mufflers rattled, and workmen shouted orders. Down the street, Traister's sedan was gone from in front of the apartment building. City life was moving on.

But not for Ben Kirschner.

Reporters dug into lots of people's secrets in the search of a good story. What had Ben uncovered that would have drawn the interest of a professional intimidator? Who was baseball guy protecting? Professional thugs had patrons.

It was only noon, but it already felt like she had put in twelve hours.

Chapter Seven

Through the windows high in the Javits Building, the FBI's New York headquarters, an afternoon sun beamed over lower Manhattan. Yves Fontaine, the Assistant Director in Charge, or ADIC, was a wiry black man with thick, black-framed glasses and a bald head. Normally, his eyes were intense and inquisitive. But as Dom stepped into his office, he was setting down the phone's handset with a distant and sad gaze.

She paused in the doorway and said softly, "Is this a bad time?"

He blinked, waved her in, and slipped off his glasses. His shoulders sagged. "What's up, Walker?"

Despite being a political beast, Fontaine had proven a reliable and honorable leader. It was a tough balance to keep for the ADIC of FBI's largest field office.

"I can come back if this is an inconvenient time." Normally, Dom reported in to Special Agent in Charge Butler, but Fontaine had gotten directly involved in her last two cases and they'd established a familiar working rapport.

He was a prickly personality but a straight shooter and believed in letting an agent run after leads. When her actions in the recent child sex trafficking case had led to an internal investigation, he had been her staunch supporter.

He rubbed his face. "I'm not sure I'll have a convenient time anytime soon."

Something was definitely bothering Fontaine, and it wasn't something good. She stepped into the room. "You want to talk about it?"

He closed his eyes slowly and shook his head. "Sometimes life just gets heavy." He had a light French accent from Haitian roots.

When he didn't continue, she said, "I'm pretty good with confidences."

"I'm dealing with a family issue that doesn't appear to be resolving."

"I hear that. Family can be tough." Sharing painful truths could build trust. She leaned back against the wall. "You know the story about my father?"

He nodded with a questioning look.

"The other half of the story is that our mother left us just after he died. My aunt should have taken us in, but she had her own problems and, frankly, had no interest in taking on two more mouths to feed. So, she enrolled us in school using her address but set my brother and I up in our own apartment. She paid the bills. Checked in a few times a month. We all pretended to the outside world that we lived with her. I was fifteen, Beecher was ten."

He raised his eyebrows. "Just the two of you? You were fifteen?"

She grimaced. "Beecher and I survived."

"I'm sorry to hear that."

"There wasn't much to be done. It wasn't like I was

going to report it to anyone official. They would have separated us and put us into foster." She shrugged. "We turned out OK."

"You turned out just fine. I'm sure your brother did too." He turned in his swivel chair and glanced outside. "My son is twenty-two years old. He's in his second year at Iowa State. But we're going to have to bring him home. He's gotten mixed up in drugs and hurting himself. My wife and I are flying out tomorrow morning." He turned back to her. "It's not the sort of thing you'd expect from an FBI family."

"I hope the trip goes smoothly"

"Yeah, we'll see." He placed both hands on the desk. "So, what can I do for you today, Agent Walker?"

"Apologies upfront for adding to your burdens."

"Get on with it." The prickly was back.

"I've got a favor to ask."

"No."

Not unexpected. "Can I lay it out?"

"Let *me* lay out what I know. Up until a month ago, you were on administrative leave for an internal investigation. Two weeks ago, you returned to work and landed the Hettie Van Buren case—one of the most prominent and complicated investigations we've had in a few years—and you closed it successfully. So, well done on your return to a productive and effective member of the FBI. But I know for a fact that Butler has not assigned you a new case—"

"But I—"

He held up his hand. "Because I told Butler to give you at least one week of downtime. I specifically told him not to assign you anything. Which means you've gotten yourself into something you should not be involved in. And this is why you are in my office."

She watched him.

He squinted at her. "How are my skills of deduction?"

She nodded reluctantly. "Good."

"What the Bureau needs is for agents to take what they are given, when they are given it. That includes recovery time." He steepled his long fingers. "Furthermore, we've got the New York City marathon this coming weekend and we'll need your idle hands. Counter Intel is strapped. All *extra* hands will be put to work."

She cleared her throat and said slowly, "It's an NYPD case, possibly homicide."

He glowered. "Then make that a vociferous *no*."

"I'm pretty sure the NYPD detective is not going to solve it."

"Why do you care what an NYPD detective is doing?"

"A family friend is involved."

He shook his head slowly. "I'm sorry. The answer remains *no*."

"Sir, given my background, I will always be indebted to the kindness of this particular family. They assumed correctly that we were poor and they often helped out in ways that made a big difference. Later, when I was old enough, we told them about our situation. They came through big time, helped Beecher out with college. It's a debt I can't ever fully repay. If one of them is in trouble in a way that I can help, then I need to do that. Which means I need to make sure the case is solved." She cleared her throat. "I don't know how else to explain it."

His eyes turned sad again. "You just did a pretty good job of it." His fingers tapped the desk. "You realize, as ADIC, I can't assign Bureau to an NYPD without cause…"

"Yes, sir."

He slipped his glasses back on. "But I can allow you to take some time off."

She pushed off the wall. Take the offer and skedaddle.

He stopped her. "But it means there will be no official Bureau support—"

"Uh, sir—" She'd already sent items to Becky Turnball down in Forensics.

"That I hear of. If I don't hear of you using Bureau resources, I can't forbid it."

He was telling her to use her internal relationships – no forms, no requests, no signatures. FBI backchannels had been alive and well since the formation of the Bureau in 1908.

She nodded.

He pointed at her. "That also means no Lea Peck. Officially."

Staff Operations Specialist Lea Peck had worked with Dom on two recent cases and they had proven to be an exceptional team. "Copy that, sir."

"And stay out of NYPD's hair. Do we understand each other?"

She nodded.

"If you get in trouble, I'm your first phone call. I think I've earned that."

"You have."

"Ok, get out of here," he said with a wave of his hand.

"Good luck tomorrow, sir."

He gave her an appreciative, but curt, nod.

Chapter Eight

Viv stood at the kitchen counter listening to the coffee machine spit out the last of its brew. She'd slept for seven hours, but her mind still oozed molasses and her limbs tingled with numbness.

Five minutes later, she added milk to her coffee, padded into the living room, and sat on the couch, letting the caffeine hit her heart. Breathing in deeply, her lungs pushed against a dull, heavy chest. In the internet search bar, she typed, *Ben Kirschner*.

At Business News, he had published often and his stuff was good. There were hundreds of articles. In addition to headlines at Business News, she discovered his articles had appeared in Bloomberg Businessweek, Los Angeles Times, the Globe and Mail, Yahoo Finance, *and* the Boston Globe. Ben had never turned it off—the list was impressive.

She returned to the Business News site and clicked on Ben's bio. In the professional photo, Ben smiled with thoughtful eyes. He should have had a haircut before that photo because it looked unkempt. His mother probably hated it. She must be catatonic with grief. She would call her tomorrow.

She took a hit of coffee and focused on the most recent articles. He'd published six in the last two months. Two biopic profiles of wealthy men had been co-authored with a reporter named Trevor Witherspoon. The first, titled "Maverick Investor Seeks Redemption in Wind," examined hedge fund CEO Peter Wilson, who had made billions before investing solely in wind power. In a photo alongside the article, a clean-shaven man with narrow blue eyes held the steering wheel of a huge sailboat, full white sails across a blue sky.

On notepaper, Viv jotted, *Peter Wilson – subject/bio* and *Trevor Witherspoon – journo.*

The second biopic was of Jason Lui, a startup billionaire who had recently invested in the technology used to trace sourcing in supply chains. "The Latest Fad: Saving the Planet through Supply Chains" was accompanied by a photo of Jason Lui, a smiling, bald Asian in a red sweater and jeans on the stairs of the Met.

Viv jotted down *Jason Lui – subject/bio* on her notepad.

She toggled between the articles. Was it her imagination or did the choice of photos make them both look smug and condescending? There was nothing more pretentious than a man sailing a yacht, smiling against a blue sky, or a man looking down from the Met's grand staircase. Had Ben purposefully chosen condescending images? The words in the titles – *redemption* and *saving the planet* – almost felt as if they were mocking their subjects. Had they disapproved of the way he'd written about them? Her suspicion kicked up a notch, and she scribbled, *unhappy subjects?*

She thought of Ben's dry wit and fiery moralism and concluded, yup, he'd been mocking them. But it would have had to be far more sinister than simply a mocking article to have warranted the visit from the intruder. Had Ben uncovered something sinister about one of these men?

She cracked her neck. Research was an instinctive process – chasing down possible rabbit holes based on guesses. Maybe Ben *had* found something sinister. It was as good a guess as any. Time to start dropping down rabbit holes.

She typed in *Ben Kirschner*.

Three hours later, her eyes burned and the back of her neck ached. It occurred to her that she hadn't eaten anything since morning. She stood, stretched, and padded into the kitchen, where she pulled a Trader Joe's chicken Tikka Masala dinner from the freezer and threw it in the oven.

At BuzzFeed, she regularly published articles on topical issues: fires, local politics, fashion week, and metro area special interests. In contrast, Ben's topics had been dense: financial regulation, notable Wall Street deals, leveraged buyouts, and corporate financial reporting.

Ben had published three articles in the last month about corporate financial reporting using terms like balance sheet, cash flows, debt, and stockholder's equity. Corporate financial reporting was about a standard report that publicly traded companies used to disclose the health of a business. The reports allowed for investors and creditors to make informed decisions about investing or lending to a particular company. While Ben's writing craft had been excellent – sharp and concise with his hallmark of an exceptionally large vocabulary - to a layperson like Viv, financial reporting was a dry and complex topic.

Ben, what were you chasing? She jotted down, *why corporate reporting, so dry, had he found a scandal?*

Two years earlier, over a white laminate table in a loud diner in the Lower East Side, Ben had castigated the lenders that had caused the financial crash of 2008.

She'd been chomping on a French fry. "Yeah, yeah, I read all that. I totally get there were financial shenanigans even on top of those bad loans, but I'm just not sure I care."

He'd sat back against the booth and pressed his lips together.

"What?" she'd asked.

"That's just it. Way too many people don't care."

She shook her head. "Don't even start with me on that."

"No, listen, Viv. Smart people like you give up too early. It's not that complicated. It was a huge global tectonic shift that impacted the way money moves around the system, the way we do banking, the way people get loans. For crying out loud, it impacted the way Congress and regulators control banking… or don't, as the case may be. But so many people said it was too complicated. People lose curiosity when a subject gets longer than what can get covered in a ten-second social media sound bite."

She'd dropped a fry on the plate. "Hello, soapbox. That's unfair."

"I'm just pissed that journalists don't realize how easily people tune out."

"So you've just jumped from I'm intellectually lazy to it's all the fault of journalists?"

He'd shaken his head, his shoulders sagging. "I just know that people like us – us journalists – need to be doing a much better job. And readers need to be a bit, just a bit, more curious."

She'd stared at him.

"Don't you see, Viv? This isn't just about finance. Or subprime. Or banking. It's about the whole system. One shift in a corner of the map rewrites the whole map. We're all on that map. But none of us are paying attention to where that map is leading us." His fingers had clenched.

She'd smiled at him.

"What?"

"That. That right there. That crazy righteous impassioned fervor is what's gonna get you those awards."

He'd shaken the compliment off. "Maybe."

"No, it will."

"But I'm still sad about the pervasive lack of curiosity."

"Yeah, well. Stick with the world you can impact. Which is yours." She'd eyed his plate. "And eat those pancakes before they go cold."

The oven buzzer pinged. She pulled out the hot baking tray and pried the plastic film off the meal with a fork prong. As the steam rose, she gazed into the distance and tapped the prong softly against a front tooth. Ben's topics were boring and technical. But that didn't give her an excuse not to try to understand what he'd been researching. She pressed the fork's prong against her lip.

Ok, Ben, you don't have to tell me twice.

She moved back to the laptop, spooning curry over rice, to dig further into corporate reporting.

Chapter Nine

The NY FBI Forensics department was on the second floor of the Javits building. Rows of white Formica tables overflowed with purring machines. The thick smell of rubbing alcohol hung low across the room that was as bright as the inside of a lightbulb. Outside, the streets were dark.

Becky Turnball had been with the FBI for ten years. She was bright, committed, and methodical. She wore a white lab coat over green jeans and orange Crocks. Her long blonde hair was knotted on the top of her head; the ends had been dyed bright green. Forensics often attracted people whose minds worked differently, who came at problems from odd angles, who thought outside the FBI's normally rigid culture.

Becky turned as Dom approached. "Dom, what's up?"

"Hey, Becky. How you doing?"

Becky flashed her two raised thumbs and bobbed her head. The green hair wobbled. "Congrats on the Van Buren case. That was some crazy shit."

"Thanks. Your work helped crack it."

"We do what we can." Becky turned to the counter. "On that note, I got your stuff—"

"Yeah, Becky, uhmmmm…"

"Uh-oh. What?"

Dom lowered her voice. "I just came from Fontaine's office."

"Uh-oh." Becky grinned.

"Yeah, my access ain't always a good thing." She moved in closer. "This one is unofficial. For now."

Becky looked around the room. No one was watching. "I am down with that, Dom. What happens on the QT in Forensics, stays in Forensics"

"Thanks."

Becky turned back to her counter and woke her computer. "So, first let's go over those videos you sent. Let's start with the last one, where your perp got in the SUV." She started up the feed. "I agree with you; he clearly has a driver and that's unusual. Also, we've got this." Her finger worked the mouse, slowing the video and enlarging the image. It was a view of the rear of the SUV as it pulled away and a direct image of the license plate. "I'm running the plate number. I'll let you know. But, if he's professional, these can be fakes. That being said, what's potentially a good lead is the auto dealer's vanity plate." On the screen, the enlarged image read, *LARRY'S GMC*. "Sometimes it helps, but not always. It depends on how many models they sold in what year." She glanced at Dom. "And if they resist, you'd need a warrant."

"Which I don't have."

"Ok, let me see if I can sweet-talk him."

"Thanks, Becky." Dom pointed to the curb. "I've got a

print from the mud right where our perp stepped into the SUV." She opened her cell phone and emailed Becky the photos.

Becky moved the video image by image, back and forth, three times, watching the perp's foot. "Yup, that's definitely the spot." Becky flipped through images of the shoe print. "Nice work; you've taken tight and wide angles. I can use these."

"From your lips to Lady Justice's ears."

Becky waved Dom to a side table where two desktops supported five monitors. "Now the Alexa recording."

"Amazon sent that already?"

"Oh, yeah. Quick, quick. Your recipient—Vivienne Preston—approved permission, so we didn't have to get into a warrant." She woke the computer with the mouse and an audio file filled the screen. She handed Dom high-definition earphones and slipped a set over her head. "There are two very interesting wrinkles in the audio." Becky hit *play*.

The sound was loud at first, like from inside a wind tunnel, with indistinguishable white noise, maybe street traffic.

Ben's voice cracked with fear. "Who are you? What do you want?"

Steel pots clanged and glass shattered.

Feet slapped against the floor and Ben yelled, "Get out now! I'll call the cops!"

A door slammed.

His yelling was from behind the door. "I'm calling the cops! Just get out! I'm calling the cops!"

Bang, bang.

A muffled thud.

Through the earphones the wind tunnel returned. In the apartment there was only silence.

Becky and Dom exchanged a look as they listened for a long few minutes to the emptiness.

Dom asked, "What's the banging?"

"I think someone banged on the door." Becky reached out and rewound the audio. "Now, let's listen again to that silence just after the banging. I thought I had heard something, so I isolated it, pushed up the treble, diminished the white noise. Eventually, I found something." She hit play. "Listen to this."

Through the earphones, Ben screeched, "I'm calling the cops! Just get out! I'm calling the cops!"

Bang, bang.

Becky pointed to her earphones. There was the sound of a low hum, as the intruder whispered, "We warned you."

Dom blinked. "He said, 'We warned you.' "

Becky nodded quickly. "Yes, that's exactly what he said." She let the audio play out.

More silence.

Then a grunt followed by a long quiet moment and a muffled thud.

Dom whispered, "The vic collapsed."

Becky frowned, nodded, and pointed again at her earphones.

There was silence.

Long silence.

A full five minutes later, muffled footsteps stepped along the floor, then softly shut the door.

Dom blinked. "The intruder stayed a long time after Ben collapsed."

"Exactly. My impression is he stood on the other side of the door, listened to your vic die, then hung around, as if enjoying it."

That's exactly what Dom had concluded also.

Becky said solemnly, "Very creepy."
Very creepy. Very, very creepy.
Chills raced up Dom's spine.

Chapter Ten

Wednesday

From the luxury of her safe, warm bed, Bernadette Hax imagined her mother cracking eggs on a griddle and spooning brown coffee grounds into the filter. Mornings had always been calm, reassuring. Her father, a contractor, would have gone out to a job early to get face time with the client. Bern stared at the open closet and contemplated what to wear to work. It had only been six months since she'd gotten the secure job in a big building in the city and her father was very proud of her.

She liked walking to the train, slipping the subway card through the reader, pushing through the turnstile, and waiting with the other commuters from Westchester. Among the crowd, she was hidden in the normalcy of everyday lives. The station was early enough in the route that she often got a seat. Sometimes she flipped through the news on her phone, but mostly she people-watched and wondered what their lives were like. She admired the clothes on the fancy-suited women with their smart shoes and colorful handbags of soft leather and brand names. She imagined they were vice presidents in companies similar to hers, with corner offices and windows on the teeming city. The fancy women had meetings every hour. They would enter conference rooms, smile charmingly to all the men seated around the table, deliver a funny joke and pull out a chair. Sitting, they would grasp the low side lever and inch the seat higher for extra leverage. She liked to imagine these fancy women, with big houses, quiet maids, and attentive husbands, would go to the gym, pick up their kids from school, laugh over wine and a salad, and then have fabulous, gymnastic sex.

Did they have secrets? Did they have scars? Did they have memories that invaded and overwhelmed their senses with no warning: the stench of a filthy body, a painful grip on a wrist, hands prying apart thighs, the burn as their insides were ripped apart? Did they have these memories sitting across from their loyal, proud father in a local deli? Had they learned that quickly squeezing lids and concentrating on breathing sometimes helped hold the memories at bay, but mostly not? Did they stay silent as the terror washed over them, because why bring down their father with them?

Bern knew that she was smart enough to have a career, fancy clothes, and the corner office. Smarts weren't her issue. Confidence was. She couldn't imagine walking into a conference room of men and smiling, let alone making a joke. The thought of gymnastic sex, sex in any way, made her tremble.

Her therapist, Rhonda, had been working with her for two years. "Bernadette, one day you will tap your deep reserve of strength and courage and you will climb out of this dark place. That's the way your recovery is going to work. You will see yourself as a survivor. Not as a victim."

Bern's mother was a shy, anxious woman with clutching hands. "Bern, don't let this one incident define you."

In the last two years, her father had spoken only twice about the horrific night. The first to break down and sob that he was sorry it had happened to his little girl. A few months later, he'd found her staring out the window. "The best revenge is to not let him break you," he'd said.

From the kitchen, her mother had yelled, "Bern, breakfast."

She slipped her feet out of the bed and stood. One foot in front of the other. *From victim to survivor in tiny steps.* A few tiny steps. That was her goal today. One foot in front of the other, she left the room.

Chapter Eleven

The twang of coffee hit Dom's nose. She rolled toward the wall for a few additional minutes of sleep, but a tiny wet tongue stroked her cheek and thwarted her plans. She smoothed down the ears of Tinks & Tongue, her rescue Chihuahua, and rolled on her back. The ceiling came into focus.

Some investigations lasted a few days. A few lasted years. The early days were messy as you chased any clue, instinct, or rabbit hole. Some efforts added solid data points to the jigsaw puzzle. Some were a complete waste of time. In theory, the more you chased, the quicker you were able to hone in on coincidences. Keep moving forward. Let the data pile up. Because coincidences often revealed patterns.

This morning she had a few working theories. First, the intrusion had been done by a professional. Second, he had been hired by someone. Which meant she was looking for someone rich with secrets – either personal or financial – that Ben had uncovered. Finally, at this stage, it was likely neither the rich guy nor the professional heavy had intended to kill Ben. So, at this point, whoever she was chasing was probably skittish. It was a potentially dangerous dimension.

Beecher and Mila Pascale chatting in the kitchen was a murmur through the door. For three years, Dom had lived alone, but now there was a full house. A year ago, Beecher had broken up with his wife and moved back in. The divorce was taking longer than anyone expected, but Dom liked having the easygoing, funny and smart Beech around. He was also a great cook.

Mila Pascale, a young college student who was odd, precise, and possibly on the spectrum, was a more recent, and endearing, addition. They didn't know much about Mila's background, other than her missing mother was an alcoholic and she had no family in the city. Mila's doggedness had cracked the biggest lead in Dom's most recent case and had garnered her attention from two unfriendly cops. Dom and Beech had insisted Mila stay until the danger had dissipated. Neither of them was in any rush to have her move out.

Dom mashed her feet into the carpet, reached for her robe, and opened her bedroom door to the divine smell of brewed coffee.

Tinks leaped from the bed and raced down the hallway.

In the kitchen, Mila's laugh at one of Beecher's jokes was loud and goofy like a turkey gobble. It made Dom grin.

Beecher looked up as Dom entered. "Glad to see you got some sleep." He scooped up Tinks.

"Coffee," Dom said, zombielike.

"I made it dark."

"Coffee." She poured a big mug.

At the counter, Mila was intently examining a glass for smudge marks, holding it up in a stream of sunlight.

Over her mug, Dom raised her brow at Beecher.

He winked back. "Mila, your lemon is in the fridge."

"Thank you."

Beecher asked, "Do you always have to have water first?"

From inside the fridge, Mila said, "Yes."

"For just breakfast or every meal?"

"Just breakfast."

"What would happen if I didn't have a lemon?"

She closed the fridge door. "I would go get one."

"At the store?"

She did not break a smile. "Yes."

"Before anything else?"

"Yes."

"Because that's just the way you need your water?"

She shrugged. "It's better if there happens to be a lemon in the fridge already."

He grinned wider. "I would think so."

As soon as Mila sat, Tinks jumped off Beecher's lap and over to Mila's.

Beecher said to Dom, "I spoke to Viv this morning."

"She's up early. How is she doing?"

"Hard to say. She seems fine, but you can tell there's something deep there…"

"She'll be in shock for a bit. It takes time."

"She said she's gonna investigate."

Mila eyed them quietly.

Dom sipped the black coffee. "She's going to *help*."

"Are you on the case? This isn't FBI territory. It's a homicide, right?"

"I've gotten a couple of days' leave."

"How'd that happen?"

"The Prestons were good to us."

"You asked Fontaine for some days off?"

Dom nodded.

"What's the case?" Mila asked.

Mila had her sights on joining the FBI.

The FBI's overwhelming consumption of one's life would come in good time—no need to rush into it. But try telling that to Mila. "Nothing you need to worry yourself with. You got classes today?"

"Yes."

"Why don't you focus on that?"

Mila shrugged and Tinks licked her hand.

Beecher grinned. "Ah, the life of a student." He turned back to Dom. "How *is* the case going?"

"We don't have much yet. I'm not ready to make any guesses."

"Viv said the NYPD hasn't called her yet."

It was an interesting data point. She was happy to have Traister out of her hair. She opened the fridge, rummaged for eggs but pulled out the bread instead. "Toast, anyone?" She dropped two slices into the toaster and mashed down the button. Behind her, a new quiet was unnerving. She turned slowly.

Beecher was watching her with sad eyes.

Mila whipsawed between Dom's face and his.

Dom set down her coffee and waited.

He cleared his throat.

She knew that throat clearing.

He said, "She's written another letter."

A combination of anger and fear punched Dom in the throat. "Esther."

He nodded.

She turned back to the toaster. *Fucking Esther. Couldn't sleeping dogs lie or zombies stay in crypts or Esther leave well enough alone?*

Mila whispered, "Who's Esther?"

"Our mother," Beecher said.

"Where does she live?"

"Florida. With her dentist husband."

Beecher could stare at her back all he wanted. She wasn't going to discuss Esther.

He said, "She's coming to New York."

She clenched the edge of the countertop. *Jesus H. Christ. Was no one interested in moving forward instead of dwelling on the past?* "No."

"I can't stop her. She said her plans are set."

Mila asked, "When?"

Beecher replied, "In four days."

Dom walked out of the room.

From halfway down the hall, she heard Beecher say, "We haven't seen her in twenty years. She moved after dad killed himself. She left us to fend for ourselves."

"How old were you?"

"Dom was fifteen. I was ten. Long ago. Different lifetime."

"You were only ten and Dom was fifteen? That's abandonment."

"You could call it that."

"What does your mom think about the Filthy Five? About your dad?"

Dom's ears pricked and she paused, sipped her coffee.

While involved in Dom's last case, Mila had researched their father. In 1999, five NYPD officers from the 9th Precinct had been arrested in a sting operation on charges of corruption and illegal conduct. The five officers had made off with two million dollars in drugs and a duffel bag of $250,000 of rolled cash that had been planted by NYPD Internal Affairs. At trial, six months later, three of the officers had been exonerated—Robert Gessen, Art Dyson, and Mike Turner. Stewart R. Walker and John Belafonte had been indicted on civil rights conspiracy, perjury, extortion, grand larceny, and the possession and distribution of narcotics. A month later, Stewart Walker had hung himself in his cell.

"I don't know," Beecher replied. "Esther isn't exactly reliable. She was always kinda dull, dumb even, and apparently, after Dad killed himself, she lost it. Wandered around a lot. I think we were lucky she left."

"Huh."

"She probably would have damaged us further."

The silence from the kitchen was thick. Esther and her desertion burned like a branding, even after all these years. Dom swallowed the coffee against a thick throat.

Mila asked, "Why is she coming now?"

"I don't know."

"You think she's coming here about the Filthy Five?"

Beecher scolded her, "I'm pretty sure you need to leave the Filthy Five alone. The last thing any of us needs is that thug NYPD officer – that bastard Robert Gessen - or his henchmen getting riled up. We do not need them bothering you again. You were lucky Dom got you out of that apartment."

"I'm surprised a Walker would say that."

In the quiet hallway, Dom cocked her head. She imagined Beecher doing the same thing. *That Mila was a sassy one.*

Beecher asked, "What? Why?"

Mila said in a matter-of-fact voice, "Based on your and Dom's past behavior, which has been consistent, you both appear to have a healthy aptitude for risk. I am surprised either of you would back down from such an important and personal mystery."

Beecher chortled.

Closing the bedroom door, Dom sat on the bed. Cold loneliness had crept into her chest. There were too many bad memories.

One morning when Beecher had been two years old, he'd started to choke on a piece of bread. His little body had jolted. He'd hacked. His eyes had bugged wide.

Esther's eyes were dazed and her lips trembled.

Beecher's face turned blue. His bare feet banged against his highchair.

Seven-year-old Dom screamed, "Mom!"

Esther started to shake.

Dom bolted from her chair, yanked Beecher from his highchair, slammed his back against her chest, and drove her fists into his ribcage. Once. Twice. On the third pump, the bread flew from his mouth.

He heaved in air.

Dom had swung his face to her chest, hugging him tightly, and strode from the room.

She sipped the coffee. They were better off without Esther.

Chapter Twelve

An early morning breeze swayed branches over the empty sidewalks of Madison Square Park. From inside a purring black Bentley Mulsanne, Chase Richter watched a leaf spin on a current. He was trying to ignore the grating, frosty tone of his boss, who was on a call dressing dress down a senior executive. Was it only a year ago that he'd been impressed by the hand-tailored suits, the shiny shoes worth more than an airplane ticket, or the perpetual sense of entitlement? It seemed longer than that. Way longer.

The soft leather seats of the Bentley allowed his spine to curve backwards and a slash of pain fragged his lower back. He straightened. The doctor had been reducing his prescription to wean him off. but Slap had found a black market guy and new meds. Doctors that never saw action could go fuck themselves.

Outside a bus chugged past.

Boss hung up the phone and immediately resumed their earlier conversation. "What hiccup?"

Richter watched another leaf spiral downward before turning to the soft, round face. "The reporter. He died."

Boss swallowed, eyes wide against pale, pampered skin.

Oh, now he's afraid. Now. After all my warnings. For months, Boss had been full of bravado about the plan, gung-ho about the escalation of tracking, intimidation, and not-so-subtle bullying. But now he swallowed with fear. Guys like Boss had never known the confines of a trailer home with an extremely violent father. They had never outrun the cops on a beat-up motorbike. In high school, they'd never gone hungry to impress the disdainful rich girls in expensive sweaters. They had never smelled the metallic spray of a buddy's brains.

"Jesus Christ. What happened?"

Richter shrugged. "I think he had a bad heart."

"What? What happened?"

In the desert, they hit each other for fun, to laugh at lips and cheeks fluttering as the head snapped sideways. For as thin, small, and consciously inconspicuous as he was, Richter served the hardest hit against the jaw with an open palm. They'd given him the nickname Slap. Right now he could slap that condescending chubby cheek, and hard. "You don't want to know."

"No. You're right. I don't want to know." Boss shook his coifed hair. "What now?"

"Nothing. The police won't find anything 'cause there wasn't anything. It was a bad heart. That's what they'll find. Over. Done."

"Are you sure?"

"Pretty sure. If something changes, I'll let you know."

Boss nodded.

The pain blazed to his heels as Richter stretched from the car onto the sidewalk. With a grunt, he tapped the roof twice and the Bentley pulled away.

The whiff of burnt chemicals from the car's exhaust teleported him to Fallujah.

Suddenly it was November of 2004 in vivid color and potent stench. Captain had assigned him to the building roof. He was used to doing lookout alone. By nature, snipers were quiet types. He scanned the neighborhood through the scope of the M24, swinging left and right, within an easy 1500-meter perimeter. There were hundreds of tan buildings in this city of fucking mosques with thousands of pointy minarets and hundreds of thousands of hidden insurgents. To the north, columns of smoke plumed upward and rounds of mortar echoed.

His gritty eyes burned. They'd been advancing for five hours into the industrial district in the southeast, taking their time looking for tunnels and spider holes. They'd chosen a mechanic shop for a rest.

Captain had grunted to Slap. "Just lookout. No potshots. We're holding this position quietly." He knew Slap liked to target practice on cats and the rare dog.

Slap had nodded, hoofed it up the stairs, laid on the roof, and took up position.

Downstairs, in the abandoned shop, he knew the three other guys were eyeing Captain. The squad hated him. He had failed them too many times. Today, he'd gotten them cut off from the main battalion and he didn't have a fucking plan. They were down to four grunts. It was a total clusterfuck. And they'd been under his catastrophic shit-brew command for way too long.

On 26th Street along Madison Square Park, a taxi honked.

Richter blinked in the sun, waved off the taxi, then brought his hand up to his face. Focus, Focus.

His fingers rattled like a fly's antennae on a piece of shit. Focus. Focus.

His heart rate slowed.

His fingers calmed.

The last few weeks, the flashbacks had gotten more frequent. He blamed it on the new black market meds. But in the last twenty-four hours, the flashbacks had been coming once an hour. That wasn't good.

He knew why. Yesterday morning, he had pressed his ear against the thin wood of the journalist's bedroom door. He had held his breath, eyes fixed on a speck on the hallway wall, as still as a sniper, and listened to Ben Kirschner gurgle at the moment his life dissipated.

Chapter Thirteen

Dom looked out over the frenetic chaos of the bullpen of Business News. Phones rang. Keyboards clacked. People yelled across the open floor. Twenty feet away, a bank of televisions flashed all the news stations.

A young male assistant in a button-down shirt over khakis approached. "Ms. Bisset can see you now."

She followed him through the doorway into a brightly lit room, two walls covered in books, the third a window looking out over Midtown. A fifty-year-old white woman with a sleek, brown bob and a trim body in a form-fitting navy dress held out her hand. "Nora Bisset. Welcome, Agent." Her heels clicked as she led her to a glass conference table.

Dom took a seat. "Thanks for meeting with me."

Bisset shook her head. "Horrible. Just horrible. I can't believe it. How did it happen?"

"It's not clear. But it appears there was an intruder in his apartment."

"What can I do to help?"

No hand to neck, no tick, nothing. Straight eyes ahead. She was tough, no-nonsense. Even death didn't make her nervous. "Can you describe Ben for me?"

"He was one of my most indomitable reporters. His work was penetrating. He was sagacious, perceptive, tenacious. He could be a sanctimonious shit – not supercilious, more cocksure – and excuse me for speaking ill of the dead."

Seriously? "So, he was persistent?"

Bisset nodded.

"How much time do reporters generally spend here in the office?"

"They're pretty much always on the clock, but not always in the office. They can be doing research, interviewing. But in Ben's case – he was notable. A workaholic. And coming from me, that's extraordinary."

"Was he well-liked here by his colleagues? Any issues?"

Bisset cocked her head. "If Ben's death was intentional, it would not be related to any kind of relationship issue here."

Maybe yes, maybe no. "No enemies, no jealousy?"

"That just isn't a lead for you, Agent."

Sometimes you trust the interviewee, even if they are haughty. "Can you explain to me how you worked with Ben?"

"Can you expound?"

"Did he vet the idea first with you on his next features?"

"Yes." She was in charge. End of story.

"So, he would come to you with ideas and you approved them?"

"Yes."

"Do you normally see early research?"

"No. Ben pursued his research autonomously. Once he had a first draft, we would discuss angles."

"You sign off on final copy before it goes to print?"

Bisset's lips pursed. "Yes, that's my job."

Dom reached into her pocket and retrieved the printouts of the two profiles Viv had emailed. "Looks like two of his most recent articles were about wealthy men. Peter Wilson and a Jason Lui."

Bisset's face was neutral. "Yes."

Again, no ticks, no soothing motions. These articles did not cause her anxiety. "Did you work with him on these profiles in your normal manner? Did you review an early draft?"

"You think this has something to do with those profiles?"

"Did you discuss anything about these two men that seemed... unusual?"

Bisset leaned on her elbows. "These two men are a possible motive?"

Bisset was leaning in, a cue of confrontation. "I'm saying it's a possibility. At this stage, anything is a possibility." She held up the documents. "Anything that you and Ben discussed about these two men that I should know?"

She crossed her arms over her chest. "We're a professional news outlet with a focus on business and finances. We do not publish details that may be considered muckraking."

So, he'd found something. "But in his research on these two men, and in the first draft he sent to you, he had discovered something?"

"We are always happy to work with law enforcement..."

Shit. Her resistance was building. Dom held up her hand. She didn't want Bisset to ask whether this was an official investigation. "I get it. I'm not prying into journalist integrity. I'm just considering possibilities."

Bisset placed her hands on the glass. "Let me say it this way. Ben always found a lot of information on his subjects. A lot."

"As in, you actually think there might be some dirt on these two men that would be worth a home invasion?"

"I'm saying individuals deserve their privacy, whether we publish certain information or not."

Her stonewalling had been perfected to an artform. "In the normal process of writing, like these two profiles, I assume Ben would have communicated via email with the subjects?"

Bisset hesitated before nodding.

"These emails would be in your system."

Bisset stared at her with an intentional blank face.

The resistance continued to build. Crap. She didn't have much more time. "Have you reviewed these communications?"

"I'm afraid I won't answer that."

"We're talking about the potential homicide of one of your staff."

"I respectfully suggest you get a warrant, Special Agent."

The resistance had solidified.

Outside, the sun was bright and the sky was blue. Dom took a moment to breathe. She'd gotten no new information from that meeting. A nice dead end. She hated dead ends.

Her phone buzzed with a call.

Becky Turnball from Forensics said, "Dom. I've got some news. That license plate was a dead end."

"Thanks, Becky."

She needed a new avenue. Maybe good ole boy Detective Traister had new leads.

Chapter Fourteen

The lecture hall of Wilf Hall on McDougal Street was packed. It was only the fifth week of the NYU semester and attendance hadn't started to drop. Mila had her laptop open, typing in notes. It was an interesting subject, Criminology 101, with a focus on procedural law.

Professor Irawaddy was pretty good. He spoke clearly and followed his outline, so it wasn't too difficult to keep up. Of course, her mind wandered all around, as it often did. Even on a good day, she didn't have the most linear thought processes. She'd come to understand, especially while at NYU, that there was no thing as 'normal' and that she could stop trying to find that curve in the bell. In particular, she'd learned in Psych 101 that she should be proud of her strangeness. That idea was a far cry from what they had taught in high school, where she'd been bullied for being odd, distant.

To be honest, her research on autistic spectrum disorder was far less interesting than a ton of other things, including Irawaddy's discussion on change management and the way city police needed to innovate to handle increased public demands for results. It was subjects like this that were going to help her ace the FBI entrance exam and send her on an upward trajectory into the vaunted hallows of being an FBI Special Agent. Her fingers flew across the keyboard, jotting down the criminal justice truths Professor Irawaddy was laying down for them.

She could almost feel the badge she would be able to wear, tucked into her jeans belt. The leather would be heavy against her skin. She would flash it at suspects with a hard stare. Special Agent Mila Pascale. It even sounded legitimate.

Up at the podium Professor Irawaddy began winding down. "I've assigned a fairly heavy reading load for next class. This is primarily because the issue is a thorny one for most law enforcement management teams. Next week we'll be talking about cold cases."

Mila's fingers paused. The disappearance of her brother, Jimmy. A cold case.

Irawaddy continued. "You'll be reading a recent Department of Justice study conducted with sheriff and police departments across the country. Overall, they found only twenty percent of these offices have protocol for handling cold cases and only seven percent have a cold case unit. Only one in a hundred cold cases that was reopened resulted in a conviction."

Over the years, she had learned to push the image of Jimmy's last smile far from her current day. Even now, she gently slid the image into the shadows of her mind.

Professor Irawaddy said, "The study identified three primary reasons cold cases are reopened. One: a family member presses law enforcement."

She swallowed. Jimmy's blue eyes flooded her own,

imprinting like a watery film over the lecture hall, over the stage, over Irawaddy. His huge warm face beamed as he turned and ran to the elementary school. Jimmy. She pushed a fingernail painfully into her palm and sucked in a deep breath. A family member. Yes, that's right. A family member. Mila had a plan. A four-step plan. Step one: pass the FBI entrance exam. Step two: graduate in the top percentile from Quantico. Step three: get assigned to the New York FBI office. Step four: work after-hours on Jimmy's case.

She shook her head and focused on Irawaddy's voice.

"Two: new forensic technology advances allow for new tests to be conducted. And the last most common reason a cold case is reopened is a new witness is discovered and comes forward – perhaps because of a plea bargain in an unrelated case or because a rock is overturned and a new witness found."

Mila glanced out the window. Earlier this summer, Mila's life had intersected with FBI Special Agent Domini Walker. Dom had been on the case of a missing heiress, Hettie Van Buren, who Mila worked with at the Natural History Museum. Mila had sifted through Hettie's social media to help the FBI. It had been a version of stalking. True. But what Mila had uncovered had helped Dom crack the case.

Across the street was the Center for Research in Crime and Justice of the New York University Law School building. The work on the Hettie Van Buren case had triggered Mila's keen interest in Domini Walker and the discovery of the Filthy Five story. It was inside the library across the street that Mila had unearthed data in the Police Records Project that two of the five were working together again in Precinct 9 in the Lower East Side.

A few weeks later, she had asked Dom, "Why do you think those cops came after me?"

"To shut you up."

"But why? I mean, what I uncovered isn't so hard to piece together. The Filthy Five is regrouping. That's publicly available information."

Dom had cocked her head with a look of confusion, as if she hadn't thought of this either. In the mad dash of protecting Mila, had anyone wondered why the regrouping of the Filthy Five was such a white-hot topic? "I mean, all I did was send an anonymous note to their bosses."

Dom had pointed a finger. "It doesn't matter. You're off it. No more researching the Filthy Five. Focus on school."

In the lecture hall, Irawaddy was packing his bag, students were snapping laptops shut, and hinged seats were banging as students stood. Mila stared through the window at the library. The sun flashed as the students filed past.

Esther Walker was coming to New York. Domini Walker had saved her life. What if Mila could find something that would enable the family to reopen the case and clear the Walker name?

Over the years, Mila had learned that actions speak louder than words. Maybe if she did some poking around, she could help repay the Walkers.

Chapter Fifteen

Trevor Witherspoon, Ben's frequent co-author, had suggested they meet at Manhattan Coffee Grind across the street from Business News, six floors below where Dom had met with Ben's editor. Viv had arrived early and gotten them a small two-top by the back.

Earlier in the morning, she had called Emily, the editor at BuzzFeed, and had asked for a few days of bereavement leave. True to her bubbly nature, Emily had been effusive. "Oh, God, Viv, you take all the time you need. That's horrific. I'm here when you need me."

Trevor Witherspoon arrived on time. His professional bio picture on the Business News site did not do justice to his size: he was defensive linebacker big. Unusual for a reporter. His face was disarmingly young and wide-eyed under short, light brown hair. He was a nice-looking guy. For a brief second, she wondered if he only dated white girls.

He sat down gently, but his girth strained the small

coffee shop chair as he set a bag on the floor. "I can't believe it. I just can't believe it. It's so insane."

She gave him a sad smile. "I know. I'm in shock."

"How did he...how did it happen?"

"Someone intruded into his house. I found his body behind his bedroom door." She didn't know why she just blurted that out. Maybe she hadn't given herself enough time to properly process the shock.

He blinked rapidly. "What? *You* found him?"

His face was so gentle and innocent. Viv often relied on her gut instinct about people. She lowered her voice. "I heard the whole thing."

"What?" His mouth dropped open.

"Ben had his Alexa call me when the killer was breaking into his apartment. I was on the line the whole time."

"Holy shit." He reared back.

Maybe, in the future, she shouldn't tell that part about the phone call. She didn't want that look for the rest of her life. "Yeah, listen. The case is with the NYPD. But, as you can imagine, one journo to the other, it's not in my nature to leave this to the overworked, underpaid authorities."

"Ok?" His voice was hesitant.

"I'm quietly snooping around. I'm not doing anything illegal. I'm just gonna try to figure out who may have had a beef with Ben."

"I'm listening."

"I've been reading some of his recent articles. You co-authored some of them."

Trevor nodded.

"I'm starting with the working hypothesis that something he wrote recently got him in trouble."

"That makes sense."

"I'm thinking it's probably some rich dude who didn't

want Ben to publish something about him. How did he get in to interview Peter Wilson and Jason Lui?"

"If I remember correctly, he just called their offices and they said *yes*. He started with a list of ten possible billionaires to profile, but those two stood out for their unusual turns in their careers. Ben straight-up called their offices and asked if they would be willing to be profiled."

"How long does it take to work up the first copy? With the research, interview, write-up, editor?"

"A month. A few days' research online. The interview with the subject. A few interviews of folks who have worked with them to corroborate. Then the write-up."

That would have put Ben back three months. "Have any complaints come in the last three months?"

"Hold on." He pulled out his phone and hit a quick dial with a fat finger. "Ally, remember Ben Kirschner's profile on Peter Wilson? Didn't someone call in to Nora?" He mouthed to Viv, *That's our editor.* "Yeah, that's it." He listened then hung up. "Wilson's PR firm called in to Nora Bisset and gave her an earful. So apparently Wilson's people weren't thrilled."

Viv scribbled *Peter Wilson PR* "Great, thanks."

He eyed her notes. "Be careful with these guys. They play heavy and with lots of cash."

His kindness made her chest clench. Boy, her emotions were all over the map. "I gotta be a journo, you know?"

He nodded sadly. "So what are you going to do?"

"I'm going to give it the personalized attention Ben deserves. I'm going to do a shit ton of legwork and see what I can find. I know folks in law enforcement who can help if I find anything."

"Don't you think you should be scared?"

"Yeah. I'm still trying to deal with that. But I feel like Ben singled me out to help him."

Trevor looked away, then reached into his bag and pulled out a black leather-bound notebook. "I was debating whether or not to give this to you. Ben was a voracious notetaker. One of the best. This is his most recent notebook. It was on his desk." He handed it to her. "If you want to copy the contents, I can take it back up and put it back on his desk. In case… the cops…"

She opened her phone's camera and started snapping the notebook's pages. "Thanks so much, Trevor. I'm sure this will definitely help."

He was watching her.

"What?"

"There was something else."

She waited.

"About two months ago, Ben said something about the underbelly of New York. I asked him what he meant and he only said, 'There's some weird shit that goes on in this city on Tuesday nights.' "

She paused. "Tuesdays?"

"Weird, right?"

"Do you remember exactly when he said that?"

"I've been sitting here trying to remember, and I can't remember the exact day." He nodded to the notebook in his hand. "But it was definitely within the last two months."

Chapter Sixteen

Detective Traister chewed a piece of gum loudly, smacking it between his back teeth as he tapped a manila folder on his desk. "So, it was a heart attack." The autopsy report had just arrived.

Dom asked, "So where does that leave you?|

"Where I started. Delivery gone bad. Guy buzzes up, pushes into the apartment, maybe pulls a gun, chases our vic around. Our vic runs into bedroom. Dies of a heart attack."

Seriously? She said out loud, "I'm having trouble following you. Can you say that again?"

Traister's body stiffened. "Maybe manslaughter in the second degree. Maybe. If the vic bites it from a weak heart."

His first rendition included 'our vic'. The second time he replaced it with 'the vic'." He was mentally removing himself from the case.

"Any news from your forensics guys?"

"No. It'll take them a few days. We're swamped over

here. And I just got a new case. This Kirschner will have to wait."

Better to still play nice. "I've got a copy of the Alexa audio recording."

"What the fuck? How did you do that?"

She held up the UBS stick. "I think you'll find the recording helpful."

"Jesus Christ."

"You able to talk to the family?"

"Yeah, I spoke to the mother. Dead end. No pun intended."

"I noticed surveillance cameras in a couple of the shops across the street."

"It's not that easy."

"Listen, Traister, I know all about DAS." The 'Domain Awareness System,' a public private partnership with tech companies to the tune of $230 million that accessed 6,000 citywide cameras, one third police devices and the others that private businesses provide access to the NYPD. "I also know your precinct has a pilot. So, don't give me this bullshit. We are, believe it or not, on the same team."

He pointed a finger at her. "Special Agent Walker, I don't need you running point on this. This is a NYPD, not FBI, case. You got it?"

"Listen, you need to get over to his work at Business News. Go in with a warrant and get Ben's communications going back two months. The motive will be in there."

"I'm busy." He sat back, glared at her. "Wait, why don't you do that? You got official sanction to be sniffing around in this case, Special Agent Walker?"

She stood. They were done here. "I'm just trying to find out who wanted Ben Kirschner dead."

"Robbery homicide."

"So you said."

He grunted.

"If you're wrong, you're letting the perp walk away."

He grunted again.

"It's a small town, Traister."

"Too small, if you ask me." He crossed his arms. "I'd have thought you would have learned to be a bit more respectful with the NYPD. To not raise a ruckus. Being Stewart Walker's kid, and all."

Her chest clenched and she held a blank face.

He nodded. "Oh yeah, I know who you are."

In her mind, her father whispered, *Don't take the bait. No ignorant two-bit bully is gonna scare my Dom*

"Huh. That's interesting. A bully aiming for what he thinks is a weak spot. So predictable. You're gonna have to find a better stickler than that old, tired refrain, Traister."

He glowered at her.

"While you're slow-walking this case, I'll be out finding evidence. Call me if you want any help." She turned and strode out.

Chapter Seventeen

Inside the Javits Building, five blocks south of Chinatown, Owen Whyte pushed back his chair, stood, and rolled his shoulders. He had been staring at his computer for five hours straight, working on the case for Assistant US Attorney Abigail Harris that was going to trial on Monday.

A small-time, Harlem-based mob accountant had been caught red-handed because the money trail was straight forward. The deposits, withdrawals, and transfers were crooked. Abigail Harris just needed to stick to the evidence and the movement of money. For a forensic accountant in the Financial Crimes Section of the Criminal Investigations Division (CID) it was the classic method of 'cleaning money' that he'd studied in business at the University of Maryland.

Since 99 percent of his work as the lead financial crimes investigator had already been completed, he just needed to triple-check the numbers. But twenty minutes ago, he'd lost concentration.

Owen could feel the signals firing across fibers from the

deltoids to the trapezius and he knew the muscle tension was only going to get worse if he didn't get to the gym. Pronto. He grabbed his gym bag from the floor and headed out the door.

Outside, the air was crisp coming off the southern tip of Manhattan. He breathed in deeply to fill his lungs and pump up his heartbeat. He needed the cardio work to begin even before he hit the gym because he was aiming for a ten-mile jog on the treadmill at 7:30 minutes per mile. It was about what he needed to clear his head.

It wasn't the Harlem accountant case that had distracted him. Thirty minutes earlier, a note had pinged into his email inbox from the guys in the FBI's social media group that used Dataminr to screen keywords. The email's cover note had read, *This cropped up in our keywords for SAR and Manhattan. Forwarding as an FYI.*

Below the note had been a link to a Twitter post and Owen had clicked it open.

It read, *Anyone know anything about SAR file number AA94593?*

Alone in his office, he'd let out a small whistle.

Owen Whyte had seen hundreds of Suspicious Activity Reports, otherwise called SARs, in his ten years with the Bureau, particularly with the cases he had worked on for the Southern District of New York's Attorney Office of Complex Frauds and Cybercrime Unit. SARs were lodged by financial institutions when they believed transactions were suspect. In general, a frontline staff person would notice something fishy, report it up to a bank's compliance officer, who would submit a SAR. The bank would not inform the client that a SAR had been referred to law enforcement.

Who was posting a SAR number on Twitter? Owen hovered

his mouse over the Twitter profile of one Ben Kirschner, who appeared to be a reporter at Business News. Owen opened up the Business News website and skimmed Kirschner's backlog of articles. By the looks of it, Kirschner was a savvy financial reporter.

Owen clicked back to the Twitter post, his mind racing. *Why was a legit reporter putting a SAR number on Twitter?*

He clicked open the screen for the Treasury Department's Financial Crimes Enforcement Network, also known as FINCEN. FINCEN was made up of 147 nationally-based financial intelligence units. FINCEN's purpose was to enable those law enforcement agencies, including the FBI, DEA, ATF, IRS and Secret Service, to 'follow the money' to combat illicit financial transactions. Owen logged in his user credentials and requested a report on *AA94593*. It would take a few hours, maybe a day, for FINCEN to respond. He had closed the site. But by that time, his shoulders had tensed beyond what could reasonably be called comfortable.

The low-rent, scrappy gym was on the third floor of a commercial building a block from Javits and the third one he'd tried this year. Much of the weight-lifting equipment was old, but the treadmills had recently been upgraded. No more jumpy bands and spotty speeds.

He flashed his membership card at reception and headed to the tepid men's locker room. He threw open the grated door of an empty locker, stripped from his work attire, and pulled on his running gear.

On the treadmill, he stretched his calves and quads and punched his goal and speed. The band picked up speed and soon he settled into a solid jog.

The last thing he needed was to get sidetracked from the Harlem accountant case three days before the trial. But why was a savvy financial reporter for Business News putting a SAR number on a freaking Twitter feed?

Owen jacked up the speed on the treadmill.

Chapter Eighteen

Melanie Ludrow answered the door to the Brooklyn Heights townhouse with a quick jerk. She was tiny, maybe 5'2", slender with large breasts, dark shoulder-length hair, and long red nails. Her eyes were wide against pale skin.

"Ms. Ludrow. I'm Special Agent Domini Walker. We spoke on the phone."

"Yes, yes. Come on in," she said, leading Dom into the living room. "I can't believe this. It's crazy."

It was unusual for a twenty-something to own a townhouse in Brooklyn Heights. "This your place?"

"I share it with some roommates. One of their parents owns it."

The living room was bright. Old, mismatched couches gave it a college feel.

"Thanks for seeing me," Dom said as they sat.

"Yeah. Of course. Just not sure I can help you. Ben and I—" She coughed to clear her throat. "Sorry, I just am having a tough time believing all this."

"I know. Death is never easy."

Melanie picked at cuticles. "What happened?"

It was a very common question. It was, interestingly, almost never asked by a perp. "We're not exactly sure. There was an intruder. Ben died in his bedroom behind a closed door."

Melanie looked confused. "What does that mean?"

"We're waiting on the official report, but it appears he may have died from a heart attack. Possibly instigated by the intrusion."

"Jeez." She shook her head.

"Just a few questions."

"Of course."

"When was the last time you saw Ben?"

"Six months ago. I remember 'cause it was two days after my birthday."

Dom encouraged her with a nod.

"He and I went to dinner on my birthday and we had an uncomfortable night. It was clear to both of us that we weren't going to work out as a couple."

"How long had you been dating?"

"About three months. We went out, I'd say, once or twice a week. To dinner. To drinks. Met friends at parties. We went to a comedy club once. Just hanging out."

"Did you like him?"

She looked away, collecting memories. "He was ok, nice. But just not special... to me. I mean, in the end, I thought someone would be happy to date him. But I found him kinda boring, dry, snobby... I dunno. He didn't knock my socks off in any way."

"Were you intimate?"

"As in, did we sleep together?"

"Yes."

Melanie blushed. "We fooled around but never actually

had sex. We probably should have, but he worked a lot. When we did catch up, he always had to go back to work or had to be up early, so he went home. I was fine with that, to be honest, 'cause I didn't really know how I felt about him. Three months was probably longer than I should have stuck around, but dating in New York ain't easy. When you meet a fairly normal guy with a good job, you try it out."

Melanie's demeanor was embarrassed but open. She was dissembling. The story she had presented was real. This woman was in no way a suspect. But she could be a source of good intel. "Can you describe him? Adjectives can be very helpful."

"Workaholic. I mean he worked *all* the time. Ambitious. Smart. Persistent. He would drill into a topic. We'd have discussions and if he disagreed with me or thought differently, he really dug in, trying to identify the reasons we didn't agree. Very dogged. Yeah, dogged. Otherwise bland. Didn't talk about movies or books. Didn't talk about much outside of his financial reporting, which, if I'm honest, kinda bored me."

"Do you remember anything about his work that he mentioned?"

"Not really. Just that he was chasing down a lead."

A lead? What lead? "Any more on that?"

"I mean, he'd be excited 'cause he'd learned something new that day, and he'd want to get back at it. Like uncovering a mystery or something. Yeah, when he was deep in research on someone, he got very excited about it and wouldn't let it go until the article was published."

"Any in particular that you remember?"

She looked to the ceiling, then shook her head. "Not really. Nothing specific."

Rats. What about anything that could tie to someone

with a personal motive? "Did he mention other people he dated?"

"Now that you ask, no. I remember asking him about old girlfriends and he said there were none."

"Did you get a sense that he was into anything kinky? I know that sounds out of left field, but it's a thing."

She lowered her chin, speaking quietly. "No. And can I tell you something?"

"Sure."

"I kinda got the sense from him that sex wasn't too important."

"As in, he wasn't pushing for it?"

"At all. It struck me as slightly odd. Most guys push for it all the time. And the times we did fool around, he wasn't all that into it."

No sexual motive there. "Do you think he was gay or asexual?"

"Nah, I didn't get that. Just that he was...uninterested."

Another dead end. This case was going nowhere fast.

Melanie continued, "At first, I wondered what was wrong with me. You know, like maybe there was something about me that he could tell wasn't the best?"

Dom nodded. It was a feeling most women knew. A bit too well.

"One time he slipped and said he thought the books I read were too light." She tilted her head. "I mean, super superior or what? It took me a bit to realize he wasn't the guy I wanted." She shook her head. "I'm way overanalyzing a three-month dating scenario, but I dunno, sometimes these guys—some are better on your psyche than others. Some just really can destroy you with a comment."

Oh, yes, Dom knew that too.

Melanie shook her head. "But still. I can't believe he's gone. Holy shit."

Definitely a dead end. Dom rose and shook Melanie's hand. "Thanks for this. It gives me some color to go on."

"Really?"

"Sure. You never know what will be helpful later in an investigation."

The word hung in the air.

Melanie blinked. "I hope you find out why this happened to him."

The smell of oil and gas was thick in the quiet car. Melanie was right about one thing; some guys were better on the psyche than others. Even Ben—the boring, superior workaholic who didn't know how to treat a woman well—had at least dated recently.

Her senior year in high school, she'd been sitting at lunch with a study partner when someone had invited them to an afternoon party at an unchaperoned house. Dom hadn't been to many parties. She'd spent much of her time at home with Beecher.

At the party, one of the athletic boys had cornered her in the kitchen. He'd been on the basketball team. His blue eyes had made her heart flutter. "You got a boyfriend?"

She'd stood mutely.

"I mean, you seeing anyone?" he'd asked.

She'd shaken her head.

"Why not?"

She'd shrugged.

"You don't talk much."

"I do when I have something to say." It came out sarcastic, snarky. *Why had she said that? It hadn't even made sense.* She'd cleared her throat against a thumping heart.

"So do you *want* a boyfriend?"

"Not sure how to answer that." It had exploded into the quiet room like an insult. As if she didn't want *him* as a boyfriend. *Where had that come from?*

He'd reared back. Blinked. Snorted. "I guess nobody wants you anyway. You might have suicide DNA."

Dom's cell phone buzzed.

It was Viv calling. "I found something in Ben's notes. He wrote, *Longwood Manor, Tuesday.* I found two such places in the US.

"The first is a huge building in Nebraska that looks like a cheap man's castle – two round turrets, a fake balcony, and a moat. I am not even kidding – it has a moat. It was built by a manufacturing tycoon in 1960. He died in 1991 and his family sold the house to the local government, which turned it into a museum. But ignore the Nebraska castle. That's not the Longwood Manor we're looking for.

"The twelve-story Victorian apartment building on the Upper West Side … well, that just may be what Ben was researching. In the photos, it's a lovely building. And Ben's co-writer, Trevor, said something about Tuesday nights being weird. And of course—"

"Today is Tuesday." Dom spoke quickly. "I'm on my way to you."

Chapter Nineteen

Dom stared at Viv. "No. This isn't a game—"

"No pun intended."

They'd been arguing for the last ten minutes. Viv had been relentless.

Finally, Dom had attempted to end the conversation. "Viv, you are not thinking through the seriousness of your proposal. You could get very, very hurt. You're not going anywhere. We're not discussing this anymore."

"I *am* thinking it through. I've just come to a different conclusion than you." Viv sighed. "I think we need to see for ourselves what creepy shit is going on up in Longwood Manor. We need to waltz right in and look for ourselves. I get that you want to be all 'big sister' and protect me, but I highly doubt there will be anything dangerous going on. I'm pretty sure the worst we're gonna find is a bunch of people having sex. I'm an investigative journalist, for crying out loud. I do this for a living. Two sets of eyes, one of them more intimately involved, is better than one."

Dom was losing the battle. "You are not coming."

Viv's head dropped and she whispered, "You have to let me help find who did this to him."

Dom relented with a nod. *Mrs. Preston was gonna kill me.*

Viv beamed. "Really?"

"Don't make me regret it."

"Definitely. I won't." She eyed Dom's outfit. "Let me get you something to wear."

Confused, Dom glanced down at her jeans and the white button-down shirt.

Viv pulled a face. "You can't wear that to whatever sex club or swingers bunker this place is. You're screaming law enforcement."

Dom's mouth dropped open.

"No, seriously, you can't wear that." She waved Dom into the bedroom, opened her closet, pulled out a red silk top, and held it up. "This is the best I can do with those jeans."

Dom smashed her lips shut.

Viv turned back to the closet, rummaging around in her shoe collection. "I talked to Beecher."

Good. Beecher was a good listener. Maybe he'd convince her to let this case go.

"He said something about your mom coming to town." Viv peeked a look over her shoulder.

Uh-oh. "Apparently she is."

Viv returned to pushing through the pile of shoes. "How do you feel about that?"

Here we go. "I don't."

"You don't feel?"

"No."

"Nothing?"

"Nope."

"Huh, that's weird. Most humans would feel things about long-disappeared mothers resurfacing."

I'm not like most humans. I'm a goddamned FBI agent on a case. Dom stood silently holding the red shirt.

Viv pushed some shoes between her knees. "I wonder if that comes with the training they give you guys down at Quantico? They teach you to not have human emotions?"

Maybe. Dom's jaw tightened.

"Like fear." She pushed a pair of brown pumps out from the closet. "Or anger." She set out shiny gold sandals with a two-inch heel. "Or maybe even some sadness that's since morphed into deep-seated loneliness." She turned on her knees, sat back on her haunches, and set down a pair of suede red boots with a one-inch heel. "Because most people do have that. A deep-seated sense of loneliness. It's actually in our DNA. And if someone lost both their parents in their formative years, that person probably would have an elevated sense of loneliness. I'm not saying abnormal, because, really, is there really a normal? Just more like they would have that extra depth of loneliness."

Surely, Dom thought, any judge would consider gently placed duct tape over a journalist's mouth as, at most, third-degree assault. *Only a misdemeanor in New York City.*

Viv set the boots down in the middle of the rug. "These will fit. The heels aren't too high. And, can I just say, that they're the perfect red for that shirt? Now, that shirt is pretty silky. Let me see what bra you're wearing."

Dom turned and walked from the bedroom.

Viv yelled behind her. "Your bad-bra-through-shirt-situation could out us with the swingers!"

An hour later, they walked silently through the double doors of Longwood Manor. A red carpet ran the length of the lobby, over marble floors and under a brass chandelier hanging from a twenty-foot-high ceiling. At the far end, a small marble desk was manned by a tiny doorman in uniform.

In the sports car screaming through the city's streets, Viv had worked out their plan of attack. Their cover was that they were a couple. Viv would do the talking. If things got dicey, one or the other would grab the other's hand and pretend to be uncomfortable. That was their signal to get out. Their safe word, so to speak, said Viv.

Viv smiled flirtatiously at the doorman. "Hi."

Dom stood stiffly behind her.

He hadn't warmed to her. "How can I help you?"

"We're supposed to meet friends here tonight." Viv dropped her chin to her neck, looking up at him conspiratorially. "A special meeting."

Damn it, she was good at this undercover work.

He waited.

"They told me to say 'Butler.' "

"Yes, a butler can assist you," he replied.

Viv smiled widely. Ben's notes on the code phrases were correct. "If you know what to ask of them, they can indeed."

He smiled and pulled out a large leather-bound book from below the desk. "I'll need your names and $50 each for membership."

Good lord. Kinky sex wasn't cheap. Dom reached into the red handbag Viv had lent her.

His eyes followed her hand.

She pulled out two fifty-dollar bills and placed them on the marble.

He nodded to the book and they both signed fake names.

"This way." He led them down the long hallway. Near the end, he stopped and pushed slightly on the wall and a hidden door creaked open. "Enjoy."

Viv tapped Dom's back and they stepped into the gloom.

Chapter Twenty

During the day, Bern had gotten three coffees, one at 10 A.M., one at 1 P.M., and the third at 4 P.M. She knew the caffeine would delay the hunger, which allowed her to eat the lunch her mother had packed – a turkey sandwich with mayo, crackers, and an apple – at 3 P.M. If she was going to stay late, she had to stretch out the food for most of the day. Executive assistants didn't make a lot of money and buying lunch in midtown New York City was a rare luxury.

When Bern had first gotten the job as the Executive Assistant to Sonal Kumar, Chief Human Resources Officer, they had mistakenly given her access to all of the computerized systems, but it wasn't until recently that she had innocently begun to explore. To her surprise, she had access to a huge amount of data about the entire employee population: compensation figures, salary reviews, performance reviews, promotions, redundancy plans, and hiring and firing processes. It was a dizzying amount of confidential, and surely very restricted, information.

When she had discovered the mistaken access, she had decided to not raise the alarm. Surely, they would find the mistake and lock her out. Soon enough. Until then she would claim ignorance. But six months had gone by and no one had noticed. Then a month ago, as she'd been sneakily sniffing around, she had discovered the cache of files in a folder titled *Diversity*.

Her stomach growled. It was now 9 P.M. The third floor was empty and the lights were low, timed with the workday. The exit light over the emergency door beamed brightly in red. Even though she had put on an extra sweater, she felt the chill of the air conditioner. They clearly set the temperature for the men in wool suits, not women in dresses.

She rubbed her hands together against the chill.

Like she had done three times since the discovery, she opened the folder *Diversity* and the subfolder titled *Sexual Harassment*. Over the last five years, women in the company had filed thirty-one cases of sexual harassment. In one case, a manager in Data Analytics had sent twenty harassing emails demanding blow jobs. An intern had been fired after reporting her boss for commenting on the size of her breasts. A manager in Product had failed to address a female's complaints that a colleague watched porn at work.

Bern had dug into the company's responses. In each of the cases, the company had paid out the complainant with a large sum as they walked them out the door.

One of the complaints she had read at least ten times. Sylvester Morgan, a manager in the R&D department, had exposed his penis to a Natasha late one worknight. Natasha reported, *"I was busy at my computer. My face was really at the screen. Sylvester approached me from the right. He was saying something about how his wife was going to be mad at him for working so late. There was no one else in the office. I was just kinda responding, yeah, yeah. I heard him coming closer. And he says, I guess I'll have to tell my wife no sex for her tonight. I remember it very, very clearly. I was typing when he said that. I stopped. Because what do you think when your boss says that to you? I was all of the sudden nervous because I knew by kinetic energy that he was standing over my right shoulder. It like tingled. My fingers were on the keyboard. I didn't turn around. I didn't know what to say. I didn't know what to do. He said, 'My wife is going to be very disappointed. I have a lot to give her.' I heard his zipper go down. I knew. I knew what he was doing. I had to turn. Of course, then I had to turn. His penis was right there. A foot from me. I stood up. Very fast. I walked away."*

Of the three times Bern had gotten into the system and read Natasha's account, it triggered a flashback. A huge shoulder slammed into her face, over and over, rammed her nose, battered her lips, pounded her eyes. Between heaving thrusts, her gasps for air were filled with talcum and menthol.

Her fingers shook over the mouse as she closed the file.

She had looked up Natasha in the system after the first peek. Her last day had been two months after the incident. She had gotten a year's worth of salary and a bonus. In the system, Natasha's departure was the result of *redundancy by a department merge*. Sylvester Morgan still ran R&D.

She took a deep breath and looked up and down the empty, dark floor. Tonight she would dig further into the files. She started with the file *Diversity Breakdowns*. The file was made up of spreadsheets that synced up to the top, overview table. The data sorted the entire employee population into five categories: gender, ethnicities, sexual orientation, veteran status, and disabilities. Columns calculated minority demographics across key categories such as Board composition and budget allocated to training. From a quick glance, she picked up that: 0 percent of the Board was diverse, only 1 percent of C-Suite and VPs were diverse and that only 10 percent of training budgets were spent on minority audiences.

Bern scanned the numbers in the overview table. While she wasn't an expert, these looked about right. There were only white men on the board. Her boss, Sonar Kumal, represented the only 'diverse' member of the C-Suite. Of the company's Vice Presidents, 99 percent of them were white males. Of staff that received training from the company, nearly 80 percent were male and white – either intentionally or as an unfortunate oversight. The company was heavily, heavily run by white men.

She closed the file and opened one titled *Diversity Compensation.*

This table showed promotions and pay raises over five years by the five key categories. Here the figures were also dramatically skewed in favor of white men. Of all the staff promoted in the last five years, only 3 percent had been women compared to 20 percent of men. A comparison of the same job bands showed that women were getting paid only 45 percent of their male counterparts. She knew from the news this was significantly less than the US pay gap of 78 percent.

This was really bad. The level of discrimination was off the charts.

She paused, her fingers hovering over her mouse.

The phrase 'off the charts' triggered a thought: what was the company reporting? Were they sharing these horribly discriminating numbers externally?

She clicked over to the company's website and opened

the Corporate Social Responsibility report. She scanned through the pages until she reached the section Diversity & Inclusion.

The lead paragraph read, *We take our commitment to diversity very seriously. 45 percent of our VPs are women and 35% are minorities.*

Bern leaned back. *Uh, no, no they weren't.*

The next paragraph read, *We spend an equal amount of our Human Capital Development budget creating careers through training and development for women and minorities.*

She whispered, "Uh, no, you definitely don't!"

The final line was equally false. *We are proud of the fact that we consistently promote equal numbers of women and minorities every year, our gender pay gap is nominal, and we continue to have very few complaints of gender discrimination.*

She stood and stretched, her mind racing across the implications. She wondered how many people knew the company lied about their diversity numbers? How many knew that they had simply paid off assault victims and promoted the assailants? How many people knew that the company was just flat-out unethical about anything to do with diversity? The company was just straight-up publicly lying about their numbers. Weren't there regulations and laws about that?

She wanted to report all of it. The misstatements in the reporting. The settlement. The blatant public cover-up. But what was she supposed to do about it? She was low gal on the totem pole in a huge corporation. She just didn't have the courage. Not yet.

At some point, IT security would figure out that Bernadette Hax, the EA to Sonal Kumar, shouldn't have access to these files. They would flick a switch in the back office and she wouldn't be able to see these files anymore.

Bern reached into her drawer, pulled out a thumb drive, slid it into her desktop, and copied the entire *Diversity* folder.

One foot in front of the other. Someday, when she was ready, she would find the courage to report these men running this company.

Chapter Twenty-One

The office on the thirtieth floor was a study in glass and chrome. In front of floor-to-ceiling windows over the dark city, a single glass slab sat on two chrome barrels. A slick silver keyboard and screen levitated on the shiny surface. Boss stood silently behind the desk, staring across a flickering nightscape, a bird's-eye view over the world's greatest city.

It was amazing what money could buy. A private school education in Greenwich. A college degree from Dartmouth. A business degree from Wharton. A familiar, entitled path led from wealthy beginnings to here, staring out over the city as if he owned it. But it was really just fucking dumb luck that kid got born into that rich family fifty-two years ago.

Richter stepped inside, let the glass door thud shut, and paused in the middle of the room on plush, white carpet.

Oh yeah, he knew all about this guy. He had done his homework. The whole fucking trajectory of a sheltered, upper-class life. There were three buried DUI's during

Boss's time in a private high school. During his time in the college fraternity with the other lily-white rich kids, there had been rumors of girlfriends who had gotten abortions. There was a photo from Wharton of the Boss, smiling next to a work of art from the business school library that he'd stolen on a dare. And now here he was, the CEO of a huge multinational. The perfectly preserved blonde wife in the big mansion in Old Greenwich and the sassy dark-haired mistress in the Soho apartment. Even the late-night gambling where he lost millions. So foreseeable. So expected.

Richter straightened his back and pain shot to his toes. "We've got a small issue."

Without turning, Boss asked, "How small?"

"Small. But it could metastasize."

"Why?"

"Others are sniffing around."

Boss turned. "I'm not liking where this is headed. What others?"

"There's a Fed sniffing around."

The pale, smooth skin grayed like a shroud. So unprepared for the real difficult stuff outside the bubble. These guys never expected their lives to go in any direction other than the one they commanded.

But that's not how life worked. Sometimes the entitled ones don't get to their destiny. Like Captain.

Richter shrugged. "I'm on it. You hired me to take care of issues. I'm taking care of it."

Boss narrowed his eyes before turning back to the window.

Richter turned and pushed through the glass door just as the flashback blew through his brain.

It had been a dark night over the minarets and the ricochet of bullets. The explosions up north blossomed neon green through night vision. The squad had held down the mechanic's shop for two days and had run out of MREs 12 hours ago. From below, he had recognized the loud voice of John O'Dore. It was always O'Dore stirring shit. A lumbering football player from Minnesota with a mean streak and zero common sense, O'Dore had constantly cursed and grumbled, and early in their tour, O'Dore had been the first to openly defy Captain.

Then John Martin, aka John-John, started hollering. John-John was slow to burn, but when he boiled it meant there was trouble.

Slap pulled back his rifle and slid along the roof. Reaching the door, he lowered himself into the second floor.

From below, O'Dore yelled, "That's it, you motherfucker! We're moving out. You're staying here."

Slap tiptoed across the wood floor and peered down into the open space.

The fourth grunt, Adam Morgenstein, kept a look out by the front door, his right hand holding the M4 angled up to his shoulder.

Captain tried to project authority, but there was a crack in his voice. "No. We're not. We're waiting for backup."

John-John yelled, "Fuck you. We're gonna die here."

O'Dore's Gerber flashed green as he pulled it from its sheath. O'Dore moved in two swift strides, grasped Captain by the jugular, spun him around, slammed him against his huge chest, and slashed the Gerber across his neck.

John-John yelped, "Fuck yes!"

Morgenstein returned his stare down the alley. Morgenstein always stayed out of trouble.

Slap sat down, his feet on the top step of the stairs, and slowly took off the night goggles.

Outside, five hundred yards out, a mortar round hit.

O'Dore looked up at him, "I'm sorry, Slappy, but it had to be done."

He shrugged.

O'Dore let the body slump to the floor.

The blood gurgled from Captain's wound, his lips spluttered, and his eyes darted across the room. Eventually, the eyes went still and life dissipated.

Chapter Twenty-Two

House music thumped down the dark hallway, bouncing off the walls. They moved in time, Dom slightly in front of Viv, toward an open doorway under a flickering red light.

Dom Walker had seen a lot. She knew human nature went bad. She had broken up a child sex trafficking ring. She had discovered an online retail store for young teen girls. She had chased down a husband who had kidnapped his wife and kept her in a box for a year. She tapped the Glock 17 in its holster on her belt under the red shirt. She wouldn't hesitate to drop a bullet into this ceiling to shut down any nonsense.

They stepped into a large room. Overhead lighting covered in red cast a scarlet glow across a small, empty dance floor circled by ten empty cocktail tables littered with flickering candles. Across the far side of the room, six red velour booths were arranged in groups. In one group, three couples dressed in work clothes sipped cocktails and spoke in hushed tones. It was early in the night.

To the right, behind a long, empty wooden bar, a bare-chested Caucasian male wearing an outsized dog collar chatted to three cocktail waitresses in skimpy maids outfits — one Caucasian, one Asian, one black.

Along the left wall a gorilla of a Caucasian male, arms crossed over a black suit, stood next to a pretty woman in a creamy, transparent latex dress on a barstool with a clipboard in her lap.

What's behind that door, my friends?

Dom led them to the bar and ordered a whiskey on the rocks with a soda back.

Viv nodded for the same.

Bare Chest set the drinks down. "You want to keep a tab open?"

Dom asked, "What else can go on that tab?"

"Your first time here?"

She nodded. "For both of us."

He shrugged. "You only pay drinks. Everything else is between consenting adults."

Dom sipped her drink, eyeing the room. "When does it fill up?"

"Not till late. Maybe another three hours?"

Viv set her drink down, leaning in conspiratorially. "How does it work?"

"The way any bar works. You chat with another couple."

"And then?"

"You go through that door."

"What if you want something specific?"

He shrugged again. He'd heard it all before. "Everything here is between consenting adults."

"But," Viv pushed, "how do we find similar interests… I mean, when it gets crowded?"

He nodded to the Asian maid. "Cassandra is good at introductions."

Viv grinned. "Got it."

They moved to an empty booth and sat facing the door and the long hallway.

As she sipped, Viv said, "Ben discovered this in the course of his work. Someone he was studying comes here."

"Agreed." Dom glanced at the Gorilla. "My bet is they take video of everything that goes on back there."

"So we wait, get a feel for the place." Viv leaned back, tried to relax. "I don't even want to think about what is mashed into this fabric."

Two couples laughing loudly, stumbled out of the hallway, weaved across the dance floor, and tumbled into a nearby booth. The Caucasian waitress approached and took orders. One of the women stood, gyrated to the music, and shoved a hand inside her skirt. The boyfriend laughed and pulled her back down on the seat.

Viv's voice came out low. "There's something I meant to call you about a while back."

This better not be about Esther.

"You know how I mentioned yesterday that I'd written some articles on the NYPD?"

Or her father. Dom nodded.

"One of the cases I researched… it had a lot of similarities to the Filthy Five."

Seriously? Now is not the time. "I'm not sure this is the right time to be discussing this."

"I think you should hear me out. I'm just providing a data point for you."

I don't need more data points. That's history. Stewart Walker and the Filthy Five had been arrested twenty years ago. *We all need to move forward.*

Viv said, "Ten years ago, out in Los Angeles, a rogue team of cops conspired together to steal evidence."

Jesus H.

"Money, drugs. Very similar to your dad's group. They were called the Die Hard crew because they loved the movie *Die Hard*. The whole John McClane character. There were four of them in the Die Hard crew."

Dom waited.

"In the end, two of the cops were jailed. They're still in jail."

"Ok?"

"Here's where it gets interesting. The two wives of both the guys in jail have been battling the courts. I interviewed them. They're totally convinced of their husbands' innocence."

Dom waited.

"At the end of my research, I concluded the wives were correct. I think Los Angeles Internal Affairs framed two innocent officers. But I didn't publish it because BuzzFeed's editors didn't think I had enough to go on."

"My father wasn't framed. He was at the scene surrounded by money and drugs. Charged. Indicted. Imprisoned."

Viv held up her hand. "Just giving you a data point. It's interesting is all I'm saying."

"OK."

From the long dark hallway, three men in dark bankers' suits stepped into the red glow. They scanned the area. The one in front nodded to the bartender before striding to the Gorilla, who swiftly held the door as they filed through.

Viv whispered, "Here we go."

"Tuesday regulars. Just on time."

Dom stood.

Viv hissed, "What are you doing?"

"Finding out what that's all about."

Dom headed to the side of the bar where Cassandra was staring vacantly into the room and rested on the other side. "Hey, those three guys in suits were hot."

"Oh yeah?" She seemed bored.

"Yeah, the ones who went right away into the back. Those banker types."

"Hmm."

"What's their story?"

"No story." Cassandra was good at ignoring the unbridled desires surrounding her.

Dom smile innocently. "I mean, we're here right? Aren't we supposed to be curious?"

"Sure."

"So can we go back there?" She gave a sexy wag of her eyebrows.

Cassandra gave her a warning look. "You don't want those guys."

"I don't?"

Bare Chest interrupted with a round of drinks. Cassandra took a moment to load them on her tray, then said, "Those guys never mingle. I don't recommend them."

"Never? So they're regulars?"

Cassandra ignored her as she swept past.

Back at the booth, Dom said, "Ok, let's go."

"What? Wait. Why?"

"I'd rather my next move be outside. This place gives me the creeps."

Viv jumped up. "You and me both."

Chapter Twenty-Three

Two hours later, the three bankers pushed into the night air outside the Longwood Manor building.

Dom touched the holster and pulled the sports car door handle. "Stay here," she said to Viv.

She straightened the FBI navy jacket over the red shirt and crossed the street.

The bankers looked spent and slightly drunk as they walked toward her on wobbly legs.

Dom stepped on the pavement and waited as the men approached. The leader slowed, his eyes glazed as he took her in.

"Gentlemen."

The bankers stopped in unison four feet in front of her.

She held up her badge. "FBI."

Three mouths dropped open.

"I've got a few questions for you. Please stand still."

The short one in the back leaned forward.

Don't do it.

Both his heels lifted off the cement.

Don't do it.

He leaned farther, his eyes charting a path to the right, around his friends and past her.

Seriously, you don't want to do that.

He lunged and took off at a full sprint, a wobbly blur as he passed his friends.

Dom stepped into his trajectory and pushed out her foot.

His right ankle hit her foot at speed.

She jacked her foot upward, yanking his foot behind while his mass continued forward, careening over his knees, both arms flailing.

She pulled back her foot.

He fell hard on both hands; his wrists gave out. With a thud, his chest crashed onto the cement, his chin bounced off the sidewalk, and he was still.

The leader sputtered. "Yo. You can't do that."

Dom cocked her head at the remaining two. "Do what?"

"You tripped him."

She ignored him. "Gentlemen. Like I said, I have a question. How was your regular Tuesday visit tonight?"

Both sets of eyes bulged, but their shoulders sagged.

Dom moved in close to the leader. "What's your name?"

"I need to see your badge."

"Sure." Dom held it for him to see under the streetlamp. "Special Agent Domini Walker. Take a photo if you'd like." She'd take the lumps from Fontaine later.

He pulled out his phone and took a photo with a smug glare.

She smiled. "Now *your* ID please."

"You don't have the authority to do that. You need a warrant."

"Clearly, you're not a lawyer. I have suspicion there has been a crime committed inside this establishment and I'm demanding your identification." She held out her hand.

He gnashed his teeth before pulling out his wallet and handing her his ID.

Matt Campbell, West 78th. She demanded the ID from the guy behind him. *Roger Abe. East 58th.*

"Well, Mr. Campbell and Mr. Abe, how was the club tonight?"

The banker on the ground groaned.

"What club?" Campbell resisted.

"The sex club in the Longwood Manor where there is surely a video of you idiots up in there. Very likely videos of a criminal nature. The least of which, I imagine, would be prostitution."

The two blanched.

Campbell rose to the occasion. "It's all consensual."

"You can tell that to the NYPD when they lock you up for the night."

He swallowed.

The banker on the ground rolled on his back and opened his eyes.

Dom leaned over him. "Do me a favor; stay down there for a bit." She looked back at the two. "Tell you what. I'll make this easy. I won't take you in, I won't file reports on you, if you cooperate with me tonight. None of you are actually of interest to me."

Campbell's chin jutted out. "What do you want to know?"

"What do you do inside the club?"

He hung his head for a moment, then said, "It's different every week."

"Sexual?"

He pulled a face that said *clearly, it's sexual*.

"With women?"

Both nodded quickly.

"How long has this been happening?"

"About a year."

"Any violence involved?"

Campbell shook his head slowly.

"Sometimes violence?"

He hung his head in defeat.

"Some rough stuff?"

He nodded.

"So not always consensual?"

He glanced away. "No. Not always."

"Which one of you set up Tuesday nights at Longwood?"

Campbell snapped his head up. "No one here."

"Then who?"

"We were approached separately. We all met here."

"Who approached you?"

"I don't know. He sends emails."

"What's his name?"

"Aristophanes." Campbell held up his phone. "I've got an email here. About tonight."

"Forward it to me." She gave him her email address, then leaned over the banker on the ground. "You can get up now." When her phone vibrated, she said, "I'm gonna let you go with a warning. Block this guy Aristophanes. Don't come back here. The FBI is up on this place."

Viv's apartment was dark. She hit the lights and headed for the kitchen. "You want a drink?"

Dom replied, "No, thanks."

Viv pulled down a bottle of gin from above the refrigerator, clinked ice cubes into a tumbler, and added the gin.

"Aristophanes doesn't strike me as a dumb person. I'll take the email to the techs tomorrow, see if they can trace it, but I doubt it."

From the refrigerator, Viv pulled out a bottle of soda and splashed the drink with it. "So, we have to draw him out. I've got a plan."

Dom glowered.

Viv took a long draw on the drink.

"No."

Viv smacked her lips.

"No."

Viv walked past her and dropped on to the couch. "It's a pretty straightforward plan. I publish some articles on BuzzFeed. They cover all the topics Ben was researching. I make sure to mention Ben's name. And I throw around the word *Aristophanes*. I mean, it's not the best plan. It's a bit of a long shot. But if this stalker is a professional and there is money behind him, then my bet is he's watching the internet. We hit all the words he's looking for – Peter Wilson, Jason Lui, Ben Kirschner, Aristophanes. Hopefully he sees one or more and slithers out." Viv took another slug. "But that's the best I've got at the moment."

Viv should have been scared. She should be terrified. But for the life of her, Dom hadn't seen any fear in this young woman over the last twenty-four hours. It was as if the death of Ben had made her audacious. And relentless. The combination was disconcerting. Dom had to keep an eye on her. She would never let anything happen to her.

It was a decent plan, actually. They would be searching down a number of rabbit holes, trying to find a connection.

But clearly there were problems with the plan. Dom settled in the armchair with a sigh. "Of course, we're not going to do that. You are not going to be bait for Ben's killer."

"Is the NYPD doing anything to catch him?".

Relentless rebel. Dom shook her head.

"Well, the longer nobody draws him out, the better the likelihood he'll get away with it. Them's the facts." She held the tumbler against her lower lip. "Dom, we can't just let him get away with it."

The traffic outside was thinning this late at night. In the distance, an ambulance wailed.

Dom scratched through her hair with fingernails. The concept of bait had merit, but it sure as fuck was not going to be Viv.

The room was silent.

Viv glanced up quickly, with hopeful eyes. "What if I use a pen name? At work?"

"Do you guys do that?"

"Not often, but I know others that have." Viv spoke rapidly. "I'll create a fake profile on BuzzFeed and pad it with some backdated stories. No one will know it's me. I'll get a throwaway email address at BuzzFeed. I'll get a cheap cell phone."

Dom stood and walked the room as a compromise solution formed. Fontaine was gonna have her hide. *Take the lumps later.* The compromise wasn't a hundred percent safe, but it would keep Dom between Viv and the killer. That was the most important aspect. By far. "I have a thought."

Viv waited.

"There's an apartment building up on Houston and Elizabeth. I know the super. I've helped him out in the past. They have a solid security system; both elevators are covered with cameras and the long hallways on each floor have their own cameras. I'll ask him if I can use a vacant apartment. I'll man the apartment."

Viv sat forward. "I'll plant that address online, so if someone does an internet search on the pen name, it will pop up. But it won't look like I put it there. We'll let the stalker feel like he's found me out."

"And we see who comes sniffing."

Viv grinned.

Dom pointed her finger at her. "You will stay far away from this."

"Far, far away." Viv cracked her knuckles. "I'll start drafting tonight. I'll get the articles published tomorrow."

"You set the virtual traps, but *I'll* be the physical bait."

Viv rolled her eyes. "Dom, I got it. I'm nowhere near this."

Chapter Twenty-Four

Thursday

Early mornings in the empty office floor were agreeable– no loud chatter, no phones ringing, no keyboards clacking. The quiet calmed Bern's bad nerves. Every once in a while, Rhonda, her therapist, suggested a new drug for anxiety, but she refused them, afraid to lose control of her mental capabilities. And after six months with this new job, she felt very accomplished. She'd made it this far. *From victim to survivor in tiny steps.*

She took another bite of the bagel and returned to her internet search. She had been reading about an ongoing court case around workplace gender discrimination. What did such cases look like? Had other big corporates been forced to pay out huge amounts to minorities if they had discriminated against them?

In one case, three women had filed a class action against a technology company for a clear pay disparity based on gender. They alleged women with the same job, title, and role were paid less than their male counterparts. If successful, the suit could cost the tech company over $100 million. A tech company spokeswoman had said, *"We focus on diversity and inclusion at every level every day. We want everyone to bring their full selves to work. We use rigorous methodology to ensure we're making decisions with the right focus on diversity. We refute these claims and will be vindicated in court."* One of the women plaintiffs had said, *"Of all the things I planned on doing in my career, I did not predict I would be considered the girl in the playground who cried too much. That's not who I am. I didn't go seeking this out."*

$100 million was a lot of mullah. Bern chewed the bagel. But the plaintiff's words rang true. Who seeks being a very public crybaby, who chooses to be a victim? The phantom smell of talcum and menthol filled her nostrils.

In another case, the plaintiff's lawyer sought $15 million in compensation and lost salary. The client, a senior woman at a large accounting firm, had been harassed by her boss. He 'loved her juicy ass' and repeatedly asked her on a date. She had lodged a formal complaint. While the firm had reassigned her and months later the harasser had been fired, she'd faced blowback: taunts and harassment from her new teammates. They'd gone so far as to sabotage her work in what was described as "retaliation, pure and simple." In the court documents, the woman said, *"I should have stayed silent. I lost my job and my career because I rejected one man who asked me out."*

$15 million. Again, a lot of money. Bern stopped chewing. Surely this was the reason her company was hiding the Human Resources numbers that very clearly outlined discrimination? Quiet settlements avoided courtroom drama, astronomical payouts, or publicity. Yes, that's what they were doing: hiding a dirty huge secret to save their own hides. But what about the victims? What about the women she had read about? They were silenced. They didn't have a chance to prove their innocence. And nobody chooses to be a victim.

She looked up to see her boss, Sonal Kumar, striding across the floor, his dark hair swept up over a high brow and dark intense eyes. She closed the websites as he neared her desk.

Never effusive, he nodded with an impassive look. "Good morning, Bernadette. You're in early."

She swallowed, couldn't bring herself to smile at this man in charge of systemically silencing women across the whole company. She whispered, "Good morning."

"I've got that presentation later this afternoon to the C-Suite. High priority. I need you to clean those slides. Also, I think you had better come with me and make sure the laptop is working. I don't want any tech glitches today."

She nodded quietly.

He strode into his office, hit the lights, and dropped his briefcase by the chair.

She imagined the conference room on the thirtieth floor. Chilled. At least ten men in suits, chatting and laughing. She visualized herself leaning over the table, hooking up wires to the laptop while the men watched her with critical eyes, inspecting and evaluating. The fabric of her shirt felt rough against suddenly raw skin, as her traitorous mind replayed the screech of ripping cotton.

She tossed the rest of the bagel in the trash can.

Chapter Twenty-Five

Owen Whyte hit "send" on the brief email to Abigail Harris. *"Everything is in order."* Finally, the Harlem accountant case was off his desk.

His phone rang just as he was going to take a nice, long, relaxed sip of his hot coffee. He knew who it was. Assistant US Attorney Abigail Harris was good at her job, probably because she was a pit bull. He picked it up. "Whyte."

Her condescending tone grated. "No reason I should be nervous about court on Monday?"

"Like I said in my note, you're good to go." In the two years he'd worked with her, he'd come to respect her laser sharp focus, but her people skills left a lot to be desired. A lot.

"You're confident?"

"I would not have signed off just now if I were not confident. My work is clean. The case is good. Follow the money, follow the evidence, you're solid."

"Ok." She was gone.

He cracked his neck and took that long sip just as his inbox pinged. It never got quiet around here. He pulled up the inbox. There was an email from Financial Crimes Enforcement Network, FINCEN. He clicked it open.

The email's cover note was the standard overview of his request. It included the original Suspicious Activity Report (SAR) number, AA94593, and that it had been filed by the Bank of Northern New York. Apparently, there were no other SARs in the FINCEN system in relation to this bank's particular client.

Owen clicked open the attached file and skimmed the paragraphs. Marquicio Moreno with account #12345678910 had been a bank customer for two years. The Bank of Northern New York did not have any identifying information on file about Mr. Moreno other than his social security number. The compliance officer in the bank had filed the SAR and noted, *Mr. Moreno's personal checking account was opened with an initial deposit of $10,000. Monthly deposits have been consistent, once a month, over the last two years of approximately $25,000.*

Owen whistled. This Moreno was on a fat salary, probably close to $400,000 a year after taxes and social security deductions. Shame he'd risk that for whatever he'd gotten flagged for.

However, in the last five months, his monthly deposits have increased significantly upward to $50,000. These payments are followed by immediate wire transfers of $10,000 to $15,000 to Bank Cainvest in the Cayman Islands to a single beneficiary, M. Moreno, account #381012345.

Owen blinked and read the paragraph again. Somebody had started paying out Moreno in big chunks, and Moreno had been moving those in smaller chunks to the Cayman

Island, a haven of sloshing dirty money. *My, my, my this was getting weird.*

He scrolled down through the SAR.

The volume and frequency of the deposits is not consistent with previous banking transactions conducted by Mr. Moreno. Specifically, the following activity has been observed. The compliance officer listed the deposits going back the last five months:

Deposits:
$51,000.00 (03/15)
$49,000.00 (04/18)
$52,000.00 (05/16)
$52,000.00 (06/17)
$48,000.00 (07/17)
$61,000.00 (08/15)

The compliance officer had also listed all the wire transfers to Bank Cainvest. The month of March alone accounted for four transfers:

$16,000.00 (03/16)
$14,000.00 (03/19)
$15,000.00 (03/21)
$13,500.00 (03/24)

Oh yeah, Moreno was moving money offshore. In increments he had hoped would go undetected.

Owen pulled up the National Crime Information Center database of criminal files and stolen property and typed *Marquicio Moreno* and hit "return". Nothing was returned. That meant Moreno was not associated with any missing guns, boats, or vehicles, or to any missing person, terrorist, fugitive, protective order, or sexual offender. If Moreno was a criminal, he was smart enough to not have been caught. Yet.

Owen picked up his phone and dialed Marty two floors

below with access to social security numbers. "Marty, I need to find someone."

"Hit me."

He relayed Moreno's social security number.

Through the phone, Owen could hear Marty banging on his keyboard. "Marquicio Moreno?"

"That's him."

"Not much. Looks like he was in the Army, 2002 thru 2004. Enlisted based on his pay. But then nothing through to two years ago when he started paying taxes." Marty was scanning what he had. "Looks like he is claiming to be self-employed. You let me know where I can get that gig. This cat is pulling in some big money. You'd have to pull the records from IRS to get his clients. That will take about a week if you're lucky… "

"A week?"

"Hold on." Through the line, more clicking. "I'm sending in a request to the IRS liaison office. I'll let you know what I find out. It's weird that your cat is a ghost for almost ten years after the Army. No income. Usually I see credit cards, credit scores, that kind of thing. Nothing here. So, he's off-grid for ten years, probably using cash. Your guy has made a concerted effort to be invisible to the authorities." There was a pause. "Wait. I've got something. He's listed an address here in the city on a social security database. I'm sending that to your email."

This mystery was getting weirder by the moment. "What's your gut feeling on this guy?"

"Uh. I'm feeling mercenary. Some stinky shit. He got out of the Army. Didn't get a job in the US. I'm guessing he signed up with one of those outfits, those security firms. They hire grunts and pay them in cash in whatever hell hole they send them to. All overseas. Not reported. Very sketchy, if you ask me."

Marty reviewed profiles of hundreds of people a day, so his instincts were legitimate. And extremely interesting. "Great, thanks, Marty."

"Just a hunch."

"But probably a good one."

Chapter Twenty-Six

The Javits Building was quiet before 7 A.M. Prime chaos was 7 P.M. after the evening news and arrest warrants or cases had been filed in the various offices. Dom made her way through the quiet cubicles to the desk in the far corner under the huge AC vent and set down two Styrofoam coffee cups and a brown paper bag with donuts.

Lea Peck looked up and a grin broke across her face. "My girl! Where have you been?"

Lea had worked with Dom on previous cases. They were close and their work styles balanced each other out. Dom gravitated to the action on the street while Lea was one of the finest young researchers in the NY office. She was confident, intelligent, quick on her feet, and exceptionally persistent. She could find a needle in a picture of a haystack. The younger black woman was also fiercely moral and loyal.

Dom settled into the cold chair by the desk. "You know, around. How you doing?"

Lea scooped up the coffee cup, ripped off the lid, and

took a deep inhale. "I cannot complain. I want to whine about this crazy-ass traffic, this fucking marathon, the gray fucking skies, and the fucking lack of men. Mostly about the lack of men. But I can*not* complain because my life is just too good. Really. And I have a hot-ass coffee in my double fist." She'd been raised by a Baptist minister father and an English teacher mother, which resulted in a rebellious curse words and sex talk embedded in a strong moral compass. Lea Peck was that rare animal: super-intelligent who just did not give a shit what others thought of her. At 5'10" with long braids, she was retained very bit of physical track-and-field star prowess she had earned at Louisiana State.

Dom picked up her coffee and grinned.

Lea blew on the coffee. "And you, my boss sister? What brings you in this fine gray fucking morning?"

"You know. I caught something. A mystery."

Lea sat straighter. "What? Without me?"

"It's unofficial."

Lea winked. "So says Fontaine, eh? That why you're down here? Plying me with coffee and filling me in on the case I'm not supposed to work on?"

Dom filled her in on the case. She ended with the story outside the Longwood Manor and Aristophanes' email.

Lea put out her hand. "Go on, then. Hit me."

Dom faked surprise.

Lea bounced her hand in the air. "Give it to me. You need me to trace that email, yes?"

"That's exactly what I need."

"But Fontaine's got you on some tight leash, so you can't officially ask me. I get it. I'll put it in under cover of this other case I'm working on."

Dom swiped open her phone and forwarded the Aristophanes email. "So, this is part of that official investigation you're working on…"

"That shibacle of a Russian restaurant over in Jersey City, obviously. The one that's money laundering for the crooks out of Cyprus. That one. Clearly."

Dom nodded vigorously. "Yes. That investigation."

"You want origin, account owner, what?"

"I want anything on that particular email and anything on the sender."

"Roger that." Lea's eyes scanned Dom's face. "You're doing this on personal days? Tell me why."

"Family-related."

Lea shook her head. "Those are the worst. But at least Fontaine likes your shit."

"So far we've had a mutually beneficial relationship."

"Because you solve his troublesome cases for him."

"And that."

"Girl, you've got a killer close rate. Makes his ass look stellar."

"I guess." Dom shrugged.

Lea licked her lips suggestively. "Speaking of stellar asses, how's my Beecher?"

Dom laughed. "Good. All good. His divorce is close to being finalized. It's a long time coming. They just didn't need to drag it out the way they did. Two relatively young people with not much to split up."

"Women. We're never easy."

Dom relaxed against the chair, sinking into easy banter. With Lea there was no reason to be restrained. "Normally, I would have agreed with that statement. It's easy to blame one person when the relationship falls apart. But, you know what, we all have our faults. We all can have our bad sides. Who knows what combination of weird mixology got involved in their relationship? I don't necessarily like her. I think she's a social climber and gold digger. But she was never shy about it. She told him from the get-go what her interests were: money and society. My brother just didn't want to admit that."

Lea rested her chin on her hand. "Special Agent Domini Walker. Look at you turning all philosophical on me. Will wonders never cease?"

"I'm rethinking stuff that in my twenties seemed black and white."

"Like what?"

Dom shrugged. "I was involved with a guy in my late twenties. It ended. No big deal."

Lea leaned back into her chair with a grin. "Hallelujah, now we get to the fun stuff."

Dom kept her personal life very personal. After Esther had left, she had learned in high school to keep their secrets safe. God forbid they take Beecher and put him in foster. But later, while attending college in the city, she'd let her guard down. She'd had two close friends. Denise now lived in Washington, D.C. and worked on Capitol Hill. Karen had moved out to L.A. and was a lawyer for a big corporate. Dom chatted with them by phone every few weeks. That was it. She wasn't one for chitchat about personal issues with other people. "No, seriously. It was no big deal."

"So I'm sitting here, minding my own business, and you ramble on up like you're on a Sunday stroll through the neighborhood, you hand me a quite fine cup of coffee, and then start chatting like we're in the salon. You had better start talking, sister."

Dom glanced at the ceiling. "We met at Quantico—"

Lea chortled. "Oh no, you didn't. A Bureau guy?"

"I know, right? First mistake."

"Everybody, and I mean, everybody knows not to shit where you eat. That's like life lesson 101. No, like life lesson 95."

"Look, I know. But who else are we supposed to date? At least they don't get scared of our lifestyle."

"My girl, you got this all wrong. You need to find a man who thinks this situation is the tits. Who thinks a smart, sassy baller of a hot-ass female is exactly what he needs in his life."

"Where are those guys?" It was a legitimate question.

"I'm working on my certified list of venues."

"Oh yeah? How are you making this list?"

"With the scientific method. Process of elimination. I visit and assess. Different neighborhoods, types of bars, time frames. I've got a nice old spreadsheet. Working my way through the city."

"Seriously?"

Lea wagged her head. "If I can track down some half rate mob guy out in Jersey City in twenty-four hours, I can sure as hell hone in on the prime locations of available men in this city."

"Wow. Uh, ok."

Lea pointed, "You could help!"

"I'm no wingman."

Lea sat back. "See, that's just what I'd expect you to say."

"What?"

"You need to let your hair down. You're all up in this J.O.B. You get on a case and you go full throttle. You don't sleep, you don't rest. It's definitely one of the reasons I look up to you."

Dom glanced away. Compliments made her uncomfortable.

"But you don't know how to relax." She pursed her lips. "Tell me about this guy from Quantico."

Dom crossed her arms. "My age. From Florida—"

"Oh, God help the baby lambs."

"No, seriously. He was a solid guy. When we finished training, we both got assigned up here."

"I've never heard any gossip about you with a dude up here." She wagged her eyebrows. "And trust me, a lot of these idiots have asked me about you."

Dom ignored the inference. "Yeah, we kept it quiet."

"What field office is he in now?"

"Sacramento."

"What happened when you got here in New York?"

"We were together for a year." Dom looked away.

"And?"

Exactly. And. The painful memory pushed through.

He had dropped heavily onto the barstool in a local wine bar. He'd rubbed his face. "I've gotta tell you something."

Her stomach gripped tightly and she had given him an awkward grin. "Please don't say you've cheated."

He'd closed his eyes. "I've cheated."

Even now, sitting in the office, she could feel the gut punch. She exhaled, looked at Lea. "He cheated on me."

"And him who dishonors you I will curse. Motherfucker. Genesis 12:3."

"Listen, I wasn't an angel. I worked a hell of a lot and wasn't available. This is what I was saying about Beecher's divorce. Everybody has a responsibility in a relationship. Fifty-fifty. It's up to each, to both, to get healthy or get out." She swallowed. "Anyway, I walked. He broke my trust. Never date a Bureau guy. Life lesson learned."

They sat in silence for a long while before Lea said

gently, "You know there's nothing wrong with you. You know that, right?"

Ouch. How could someone so young be so wise?

Lea reached out, grasping her wrist. "That's the past. You gotta dip your toe back in that water, honey."

Not just yet. Dom snorted. "I wouldn't know what the water looked like."

Lea's eyes widened. "Oh, lord, how long's it been?"

Oh God. "Since what?"

"Since you had some hot, sweaty, thumpy-bumby, jungle-gym sex?"

"So long I don't remember?"

"Since the FBI guy?"

"No. There have been some short flings."

"Oh, thank Baby Black Jesus." Lea grinned. "To prove to you that there is nothing wrong with you, I am officially recruiting you into the Dr. Peck Love Locator Inquiry. As a guinea pig." Lea tapped her flimsy coffee cup against Dom's.

"Oh no, you're not."

"Oh yes, I am." Lea swiveled to face her computer, set down her cup, and started clacking.

"Dear Tech Department. Please send me all you can find on this email. Thanks so much, I owe you, SOS Lea Peck." She hovered her finger over the *enter* key and peeked at Dom. "You are officially a lab rat in the Dr. Peck inquiry, yes?"

Dom laughed. It felt good. "All right, all right."

Lea hit the key.

Chapter Twenty-Seven

Viv had worked well past 3 A.M. the night before and her eyelids scratched as they opened. For a moment, her bed felt safe and warm. Then the memories of Ben's apartment rushed through her like a tsunami in horrifyingly high-definition colors, sounds and smells. The twang of the wine over the smashed bottle in the kitchen. The thumping of her heart as she slipped down the dark hallway. The heavy, horrible resistance of the bedroom door. Then a bright flash of Ben in the sun on the Washington Square Park bench, smiling at her.

Gnawing grief punched against the inside of her chest. She seized the cool sheet, rammed her knuckles into the mattress, stretched her mouth wide, and released a tortured silent scream against a distended neck. Relief was fleeting. She slackened against the bed and rolled on her side. For a long few moments she allowed the tears to fall unchecked.

She wiped her cheeks and her snot, pushed herself up, and shuffled into the kitchen. She powered up the coffee maker.

With a steaming mug, she sat at her desk and opened the laptop. Last night, she'd transferred all the photos she had taken of the most recent six months of Ben's notes, opened them, skimmed them, and arranged them in chronological order. Then she'd reread from the beginning.

He'd written in script using a personalized shorthand with brief commands and instructions for later research. He used dashes to set off a new set of ideas.

- Trevor, ask, research last year
- March 23, Wilson, PW, look up father
- PW first million?, find
- Jason Lui, JL, hiding wealth, dig

She had highlighted any note pertaining to Peter Wilson, PW, Jason Lui, or JL.

She took a deep sip of coffee. She would start with Peter Wilson, per Ben's instructions: *dig, lookup, find*.

Peter Wilson was #109 on Forbes' Wealthiest Americans. His hedge fund, Arabian Management, managed $12 billion in assets and outperformed its peers five years in a row. He made a killing by betting on distressed, even bankrupt, companies and stayed on those bets when the fainthearted would have sold – it was a strategy called "vulture fund." The general opinion of Wilson was that he'd made some unusually lucky investments around the time of the 2008 financial crisis that had built him a war chest. Commentators likened Peter Wilson's stubborn confidence to brass balls. Arabian Management had offices in midtown and all but one of its employees were white men. Peter Wilson was on his second wife, Pricilla, a former *Playboy* model, and had five sons, three from the first marriage, two from the second. He owned a small island in the Caribbean and loved to sail. One of Ben's notes read *Vanessa – contested – aggressive.*

Viv found an article about the first wife, Vanessa Wilson, in the society section of a gossip paper from the South Hamptons. The Wilsons' divorce had been acrimonious. During court proceedings, Vanessa had accused Peter of 'aggression, both verbal and physical.' In the end, Peter Wilson had paid her $10 million in alimony and $500,000 a year in child support.

The second wife was far less infamous. Originally from Brazil, Pricilla was fifteen years Peter Wilson's junior, a gorgeous black-haired beauty. The second time around, Peter had forced Pricilla into a prenup.

Nothing new there. Acrimonious first divorce. Billionaire. Prenup.

She rose and got a third coffee, her brain chewing on the seed of an article for the Aristophanes pen name that would hopefully enrage Mr. Peter Wilson.

Thirty minutes later, she reread the draft of a short, gossipy paragraph for the tabloid section of BuzzFeed.

New York Billionaires Shafting First Wives

There seems to be an illness among New York City's billionaire men. In the last ten years over twenty of our richest playboys have gotten divorced. That's not utterly surprising. 50% of all couples end up in divorce. But we mere mortals don't spend months contesting billions. And when that happens, it's almost always the first wife who loses. Let's take the example of one of our homegrown dilettantes. According to Business News *reporter Ben Kirschner, Mr. Peter Wilson of Arabian Management was valued at $12 billion at the time of his first divorce. But after much legal wrangling, he was able to make out only paying his first wife $10 million. That's a small portion of his net worth. That just doesn't seem fair. – Aristophanes Smith – taking on the system.*

She opened an email and sent the article to her editor. Time for the next one.

Chapter Twenty-Eight

At 9:30 A.M., the hallways of the New York University Law School building were quiet because most normal students were happily sleeping late. But Mila Pascale wasn't normal and she was fine with that. *Abnormal* also meant *exceptional*. No, Mila was excited to be in a deserted library all alone because she loved research. She loved discovering leads, chasing down new theories. She loved imagining she was close to an answer, only to find that she'd hit a dead end and was totally wrong. How exhilarating to have to reevaluate preconceived theories, backtrack, and find new paths.

Through the door with the frosted window that read *Center for Research in Crime* was a long, thin room crammed with full bookshelves that smelled of slowly disintegrating paper. At the nearest table, she set down her backpack, unzipped the top portion, where ten pens were neatly tucked, and slid out two. One always needed a spare pen. You never knew when one would fail, right in the middle of something very important, and you could lose your train of thought if you had to go retrieve a new pen. She slipped out a spiral notebook. Earlier, she had written on the front cover *"Stewart Walker: Research"* in thick black ink.

She breathed in deeply in the heavy silence. Mila loved the logic of research. What were the percentages that the answer was one or the other, and how to cross off possibilities in order to narrow those percentages? For example, last night she had started a new line of inquiry: what were the odds she could turn up a new witness in the Filthy Five case?

It had been a high-profile case in 1999. At the time, it didn't appear there were many defenders of the five cops. Many had assumed the cops had been dirty. From her research, she knew the local news had been incendiary. *"DIRTY COPS CAUGHT!" "FILTHY NYPD OFFICERS BUSTED."* It also appeared that many within the NYPD had assumed their guilt. The head of NYPD Internal Affairs, a guy named Dartanian Velk, had initiated the surveillance eight months prior to launching the sting operation. There hadn't been a lot of folks trying to find additional witnesses to help prove the suspects' innocence. She put her odds at finding a new witness at 50/50.

Last night, during her initial internet research, she identified stories in *the New York Post*, *the Village Voice*, *the Villager*, and *the East New Yorker*. The Center for Research in Crime library had hard copies of those papers only for the last ten years. She would have to use the microfiche machines.

But before she put the work away for the night, Mila had typed in *James Pascale*.

As the headlines scrolled past from 1999, she hit return.

His smiling, rabbit-tooth grin leaped from the screen above a *Brooklyn Times* article titled *A Ten-Year-Old Boy Missing*.

She was instantly catapulted back in time, watching

Jimmy's lanky legs spinning down the street toward the brick elementary school. In her mind, he had stopped at the corner, smiled up at the retired policeman in the bright orange vest, and turned to give Mila a goodbye wave.

He was last seen yesterday morning on his way to school.

She had waved back.

A search party has been combing the neighborhood.

Mila had crawled into Jimmy's bed and curled up with his ratty bear, Rugby. The lights from police cars blinked against the wall.

A reward has been offered by the family.

From the living room below, the wails of her mother had pierced through hushed, panic-stricken voices. Mila had slipped off and under the bed. LEGO pieces had dug into her skin. She'd plucked each piece, counting *one, two, three*. Her mother's wails turned to screams. With twenty-eight lost LEGO pieces, she'd slid tightly to the wall and begun placing them in a line. A straight, logical, orderly line. One. Two. Three.

The door to the NYU library opened with a rush of air.

She blinked, clicked out of *The Brooklyn Times* article, and typed in *Filthy Five*. I'm not searching for Jimmy, she thought. Yet.

She moved quietly down the center aisle toward the microfiche storage area.

She started with *the New York Post*. Of the three officers who had been acquitted – Robert Gessen, Art Dyson, and Mike Turner – she had discovered three new references. In a 1980 photo, a young Robert Gessen shook the hand of an older officer above a caption that read, *NYPD blue family.* Mila wondered if NYPD "family loyalty" or backroom deals had somehow spared Gessen from prison. The second photo was from 2000 and captured Mike Turner in a red hat dressed as Santa Claus handing out Christmas presents in a hospital's children's ward. She zoomed in the photo. His smile didn't reach his eyes. *I don't believe you. I don't believe you as Santa and I don't believe you weren't dirty.* Mike Turner had also turned up in a second article at a local NYPD baseball game played in Brooklyn and hosted by the law firm of Baker and Kemper. She jotted down the name of the law firm.

It was the microfiche search through *the Village* that turned up the goods. The fifth article was only two paragraphs long, but it mentioned that the Baker and Kemper lawyers had argued that their clients had been instructed to commit the crime by Stewart Walker, the more senior officer. Their clients were Gessen, Dyson, and Turner. All three of them. Belafonte had been represented by his brother, Antonio Belafonte. Did Belafonte trust his own brother over any other lawyer? That was probably good reasoning. The article noted that Walker's lawyer, Simon Bigg, had downplayed the more senior role of Walker, but, surprisingly, Bigg did not put up a lengthy defense of his client.

She sat back. Baker and Kemper represented the three officers who had been acquitted. No way was that a coincidence. And Stewart Walker's lawyer hadn't put up much of a fight.

She made a note and returned to the empty table and her book bag. She pulled out her laptop and looked up Simon Bigg of Myer and Bigg. Their home page described it as *a boutique firm established to provide legal services to its primary client, the New York Police Benevolent Association.* They represented individual police officers on administrative complaints, Civilian Complaint Review Board, Police

Department Trial Room, and Internal Affairs. Jayson Myer had retired, but the website said nothing about Simon Bigg.

How had Stewart Walker found this firm?

Something smelled illogical. Quite illogical.

She jotted down *Find Simon Bigg*.

Chapter Twenty-Nine

The executive floor of the building was a large stretch of beige and towering views of the New York City skyline. In the thick silence, the air conditioner was set very low. Bern's skin puckered and she pulled the sweater tight. Up ahead, a long reception desk dominated the center of the space. A young Latino woman with a slim headpiece watched her approach.

Bern's heels tapped loudly on the marble, making her feel awkward and clumsy.

The receptionist nodded. "Can I help you?"

"I am...uh..." The words caught. She started again. "I am here for the meeting. I'm the EA for Sonal Kumar."

"Last conference room on the right."

Bern cornered into the empty conference room. It smelled singed dust from the fans of tech equipment. She set her laptop at the end of the long table, reached into the cubbyhole in the middle, and pulled out wires.

A lanky IT tech with greasy hair and stubble appeared. "You setting up for the 3 P.M.?"

She nodded.

"You ever done this before?"

She shook her head.

He took over the setup, plugging in the laptop and testing the presentation on the huge screen. "There are three guys coming in via video conference. They'll be up there." He pointed to the huge television screen. "A couple will be dialing in and not on VC." He pointed to the speakerphones in the center of the table.

She nodded.

He checked a couple more items on the laptop. "Ok, you look good to go. Does your guy know how to click through the slides?"

"I think so."

He left her alone, cold, and anxious.

An excruciating fifteen minutes later, a man in a blue suit entered, glanced at her, and settled into a chair. He slid on reading glasses and opened a document. The lights glinted off his unusually slick hair.

She sat silently, awkwardly, at the table's far end.

A minute later, another white guy in a blue suit arrived and the two men chitchatted.

Sonal Kumar arrived and headed toward her. "Is it set up?"

She showed him how to walk through the slides. Four more men entered and sat around the table.

The VC screens lit up with three additional men.

Sonal said, "Ok, just sit by the door, and once my presentation is working, you can go."

The speakers on the table rang and Sonal pressed buttons.

A voice boomed. "Hi, all. Everyone here?"

Sonal Kumar leaned toward the star phone. "Yes, Malcolm, we're all here."

Malcolm. It must have been the Chief Operating Officer, COO, of their company.

Bern's throat constricted. The maleness of the room was overpowering.

The COO boomed, "Good, good. Thanks, Sonal. So, before we kick off with Sonal's presentation I just want to say, I've just got our third-quarter results in and we're looking very, very good."

All the men smiled.

Bern wondered how many of them knew about the discrimination in their ranks, the cover-ups, and the payouts? Had they been in a similar meetings, winking at each other and laughing about ethics?

The COO continued. "I'm glad to say our numbers are stellar. Well done, to all the teams. We're killing it. This firm is killing it."

Around the room, heads bobbed supportively. Literally, they were yes men.

She snuck a peek at the guy with the slick hair. *Did he know? Had he been part of the decision?*

The COO's voice was strong, confident. "Now, let's walk through the numbers."

A short, squat man at the end of the table in a pink button down shirt and a blue suit droned on about numbers. Returns, percentages. Her mind could not follow. *Did he know? Of course, he did. Did he care?*

She glanced over at Sonal. He was smiling that the

meeting was running well. *Definitely, her boss knew. He was in charge of the numbers.*

What would happen to Bern if she pushed up from her chair and yelled, "I know your secret!"

The thought sent her heart into overdrive and her bladder squeezed. If she urinated now, it would first be warm across her crotch, before it fanned out and soaked into the chair. Her throat constricted. Her bladder ached.

She jammed her nails into her wrists and imagined Rhonda the therapist speaking calmly. "Breathe, Bern, breathe. Count to ten." 1. 2. 3. The panic was beginning to recede. 4. 5. 6. 7. 8. Bern found her breath, felt her senses return to the room.

The COO picked back up. "I want you to know that this year's bonuses will be solid. I promise you. Can we talk about our expansion?"

A tall man with thin shoulders leaned forward. "Given the great numbers we've had over the last two years, we're moving forward on new hirings with a focus on North America. There will be thorough searches at all levels. As most of you know, the renovations on the twenty-fifth and twenty-sixth floors are proceeding on schedule."

The COO began to wind the meeting down. "Great, great work. Ok, Sonal. Over to you."

Sonal moved his hand to the laptop's mouse and clicked to the first slide. The screen lit up.

Bern leaned forward, ready to stand.

The slick-haired man held his finger in the air. "Sorry. Before we move to Sonal, have we heard anything about BAM?"

Everyone went quiet.

Sonal's eyes flicked nervously to Bern. He jerked his head for her to leave.

She stood and rushed from the room.

Chapter Thirty

Stepping from the shower, Viv heard her cell phone chiming in the living room. She made a mad dash and scooped it up. It was her editor, Emily. "Viv. We just got something. I'm sending it to you. Read it. I'll wait."

Emily hadn't questioned the plan to bait Ben's intruder. Emily. Always stand-up. A really solid person and a great editor.

"Hold on, Em." Hair dripping on her robe, Viv sat down at her laptop, opened Emily's email, and read.

Finch & Ludwig Lawyers
8 Park Avenue
New York, NY
Dear BuzzFeed,
It has come to our attention that you have published an article or similar that mentioned our client, Mr. Peter Wilson. This letter serves as notice that you are to cease and desist all harassing activities against Mr. Peter Wilson in the immediate. We believe you are infringing on his rights in terms of character assassination, slander, libel, and

defamation. Your actions are aggressive and unwanted. As a result of your harassment, Mr. Peter Wilson will suffer substantial harm to his reputation and business.
If you do not cease and desist the harassment, we will be forced to take appropriate legal action.
Sincerely, Talbot Sinclair

Viv grinned. "Interessante. Aristophanes Smith has hit Mr. Wilson's nerve."

"Keep going, but do it quick. If we get a second complaint about Aristophanes, our lawyers say they want to shut the pen name account down in twenty-four hours."

"Thanks, Emily!"

Next, she texted Dom. *We got a cease and desist on Peter Wilson article. I'm working on the second one on Jason Lui.*

She cracked her knuckles and watched for a third time the video she had found. On a dark stage, Jason Lui, dressed in black with red sneakers, stood in front of projected images of molecules and blood cells. A wireless mic looped around his ear and jutted out along his chin line. His bald head glinted in the spotlights. Walking back and forth the width of the stage, he gestured to the images overhead and spoke animatedly about applying information techniques to molecules as the image morphed into a snow-covered mountain.

He paused, looked out into the audience. "We're going to do this on a large scale."

Jason Lui's expertise was Bioinformatics – addressing biological problems with computational techniques. His company, BIOTECH, based outside Boston, had grown leaps and bounds with a recent breakthrough in proteomics and the study of proteins and disease. Recent articles discussed a rumor that the company would be receiving additional rounds of funding.

On stage, he had a lot to smile about. Jason Lui had a net worth of $500M.

For two hours, she had been looking on the internet for dirt. She had come up empty-handed.

Jason Lui's father had been a mailman and his mother had been a social worker. They still lived in Los Angeles, where he'd grown up. His girlfriend was an associate professor at Harvard in medical ethics. They had been together five years. They owned a big house outside Cambridge. He had recently completed the Boston Marathon. Overall, there was not a lot sketchy about this guy.

Viv blew out her cheeks in consternation. *Ben, what was dodgy about this guy?*

Maybe she was chasing down the wrong leads. Dom had cautioned that this early in investigation, they were most likely pulling at the wrong threads. She needed to get dressed and look at Ben's notebooks again. Maybe a fresh review would give a hint.

An hour later her eyes paused over one of Ben's notes.

- JL, check survey, Twitter

Twitter? Did Ben have a Twitter feed? How had she not caught that?

Her fingers flew over her keyboard, opening up her own Twitter feed, and typed in *Ben Kirschner.* The same photo he used at Business News flashed up on the screen. The grief pounded inside her chest, a repeat from this morning's pain. She swallowed, letting the feeling wash through her.

Under his photo was a brief profile. *Journalist covering financial and political. Deep dives to uncover truths. Media requests: pr@BusinessNews.com*

Tips: Ben.S@BusinessNews.com
Joined September 2008

Ben had joined Twitter in September 2008 and he had tweeted 2,745 times. He'd been following three hundred others, had 30,000 followers, and had 723 tweets others had liked. It was a very decent social media presence, although she knew BuzzFeed had millions of followers.

Some of BuzzFeed's reporters used social media religiously. Had Ben used his for research?

She scrolled slowly through Ben's timeline, skimming each 280-character tweet. Some of the concepts made sense. Others were more cryptic. She knew from experience it was difficult to encapsulate most subjects and opinions in so few words. Ben had started using threads to indicate a concept that was discussed over more than one tweet.

She jumped back in time on the feed to twelve months ago and started moving forward. Ben had been using Twitter for professional research and it didn't take her long to uncover something. Eight months ago, a tweet read, *Need some assistance from the Ben Army.*

Viv cocked her head. What was the Ben Army?

She continued to scroll along his timeline and began to understand. Using keywords as clues, he would instruct what he called Ben's Army of Citizen Journos to help him research a topic. Clicking through the Army's responses, it appeared that Ben had a small battalion of wannabe researchers and journalism students who helped him out. Once Ben's keywords and requests were posted, his Army linked in websites, photos, and other clues. It was an ingenious way to leverage virtual volunteers.

Viv cracked her knuckles. In the search bar, she typed in *Ben Kirschner Jason Lui.*

The result delivered five threads. She clicked open the first in which Ben had put out a request. *Ben Army: Background Jason Lui BIOTECH.*

His volunteers had not disappointed. Twenty responses filled in a very interesting picture of Jason and his company.

He started at Caltech. Got bad grades first three years. Last year he got straight As. Peers questioned.

Caltech senior year advisor invested in BIOTECH early. Real early. Made millions.

Senior Year Advisor at Caltech. I knew him. Sexist pig. Hates women.

I heard Lui had issues with authority.

Some of the tweets appeared to be garbage.

Lui is hawt.

A few had GIFs and moving pictures of molecules.

One tweet had a photo of Jason Lui next to an older white man with a white beard. The tweet read. *Advisor at Caltech.*

She found the bio of the Caltech advisor. His specialty was programming languages.

Viv skimmed other notables from Caltech. Almost all of them were white males.

The tension in the back of her neck was starting to throb. She stood, walked to the window.

She needed to quickly get out an article on Jason Lui with a plug on Ben. But other than some random Ben Army tweets about his Caltech luck, there was nothing substantial in terms of a scandal. She sensed Jason Lui wasn't responsible for the intruder. Call it intuition. She just needed something out there that was provocative enough to get Jason Lui's hackles up. She cracked her neck before moving back to the desk, sitting down, placing her fingers on her keyboard, and starting to type.

Sexism in Biotechnology Start-Ups

Are all scientists white older males? It appears so. A recent review of the hot new unicorns in biotechnology turned up a striking finding. Of the fifty new start-ups that have blown up in the last four years, all but one are run by white males in their thirties. This is either the result of the advantages they have in their educational background and professional lives or the very similar skin tone and sex of investors out of Silicon Valley. The only star who rises above this trend is BIOTECH's Jason Lui, as profiled by Ben Kirschner of Business News. A product of the Los Angeles public school system who got a scholarship to Caltech, where, by some accounts, he didn't do too well until he was taken under the wing of a very influential professor, who, funnily enough, happens to be white, male, and older. How on Earth are we to break this cycle when even the one breakthrough was aided by the inside track? Aristophanes Smith – taking on the system.

She sat back. Even for a quick, gossipy article, it wasn't a great. Lots of conceptual holes. But time was the issue here. It was enough.

She texted Emily. *"Next one is on its way."*

Almost immediately the pain in her shoulders dissipated. Good. She needed to keep moving. Ben's killer was still out there.

The Twitter feed blinked at her from the screen.

She knew a lot about what Ben had recently published. But she knew very little about what he'd been *planning* to publish. What if the killer had been threatened by something Ben had simply still been researching? Maybe something he'd asked the Ben Army to dig into, say in the last two months? Her fingertip brushed the mouse.

That goddamned killer was still out there.

Chapter Thirty-One

Retired NYPD Officer Roger Byles lived in Park Slope in Brooklyn. He'd bought the townhouse back in the 50s before Park Slope had become a nice neighborhood. It was three floors of original red brick with a much coveted covered front porch.

Old Roger had been an instructor at the police academy and had mentored Stewart Walker back in the day. He was stubborn but good-natured, and one of the most honest cops Dom knew. At Stewart's funeral, he had grabbed Dom and Beecher by the hands and walked them down the street. "You kids can always come to me. Your father was a good man, no matter what happened. You come find me if you ever have trouble."

Later, after Beecher had graduated high school, Dom had wondered if she should have relied more on Roger. Maybe in those early days she should have trusted him, admitted that Esther had abandoned them. But the lies, the facade, had come easy – the empty apartment, doing their own laundry, fixing their own meals. More importantly, the fear of the unknown had been a strong deterrent to reaching out.

As Dom stepped up the stairs to the porch, Lea's words from a few hours earlier buffeted her mind. *"You know there's nothing wrong with you. You know that, right?"* Maybe yes, maybe no.

Roger stepped out onto the porch, leaning heavily on a cane. He looked old, gray. His skin was looser. He smiled warmly and waved her up with a can of domestic beer. "I heard that car of Stewart's. That thing is loud."

They sat in matching rocking chairs.

"How you doing, Domini?"

"Good, good, Roger. How you doing?"

"Surviving. Had a great little league season."

"You still coaching?"

He snorted. "Officiate. I don't coach no more. I watch them young guns and tell 'em how to play ball the right way. And keep the rosters and score boards. Keeps me busy." He took a sip. "How's my boy Beecher?"

"He's good."

"Divorce is tough. He holding up?"

"Absolutely. I mean, it's all but over."

"Send my regards."

"For sure."

They looked out over the park, where every once in a while a leaf would fall.

He rocked the chair gently. "What can I do for you, Domini?"

"I've got a homicide case. It's unofficial. My boss is ok with me chasing it. But, here's the thing, I get this sense the NYPD is purposefully slow-rolling their investigation and I can't figure out why."

"What precinct?"

"Captain Wheeler's"

He took a sip. Said nothing for a long time.

She looked over. "You know him?"

"Sure. Captain Wheeler has a nice house on the Jersey Shore now. On the weekend he drives a Mercedes. Thinks people don't notice. But we notice. We're cops."

"Huh. What's that all about?"

"Senior guys are always playing it somehow, some way. They meet people, go to fancy parties, the Yankees, VIP boxes, the fundraisers. It's a whole new world when they get promoted up like that. Some can handle it. Some can't. Tell me about the case."

She filled him in on Ben Kirschner.

He rocked the chair. "Focus on the case. You can't fix Wheeler."

"But I need to know if I'm stepping on toes."

"The way you tell it, your hold-up is Detective Traister…"

"Exactly."

He tilted his beer. "Focus on the case. You can't fix Traister. Or Wheeler."

"Noted."

"On that sex club connection, go meet with Detective Fishman over in the 10th. He knows about that stuff."

That was what she'd needed. Good old Roger had the goods.

She stood, leaned over, and gave his neck a hug. She could feel the brittleness of his bones and the paper-thin quality of his skin.

He hugged her in return, whispering, "You're a good investigator, Domini. You're a good person."

Jeesh, what was with everybody trying to convince her of that lately?

Chapter Thirty-Two

Richter stepped out from the elevator onto the 26th floor. Across the cavernous space, sun streamed in from all sides. The workmen refitting the floor above wouldn't get down for another month and he had the quiet all to himself.

Outside, in Madison Square Park, all the white-bread office workers were flooding out for lunch. A pack of skinny girls in tight skirts crossed the park on their way for salads so they could watch the calories, to stay thin, to attract a banker or an entitled CEO, then pretend to like sex. Only missionary sex. Nothing dirty. Nothing painful.

Richter hadn't eaten in twelve hours, but he welcomed the hunger pangs because they distracted from his frayed nerves.

The conversation ten minutes ago with Boss about Vivienne Preston had not gone well.

Boss had stared hard, "Now there's a journalist sniffing around?"

Richter had nodded.

"How do you know?"

"I've got a data scraper on anything that hits the internet about Ben Kirschner or his recent research topics."

"And?"

He had a hacker get into BuzzFeed's network. It was an easy $10,000 to get Vivienne Preston's emails. "A reporter named Vivienne Preston at BuzzFeed is throwing out bait."

"What are you going to do about her?"

"I'm actively monitoring the situation."

"That sounds extremely passive."

"I don't think we want any more attention on this. Any action would garner attention."

Boss had walked around his desk, poured himself a drink. He hadn't offered Richter one. After taking a deep sip, he turned back. "I'm not going to lie. This sounds like it may be getting outside your control. We've got an FBI Agent and a reporter, both digging in. And you're actively monitoring. But taking no action."

He waited.

"I'm wondering if perhaps I have put too much faith in you, was blinded by your military credentials."

Richter stood like a good grunt taking orders. He needed to finish this contract, get the payout, which meant he needed to stay in good graces for another four weeks. Just one more month for the final payout. He cleared his throat. "OK. I'll take care of it."

"As in actively take care of it?" The Boss glared at him.

He wanted to punch him in the nose. Instead he nodded. One month.

Boss finished his drink, set the dainty crystal glass on the chrome shelf, and dismissed him, "Well, get on with it."

Upstairs on the empty floor, Richter stepped closer to the window, into the warmth of the sun, and stared beyond the park over the entire city. For a moment, he felt like an important man. A boss. A titan. Not an imposter. Not a security flunky. Not an enlisted grunt in the US Army whose squad had just killed a captain.

That morning, he'd found a brown nondescript envelope with Arabic stamps had arrived sometime in the last month at the old address in Jersey City. Inside was a short, handwritten note from O'Dore. *Slappy, we're in Yemen and killing it. The money is bananas. The Saudis paying us big time to chase insurgents. You gotta come out. I'll hook you up. PS. The girls here are total shut-ins. They go wild when you get them alone.*

In the mechanic's shop, the four of them had stripped Captain of identifying clothing. Richter volunteered to hide it up on the roof in a chimney. After, they donned night vision and headed south, away from the mortar, away from the helicopters, away from the US military offensive, and away from the life they had known.

An hour later they crossed the Fallujah Dam and followed the road south along the Euphrates River. With the pounding up in Fallujah, the road was dark and empty. Four hours later they took off from the road near Albu Huwa and walked slowly through the streets of a farming village as the sun rose in the east. All of the dilapidated houses – all the same fucking brown cinder blocks – were quiet. Word must have spread that a squad of Americans were creeping around.

They were exhausted and in need of food. Morgenstein chose the house at the end of a dead end, the drapes pulled across every window.

O'Dore knocked with a fist. "US military. Open up."

An older woman with deep creases cracked open the door and peered out.

O'Dore pushed in.

The woman stumbled back protectively in front of four

young children, two boys and two girls. There was no adult male. O'Dore made the sign for eating and the woman sent the children scurrying. After eating fruit and dry bread, John-John took first watch by the front window, his eye on the dirt road. They slept through the day in rotations as the enormity of their actions seeped into their cells.

Before sunset they brainstormed a rough plan. Morgenstein knew a guy who knew a guy based in Karbala. This guy had once revealed a system by which one of the officers in charge of financing local government work had been siphoning off millions via duffel bags and weekend trips into Kuwait. To further the pilfering, this officer provided loans at very high interest rates. They would sign up for a million-dollar loan, pay for papers, and cross into Kuwait. They would hire themselves out as a four-man squad for off-grid mercenary work for a year or two. By then the Army would have classified the squad as KIA, nobody would be looking for them, and they'd repay the debt and the exorbitant interest. It wasn't the safest plan, but it was the best they had.

The agreed plan started with a 30-hour trek through the desert toward Karbala.

They had taken off at nightfall.

Chapter Thirty-Three

Dom was dealing with NYPD more than normal. But the reception officer in the chaotic lobby of Precinct 10 was a woman and it was refreshing.

She flashed her badge. "Special Agent Dom Walker to speak with Detective Fishman."

The reception officer picked up the phone and dialed a number. "Fishman, there's a lovely young FBI agent here looking for you."

It wasn't a surprise that Detective Fishman was old. He could easily have been the same age as Roger Byles. He shuffled on tender feet. His neck was thick and his chin flabby. He grumbled as he approached. "What on Earth the Feds gotta do with me?"

She held out her hand. "Roger Byles sent me."

He examined her, as if trying to get a read. He eventually took her hand, gave it a firm shake. "Well, stop dilly-dallying. I got stuff to do. Come on back."

The reception officer grinned to herself.

He shuffled through the door. "I've got rotgut coffee or rotgut coffee."

"That'll be fine. Thanks."

He chose the center interview room, gray and functional with bright fluorescent light. There were chips in the paint that had been painted over at least a hundred times, and she wondered if Fishman had been here for each refresh. The coffee was indeed toxic.

He lowered himself into the seat as if with a great deal of pain. "How you know Roger?"

"He and my old man worked together."

He eyed her. "Who's your father?"

Her chest clenched with the moment of truth. In her mind, her father whispered, *I'm sorry, my Dom. I'm sorry.* She said, "Stewart Walker."

Most old-timers knew of the Filthy Five. The normal reaction was a slow, sad nod, a mix of NYPD pride and shared shame, as if the law enforcement tribe understood the honorable FBI daughter was making up for the wayward NYPD father to redeem the family name, like some tragic Grimm fairytale.

He raised his eyebrows for a split second. "Ah. Shame about your father."

She simply nodded, having learned over the years it was best to say nothing. Stewart Walker whispered again, a faint murmur from another room, *I'm so sorry, my Dom. For so many reasons.*

Fishman's voice was gentle. "What do you need, missy?"

She cleared her throat. "I've got a case that may involve a sex club here in the city and Roger said you're the specialist."

"Which club?"

"Longwood Manor…"

"Sure, uptown. The case, what Precinct did it land in?"

"7th."

"Ah, Wheeler. He helping you?"

She gave him a doubtful look.

"Right, right, of course not." He had a quick mind for an old-timer.

"What do I need to know about Longwood Manor other than the obvious? High-end. Wealthy clientele. Decent security and secrecy."

"It's been around for a while. Nothing too dark. They cater to rich folks, mostly. Once in a while, I get a request to check it out, but it's from wives who need a PI. I send them to some private guys I know. Longwood is not an NYPD issue. I leave it be. I got plenty of other cockroach dens I gotta deal with, you know what I'm saying?"

"Who owns it?"

"We don't know. It's tied up in front companies like lots of these places. But the guy who runs it is legit. Small guy. Gay if you believe it. Not sure why he doesn't run a gay club. Maybe this way it keeps his hands out of the till. Who knows why people do what they do, am I right? He calls himself the manager."

Unlike Roger, who seemed outdated, Fishman was very current. Maybe staying on the job well past retirement was a good idea.

"You mind if I go chat with him?" Dom asked.

He frowned with indecision. "Tell me what you got. He's one of my regulars. Informant, whatnot."

She told him about the case and Ben Kirschner's research on prominent men.

He pulled out his phone, swiping the screen for his contacts. "I can see somebody going on up there and getting outed by a reporter. Sure. That fits. It's a nice enough place to actually be of interest. Likely some dodgy shit in private. His name is Pinocle. The manager. Give me your cell number and I'll send you his card."

She gave him her number. "Pinocle?"

"Just a name, missy. Don't get all funny about it. Just tell him I sent you. He knows I'm a clean shooter. But don't expect him to give up his clients. He runs a pretty tight business."

Other than the prostitution and possible violence against those women. "Tight business as in nothing illegal?"

"Didn't say that. Just saying it's not important enough to bust him."

Abusing women wasn't important enough. Anger flared, but she pushed it down. No time for that now. Her phone vibrated with the contact info. A retirement-age NYPD detective had just sent her the contact info for a sex club manager from his cell phone. Times were certainly changing. But not fast enough. She rose. "Thanks, Detective."

"How is Roger?"

"Good. Coaching baseball. Seems content."

"Coaching. That old goat. Good for him for staying so active."

Outside, while reaching the door handle on the sports car, Dom's phone vibrated.

The cell phone screen read, *Lea Peck*, which triggered a random thought: Did tragic Grimm figures ever find a soulmate? *Damn it.* She mashed the line open.

"Dom, the tech department got back to me. Your man Aristophanes's email was a blank. Nothing they could trace.

Nada. Your guy knew enough to use a throwaway email and TOR."

"Damn."

"But did you look up Aristophanes, by any chance?"

"What have you got?"

"He was some old Greek dude from Athens who wrote plays. He wrote comic drama, satirical plays to be exact. Father of Comedy. Says here his powers of ridicule were feared, and that one of his scathing plays singled out Socrates and may have helped bring about Socrates' trial and death. Maybe your guy is making fun of these rich white guys and their sense of entitlement. Making fun of them by getting them all worked up at these sex clubs…and then…I dunno, outing them or something?"

"It's a stretch. But I like where you're headed."

"I mean, I dunno, he chose the damn name for a reason, surely."

Lea was a top rate investigator. "Yeah, I hear that. You may be right."

"Where are you now?"

"I'm about to go dig around in those sex clubs."

"Oh joy. Have fun."

Chapter Thirty-Four

Owen was standing next to the taco truck outside the Javits building, enjoying the sun, when his cell phone vibrated. He brushed hot sauce from his lips with the back of his hand and pulled out his phone. "Whyte."

"Owen, it's Marty. I was trying your office, but figured I'd get you faster on your cell. I heard back from the IRS on your Moreno guy. I got something fresh for ya."

"Talk to me." Owen threw the remainder of the taco in the trash and wiped his lips with a napkin.

"My guy sent me a copy of Moreno's 1099. You ever tell anyone, I'll deny it."

Owen grinned. "I've got no idea what you're talking about."

"Exactly. Anyway, your guy has listed his employer as Trusted Security Services, Inc. I'll send the Employer Identification Number to your email."

Owen was already walking through the Javits lobby. "Thanks, Marty."

Five minutes later, he was at his desk searching Trusted

Security Services online. The Employer Identification Number was a Delaware reference and it looked like the business had been set up by Companies R Us. Whoever owned Trusted Security Services did not want to be known, because the owners' names were not available to the public.

But Owen Whyte was not public. He dialed a number he knew by heart.

On the other end, a deep voice answered, "Companies R Us."

"Reggie, it's Owen Whyte." Owen and Reggie Wellington spoke at least once a month on various cases. Federal law enforcement often used warrants to pierce into company privacy.

"Hey, Agent Whyte, how you doing?"

"Not complaining. You? How's the party capital of Wilmington treating you?"

"Whoa, hold that sarcasm. We had Bad Plus in town a few weeks ago."

"Really?"

"Really. Amazing." Reggie sniffed. "What can I do for you?"

Owen relayed the EIN number of Trusted Security Services, Inc.

A minute later Reggie said, "Sorry, my friend. That's gold tier. I don't have access to that."

The owners of Trusted Security Service had paid top dollar for the highest privacy package. Not a huge surprise given it was a security firm.

Owen respected Reggie. No reason to push it. Always more than one way to skin a mystery. "Alright, Reg. Thanks."

He set down the phone and leaned back in his chair. At this point, he knew a couple things about this mystery. He knew an SAR had been filed by the Bank of Northern New York on Moreno. He knew Moreno was an independent contractor getting paid a shit ton by a quiet firm called Trusted Security Services. Moreno had gotten a big uptick in his payments the last few months. Ben Kirschner at Business News had been curious about all this as well. Time to come at this from a different angle.

He leaned forward and searched the internet for the main telephone number for Business News.

The voice that picked up was upbeat and female. "Business News."

"This is FBI Special Agent Whyte. I'd like to speak with a journalist. Ben Kirschner, please."

She gasped. "Oh no. I'm afraid there is some terrible news. Mr. Kirschner has passed away."

Owen glanced around his small office. "When?"

"Two days ago?"

He let out his breath. "I did not know that. My condolences. Thank you."

He found a short article in a local newspaper that noted Ben Kirschner had passed away in his apartment near Chinatown two days ago.

The hair on the back of Owen's neck tingled. Ben Kirschner goes sniffing around Moreno, who is moving big money, and now Ben Kirschner is dead? Maybe, just maybe, it was a coincidence. But most likely not.

He looked up the NYPD precinct for Chinatown and dialed.

"Precinct Seven," said a gravelly voice of indiscriminate gender.

"This is FBI Special Agent Owen Whyte, can I speak to the detective working the Ben Kirschner investigation?"

"One moment."

It took far longer than a moment, but eventually he heard the clicks as the call was transferred. "Detective Glenn Traister speaking."

"Detective Traister, Special Agent Whyte from the FBI. I may have a case that is affected by the Ben Kirschner homicide—"

"We're not calling it a homicide."

"Was it natural causes?"

"We're not sure. Second degree manslaughter more likely."

"Is there anything about the case—"

"Listen, when we have more, I'll let all of you Bureau folks know."

All? "Are there other agents interested in that investigation?"

"You guys," Traister grumbled, "should be more coordinated. It's not like I've got spare time to sort your shit out too."

Owen waited.

"Hold on, hold on, I've got the card here. It's some hoochie agent, a piece of work—"

"We're all law enforcement, Detective."

Traister grunted. "You want the chick's name or what?"

"Yes, that would be helpful."

"Here. Here's her card. Walker. Domini Walker."

"Ok, thanks."

"And just so we're clear, this isn't a homicide."

"Uh-huh."

Traister hung up.

Owen dialed Reggie again.

"Companies R Us."

"Reg, it's Owen again. Listen. That company, Trusted Security Services?"

"Yeah?"

"There's something very hinky going on. Possibly related to a death. So, listen, got a pen?"

"Yeah."

"Take down this number." Owen recited the number for his current burner phone. "That's a cell phone in my pocket. My very private burner phone. If and when you can, I'd love the name of the owner of that company."

"Understood. No promises."

"Thanks, Reg."

Chapter Thirty-Five

Ben's Twitter feed was an ingenious research tool. He had a real, very active, and incredibly helpful following in Ben's Army of Citizen Journos. Within twelve hours of Ben asking for assistance, he often got twenty or more linked sources to pursue. And that didn't account for any direct messages he received – of which she was sure there were many.

It looked like his Army had been built over years. She knew Ben had won an award for an investigation into the German Bank, KTH, uncovering rampant corruption in their New York City headquarters. Three of the most senior German KTH executives had gone on to be indicted and jailed in Germany, while two senior Division heads in NYC had also faced jail time.

More recently one of his followers had noted, *"The person who exposed KTH gets my support."*

Smart man, Ben. Smarter journo. The world was a lesser place with his loss.

In a spreadsheet, Viv had copied and pasted the last

three months of Ben's tweets and related threads with any accompanying links and GIFs. Out of the 201 tweets, she was able to identify that ninety-seven of them were about Peter Wilson or Jason Lui. These ninety-seven tweets were clearly on topic.

"Any thoughts on bioinformatics?"

"Anyone invested in Tesla?"

"Anyone know where Ms. Wilson goes to a gym?"

She'd written the BuzzFeed bait articles about Peter Wilson and Jason Lui, but what if the motivation was actually one of the other subjects, part of the one hundred and four other tweets?

The muscles in her neck were sore, as if she'd been holding up a hundred pounds on the top of her head for hours. She wanted to rest her forehead on her arms and take a quick nap, just close her eyes for a minute. Had it only been two days ago that she had found Ben? How could it have been so recent, and yet so far away at the same time? When was she allowed to shut down this whole nightmare?

No. No. No. Time to get up. Have another fucking coffee and figure this out. You're a Goddamned investigative journo and you're finding Ben's killer.

She pushed up from the chair, shaking out her neck. How to write a quick bait article for BuzzFeed about a combined one hundred and four tweets?

She stomped into the kitchen. How many times had she already done that today?

An hour later, after pouring through the one hundred and four tweets, she looked at her notes. Seventy-two of the tweets looked personal. She felt confident she could put them aside. That left thirty-two tweets. She had discovered themes that she felt ran within four categories. She bit her lip and skimmed the four categories again.

Pending Regulation on Banks,
Diversity and Inclusion in Corporates,
New York City Pension Funds,
and something called Bureau of Asset Management, a.k.a. BAM.

An idea clicked in her brain. It may work. It wasn't great, but it may work. She placed her fingers on her keyboard and banged out a quick article.

POP QUIZ

What most concerns you as a millennial in New York City? Choose the direction of BuzzFeed's next long-form investigation. You care? We'll dig in, get to the bottom of it! Just like our friend Ben Kirschner would have done, may he rest in peace.

A) Regulations on Banks – do governments care?

B) Diversity & Inclusion in the Corporate World – does it exist?

C) Investing Your Pension Fund – New Yorkers

D) What does the Bureau of Asset Management do? Seriously. Who are they?

Any and all tips or insider information, please forward to Aristophanes Smith – taking on the system at A.Smith@buzzfeed, with a link to the Aristophanes Smith BuzzFeed bio.

She hung her head and closed her eyes. The traps had been baited. Now they waited for the intruder to find them. It was a long shot, but it was the only one they had.

Chapter Thirty-Six

The red velour club room of Longwood Manor looked a lot less upscale in bright light. There were worn spots in the carpet by the booths and most of the lighting fixtures were speckled with rust. Fishman had said that the club had been around for a while. During the day with the lights on, it sure looked like it.

At the bar, Pinocle, a small man around 5'2" and 115 pounds was dressed in a black shirt over slim black pants. Dark hair with a solid hairline was slicked back from dewy skin. He was probably fifty years old, but he took great care not to look it.

As they shook hands, he said, "If Fishman sent you, I'm ok with that. But let's be clear, this club is all legal. We're members only."

"I'm good with that. I'm not here about the club." *Yet*, she thought. "I've got a lead in a case. It may have something to do with someone who comes here often."

"Like I said, we're a members club. We don't give up information lightly. I will require a warrant—"

She raised a hand. "It's not that serious. I'm just trying to connect some dots. I think they may connect here. If not, I'll go about my merry way." When women were getting hurt, the lies came easy.

"Go ahead."

She pulled up a photo of Ben Kirschner on her phone and handed it to him. "Do you recognize this guy?"

He shook his head. "Hold on." He pulled out his phone and called someone. "How close are you?" He listened, nodded, and hung up. "My bartender is on his way. He'll be here in five minutes. We'll ask him."

Fifteen minutes later, the bartender, the tall handsome young man from last night, looked over the photo of Ben Kirschner and nodded. "Yeah, that guy was here. Asking questions. I told him not to."

"You remember what kinds of questions?"

"No. I talk to hundreds of people a night. I just remember telling him, you know, you don't want to be asking questions in a place like this." He glanced at his boss. "People need their privacy in here and we cater to that. It's our job."

She pulled up a photo of Jason Lui. "How about this guy?"

"No. I don't know him. If he was in here, I don't remember him."

Next, she pulled up a photo of Peter Wilson.

The bartender again shook his head. "Nope."

Pinocle leaned on the bar. "One out of three ain't bad."

It wasn't enough. She needed to put Ben Kirschner in this club with either Peter Wilson or Jason Lui. It was increasingly feeling like they were chasing the wrong lead.

Somewhere in a back room, an ice cube fell from an ice machine, landing on a pile of other cubes. All you need is one hit. She nodded to the door at the far side of the room. "I know you have a big guy, sits over there by that door. A bouncer-type."

Pinocle watched her.

"I need to talk to him."

An hour later, the bouncer lumbered into the club and Pinocle introduced them. "James, this is FBI Special Agent Domini Walker. She's got a couple questions for you. Agent, this is James."

James shrugged as if he were interviewed by FBI all the time—the result of a life being the biggest in most rooms.

She pulled up the photo of Jason Lui. "You ever see him?"

James pulled a face. "Nah. Don't recognize him."

She pulled up Peter Wilson. "What about this one?"

He shrugged again, said the same thing.

Pinocle spoke softly. "James, you sure?"

Without a glance to Pinocle, James got the clue. He nodded to the picture of Peter Wilson. "Yeah, now I remember. That guy. He's been in here a few times."

Peter Wilson and Ben Kirschner had both been in the Longwood Manor.

A hit! She asked, "What do you remember about him?"

"Sharp guy. Quiet. Doesn't mingle. Has a drink or two out here, then goes down the back."

She looked at Pinocle. "Down the back is where the action is?"

"Consensual action, yes."

She turned back to James. "How many times has he been in here?"

"Maybe four or five?"

"Do you remember when? Recently?"

He frowned. "Maybe within the last couple of months?"

"Did he come in alone?"

"He was always alone."

Could they connect to Aristophanes? Did it matter? She hated messy leads, but you had to throw out all the rope. "Did he happen to come in on a Tuesday?"

The bartender glanced at Pinocle.

Pinocle nodded.

The big guy said, "Yeah, he might have."

Ben Kirschner, Peter Wilson, and Aristophanes. Maybe a triple hit.

Outside on the street, the night had turned dark. Headlights beamed and flashed.

Dom called Viv. "I've got Peter Wilson and Ben Kirschner at Longwood Manor. There's also a chance of a connect to a Tuesday, which could tie him to Aristophanes. I can't get my head around the connection. Aristophanes sees Ben and Wilson at the same time? It's really messy, but it's what we've got."

"I just published the last article. All those keywords are in 'em."

It just felt so messy. Dom squinted against a beam.

Viv said, "We've got all our flags flying."

What if it wasn't enough? What if they'd chased the wrong leads?

Viv read her silence. "It's what we've got, Dom. Let's hope one of them takes the bait."

Chapter Thirty-Seven

The meeting in the conference room had frazzled Bern. All those men, all that testosterone. Even a glazed donut from the cafeteria wasn't making her feel better.

What if she walked into Sonal's office, closed the door, and told him exactly what she'd discovered? That she'd found the hidden Human Resources numbers. That she knew the culture at this company was horrendously discriminatory. That she suspected the hiding of these numbers was somehow illegal?

In all likelihood, he would look over his glasses and say, "Go back to your desk, Bern." Then he would put in motion for her firing.

Her heart pumped like an engorged octopus, tentacles reaching down her chest and up her throat. What she was considering was career-damaging. Was her job worth the risk?

The noise around the floor was peak this time of day. The shrew to her right who had been passed up for promotion about a hundred times and wore soccer mom stretchy clothes, was cackling on a phone call. To her left, the ever-cheerful Will Smith look-a-like was secretly watching videos of *Runway Wreck* episodes. Everyone else was blowing off work.

She glanced around. Sonal wasn't back yet from lunch. In the search bar, she typed, *corporate diversity and inclusion.* The search returned a new article that had been posted a few hours ago. Something about a millennial polling on the BuzzFeed site. She clicked over. It was a pop quiz with a reference to Diversity and Inclusion. From a journalist called Aristophanes Smith.

Her finger hovered over the mouse. What if she anonymously got the Human Resources data sheet to a journalist? She glanced at the writer's email. But she couldn't send the spreadsheet via email. The cybersecurity guys would have a record of that.

She did an internet search for *Aristophanes Smith*. The third result appeared to be a New York Yellow Pages listing. She clicked it open. The details included the journalist's apartment on Houston St.

She pushed back quickly from her chair and hurried to the bathroom, stepping into the last stall and plugging in her earphones. She dialed Rhonda. Her heart was thumping against her ribs. "It's me. Bern."

"How are you, Bernadette?" Rhonda spoke with a measured, calming tone. It had been annoying at first, but now Bern locked on the reassuring cadence.

"I'm having a bit of trouble. Do you have five minutes?"

"I do, in fact. You're lucky. I'm in between appointments." Rhonda called them 'appointments.' She never said 'patients.' If she was pressed, she'd say 'clients.' It was just one more way to empower her troubled flock. "What can I do for you, Bernadette?"

"I found something at work. It's pretty significant. I think it involves fraud. At least to our investors and potentially our clients."

"That does sound serious."

She took in a deep breath. "I don't know what to do about it. I mean, I should obviously tell someone, but the more I think about it, the more I'm sure the senior management knows about it."

"Which means you'd be putting your job at risk."

"Exactly."

"How do you feel?" It was another of Rhonda's calming tactics. If a patient focused on the here and now, on emotions, it soothed the physical aspects of anxiety.

"Nervous. Unsure. Anxious."

"Yes, ok. That makes sense. Those are normal emotions, given the situation. What do you want to do?"

"Relieve the anxiety."

"Yes, that makes sense. What are your options?"

"That's the thing. I've realized I can't tell anyone here. I'm not sure who's in on the fix. I need to find a neutral party. An external person." She blinked. "Like a reporter."

"Bernadette, do you have to take any of these actions right now?"

Bern thought about this. In so doing, her heart rate slowed. Alone in the stall, she shook her head. "No. No, I don't have to do anything right now."

"Does that delayed option make you feel better, feel more in charge?"

Bern straightened. "I'm not sure."

"Well, the important thing is that you're in charge of your decisions. You have agency. You get to do what you want to do."

Bern let out a small, shaky grin. "Thanks, Rhonda. That's what I needed. I get to do what I want."

"Exactly. Feel better?"

"Yes. Yes."

"I'll see you Wednesday at our normal time and we can discuss this further."

"Thanks, Rhonda," Bern said as she clicked off.

She exited the stall, washed her hands, and stepped out into the second floor. One foot in front of the other.

Chapter Thirty-Eight

The New York address Marty had on Moreno was in Hell's Kitchen and Owen had decided to check it out on his way home. He took the 1 uptown, got out at the 50th Street station, and followed the crowd up and onto the street at sunset. The sidewalks by the station were busy with commuters, but as he strode toward the Hudson, past car dealerships and warehouses, the sidewalks emptied. This was one of the last few bastions of gritty Manhattan.

He hooked a left onto 48th and the wind whistled off the river as the sun set. Approaching from across the street, he slowed as he reached the address from Marty. It was a brick, three-floor warehouse with a double-wide, heavy wood door with rusted iron hinges. An ancient padlock secured it. Nobody had used this entrance in years. From the second and third floors, dark, dusty windows stood sentry on the still street below. Rusted trash cans stood empty by the entrance of a dark alley that ran along the right side of the building. This was nobody's home. Moreno had used a fake address on his Social Security form. Even though this was Hell's Kitchen, a property this big on Manhattan was worth a pretty penny. Who was this guy and who was paying him?

This mystery was getting weirder and darker.

Owen crossed the street and stepped around the trash cans. He clicked on the flashlight on his cell phone and made his way along the alley, past empty windows and piles of decaying trash. His feet crunched ancient, broken cement. He passed through a rancid cloud hovering over a hidden corpse. Probably a rat. Along his right, an old wooden fence protected the neighboring building.

Reaching the end of the building, he peered around the corner. A rat scurried past.

He moved slowly along the back of the building. In the middle of the building there was a single cheap, modern door. Someone had recently installed it.

He turned and made his way back to 48th street, crossed the street, and gazed up and down the block. At this time of night there was almost no traffic, either pedestrian or auto.

He stared at the facade of the old warehouse. This was a great hideout. If you wanted to hide out.

A call from Marty vibrated the phone in his hand. "Hey, Marty."

"Sorry to keep finding you on your cell, friend—"

"No, no. it's fine."

"Listen, I found out some more shit on your Moreno guy. He's a weird cat."

Owen stared at the dark, empty warehouse. "And getting weirder by the minute."

"I called my friend at the Army liaison office. He dug in. He sent me a folder. On the QT. You know how I said Moreno served Iraq 2002-2004? Well, the story turns way bad in 2004. He and his entire squad went MIA in 2004. Body never recovered. Army called all five KIA."

The wind rushed his ears. "Wait, what? He's presumed dead?"

"Yup."

"But..." Marquicio Moreno wasn't dead. As they'd already surmised, he had survived Fallujah and gone years overseas, most likely working as a mercenary, then eventually come home. "But then how does he emerge years later and still have a social security number?"

"It's a weird glitch in the system, man. They don't always close out social security numbers when you're MIA. In most cases, a family request for benefits triggers the system to close out the number. But if no one asks for benefits, it just kinda sits in the system."

The stare from the warehouse windows suddenly felt ominous.

Marty said, "Uh, Owen, there's more. Moreno, your dead man walking, not only had very serious sniper training but he was one of the top five percent of shots in the entire Army."

Time to get serious about finding Moreno. This was getting too weird.

Chapter Thirty-Nine

Having been built in the 1970s, the large square apartment building on the corner of Houston and Elizabeth had the feel of Soviet-style modernity, right down to the concrete cinderblocks and kitschy lobby fountain. Two years ago, a suspect had lived in this building and Jazzy the super had been surprisingly helpful. Turned out the building's owner, a billionaire out of Beijing, had been happy to pay for the latest security camera systems so that Jazzy could keep a careful eye on the property.

Jazzy met Dom inside the automatic doors with an easy wave. He was an easygoing guy with long hair and the glazed eyes of a stoner. "Hey, Agent."

She shook his hand. "Thanks for this, Jazzy."

Inside the elevator, he pressed the button for Floor 5. "So, the apartment we talked about is a nice corner one. We're doing a little bit of work because the new tenants don't move in for another two weeks."

"That's perfect. I just need a few days."

They moved slowly down the carpeted fifth-floor hallway.

Dom said, "Thanks for letting me plug into your security cameras like you did before. I've brought my laptops."

"For sure." He stopped in front of 5H and pushed open the door. "We don't lock 'em when they're empty."

Two buckets of white paint sat on a drop cloth in the living room. The parquet flooring had a few tiles missing and a stack of new ones ready to be installed. The smell of acidic paint was strong. A single chair sat next to the kitchen island. An empty apartment, getting pretty for a new opportunity, for a new happy family.

He crossed the living room and opened one of the windows.

A Post-It note on the counter had a Wi-Fi password and login credentials to the building security cameras. Dom set her backpack on the island counter and pulled out a laptop, opened it up, and checked the passwords. The Wi-Fi connected instantly and was lightning fast. Sometimes billionaires were helpful. "Perfect."

"There's a blowup mattress in the bedroom if you need it."

"Thanks."

"Sure. Call me if you need me. I'll be here all night." He closed the door softly behind him.

She logged into the security system and the screen split in two. Video feeds from various cameras in the lobby, elevator, and hallways rotated across.

Let's do this.

Three hours later, Dom pulled up the last of Viv's bait publications on BuzzFeed. The spark plug had been busy. It was impressive.

The last bait was a pop quiz for millennials with four options:

A) Regulations on Banks – do governments care?

B) Diversity & Inclusion in the Corporate World – does it exist?

C) Investing Your Pension Fund – New Yorkers

D) What does the Bureau of Asset Management do? Seriously. Who are they?

She called Viv, who picked up quickly. "Dom, how's it going?"

Through the window, New York's skyline blinked against the inky night. "Not bad. Over on Houston." She glanced at the screen. "Anyway, I'm just reading over your stuff. What's with the last one, a pop quiz for millennials?"

"I found stuff in Ben's notes that didn't make any sense, so I threw all four topics out like that."

Shit. "So, it could be any one of these topics that got him in trouble?"

"Yeah. I know, I know. We've got a lot of fishing lines out right now."

"We need as many out as we can find."

Viv said, "Speaking of, how's it feel to be bait?"

"I've done worse."

"Oh, I know you have. You know, we never did finish that discussion about the Filthy Five."

The bright moon slid out from behind the clouds, its beam casting a blue tint on the parquet floor. Esther resurfacing in their lives was like a pesky ghost stirring up dangerous demons in a haunted house. The culmination wasn't going to be pretty. This wasn't going to end well.

Viv said, "There was some stuff I found in the Die Hard crew case that may be relevant to your situation."

No, there wasn't. Their situation was over, in the past. That was the life they'd had. Stewart Walker was gone. Literally. Esther was supposed to have been gone, too.

"Dom, I think some of the same actors involved in the Die Hard situation … I think there is some overlap with the Head of Internal Affairs--"

How long could Dom hold off the harrowing climax? "Can we do this another time?"

"Sure. Of course. Good luck over there tonight." And she was gone.

An hour later she called Lea. "How's it going?"

"Ya, know, Javits. Same, same. How's it going there?"

Dom mused, "I don't know. Something about this mix of possible motives doesn't feel right. We've got Ben Kirschner writing articles about wealthy men. We've got Peter Wilson and Jason Lui potentially being threatened by what Ben found on them. We've got some weird sex group run by an anonymous Greek dude. We've got a couple more lines out. Very messy."

"Like you told me, the early days of an investigation require necessary floundering."

"I said that?"

"Like a total-baller-swami, yes you said it."

"When?"

"The case before last."

Lea meant the child trafficking case. The one that would always haunt them both. "Huh. I don't remember saying that."

"Must have been God channeling through you. Luke 4:10 said 'He will command his angels concerning you to guard you carefully.' "

Dom shook her head. "Do you have the entire Bible memorized?"

"Nah, just the sections my daddy repeated to make a point. Which, to be fair, were a lot of sections. And a lot of points to be made. I mean, that's literally the raison d'etre of a pastor." There was a pause. "But, listen. You know what you're doing. I have U-Haul truck amount of faith in you."

"Thanks. Coming from a bible thumper that means a lot."

"Amen, sister."

Chapter Forty

Viv couldn't stay asleep. The heavy lift of the research into Ben's topics and pushing out of Aristophanes articles had exhausted her. At 6 P.M., she had stumbled into bed and slept like a drunk. But now, her eyes were wide open. She glanced at her phone. 1 A.M. Should she stay in bed and try to force sleep? Sometimes meditative breathing worked. But mostly it didn't. Did she get up and make a cup of sleep-inducing tea? That shit almost never worked. Maybe there was a mindless movie on one of the six hundred cable channels. When was there ever not a movie on one of the six hundred cable channels?

She rolled to her side, staring at the wall. The thought of Ben, dead, pushed into her consciousness. She took a deep breath, forced its retreat. She'd focused on Ben for what felt like a week. She was tired of the rawness, the tender edges to the wound that was now her heart.

I'm done with this sadness for a bit.

She pushed up off the bed. Rather go get a milkshake down the street than lie here wallowing in despair.

In the dark, she rummaged for sweatpants and a sweatshirt, then slipped on her sneakers.

In the living room, a high moon cast silvery shadows across the carpet. She grabbed her wallet and phone and headed outside.

The Lower East Side never slept and tonight was no different. College kids yelled to each other across the busy street, loud house music thumped from underground clubs, and dogs barked from Tompkins Square Park. It felt good to be walking along 5th Avenue, the sensory overload pushing away the painful thoughts of Ben.

The ice cream store near the Starbucks three blocks away stayed open for the late-night crowd. She felt alive and suddenly uplifted. Her strides were long and confident. The mood swing struck her as weird, but then, probably normal, right? What was normal when someone you knew got killed? And you hear it happening?

She shook her head, pushing the thought away.

Across the street, a taxi dropped off four young revelers in front of the Cuban place. Salsa music blared as they laughed their way into the restaurant. Must be nice to be carefree. Not trying to run down the killer of one of your closest friends.

Goddamn it. Just focus on the milkshake, Viv.

Up ahead, the ice cream store glowed on the corner with bright pink and baby blue neon lights. She'd get a salted-caramel-pecan blended. It was tough to get those nuts through the straw, but the mix was delicious.

She pushed through into the bright light. Behind the counter, a young black woman in a blue and white striped uniform and pigtails smiled. "Welcome to Blinks."

Viv grinned. "You are my hero."

The young girl grinned more broadly. Two sisters connecting. "Got a craving?"

"Oh yeah." She ordered her shake.

"Oh, that's a good one. Will just take me a sec."

Viv turned, stepped to the window, and watched the activity on 5th Avenue. A small crowd had formed outside the Cuban place. They must have been at capacity. A guy with a ponytail walked a German Shepherd just past the ice cream store. He turned and gave her a grin.

Oh God, I must look a right mess.

Across the street, a thin man stood in the shadows of a doorframe. He was wearing sunglasses. Still as a statue.

She cocked her head.

How stoned was that guy?

She watched him. He had a tight face, sharp cheekbones.

Wait, was he staring back at her?

Blood pumped in her chest.

His line of vision never left the front of the ice cream shop.

What the fuck? I am not in the mood for this.

The sunglasses didn't flinch.

Hey, stoned guy, I'm exhausted from chasing down my friend's killer and I do not have time for whatever creepy Lower East Side shit you want to throw my way.

The thin man continued to stare.

Fuck this. She lifted her phone and opened up the camera application. She held it up, pointed it across the street to the shadows, and snapped five photos before he moved swiftly from the shadows of the doorway and disappeared into the pitch-black of the park.

Good. You chicken shit. You can't just walk around creeping out women. Not cool.

From behind, the shop gal said, "I've got your fix."

Chapter Forty-One

Every time she blinked, Dom's eyes scratched. It was too dry in this empty apartment. Or maybe it was because it was midnight and she'd been staring at different the security camera views covering the lobby, elevators, and fifth-floor hallway for hours. She reached her hands over her head and stretched against the tightness in her shoulders.

In the period between 8 and 10 P.M. there had been a lot of movement. Residents of the building came and went with shopping bags, takeout restaurant bags, and dogs on leashes. At least five food delivery guys had locked up bikes just outside the lobby door and gotten buzzed in. It was a busy building.

But around 10:30, things had quieted down. A few people arrived home late from work. A woman left to walk a fat, lumbering bulldog at 11. No one had gotten off on the fifth floor in the last two hours.

She was ready if someone had. The Glock was resting on the counter by the door and she had already scripted how it would go down. In her imagination, she would watch on the screen as the single male – like the gaunt man she had on video in a dark hoodie – stepped off the elevator and glanced up and down the quiet hallway. She would rise from her chair, grab the laptop with her dominate right hand, take two strides to the counter, place the laptop facing the door, sweep up the Glock in her left hand, and transfer it to her shooting hand, step behind the door, back against the wall. She would watch as the male moved down the hallway. As he approached her position, she would raise the gun in anticipation, her finger on the trigger. In her mind, the male would stop outside her door and knock once. He would be on edge but only be anticipating a civilian reporter. From the laptop screen, she would ensure he had not drawn *his* gun. If not, she would unlock the deadbolt, step to the center of the frame, throw the door open, and aim the Glock at his eyes. In her mind, she would growl, "FREEZE, FBI!"

But as of midnight, no such drama had even come close to reality.

Her phone vibrated.

It was Beecher. "How's it going?"

"Slowly," Dom replied.

"Is your plan dangerous?"

"Beech, I'm an FBI agent. I'm trained for this."

"Right. A stone-cold warrior of justice. So some danger is involved."

Let's move this along. "How's it going there?"

"Just took Tinks out. Gonna hit the sack. Mila's been running around, head down, busy. I think she has some tests or a research project or something."

Dom smiled. "She's a unique one."

He chuckled. "You can say that again."

The lobby and hallway scenes on the laptop screen were still. Nothing was happening here.

Might as well get this conversation over with. Rather than let Esther emotionally stalk them, maybe it was better just to confront her, find out what she so badly needed to say to them. "Go ahead, Beech. Spit it out."

"She's still getting here in four days."

It was a punch against an ice-cold chest. "Yeah. Are you in touch with her?"

Beecher said, "No. She wrote a second letter. It came today."

The pesky ghost was in the house. "Jesus."

"She'll be staying at a hotel in Brooklyn."

"She gave you her telephone number?"

He assured her, "No. And she doesn't have either of ours. I say we call the hotel once she's here and arrange a meeting."

The dreaded culmination was imminent. The air left her lungs. "Agreed."

His voice was soft. "Agreed?"

"Yeah. Agreed. Let's get this over with. This is gonna be me and you and a lot of old wounds. But maybe we can move on." It was the first time she had framed that out loud.

"Yeah. Agreed." He exhaled.

"You ok with this plan?"

"I mean, I don't know how we can't hear her out. It's just too… momentous."

"Agreed." It felt good to be on the same side as Beecher again.

As if reading her mind, he whispered, "Me and you, Dom, two in a pod."

Warmth crept into her chest. Two in a pod. It had been

a child bastardization of the phrase 'two peas in a pod' that they used most of their lives.

Beecher had been four years old and she'd been nine. He had run in from the kitchen, screaming and grasping his right middle finger. Blood had streamed down his wrist. "I cut it, I cut it!"

Dom had glanced at Esther, but her blue eyes had been unfocused.

She'd grabbed Beecher and run to the bathroom. She'd dived into the cabinet, her trembling hands rummaging for bandages.

Beecher had been jumping on his feet. "Ow, ow, ow."

With a roll of bandage, she'd held out her hand. "Ok, let me see."

A deep slice had gone through the top of his finger to the bone. She'd wrapped the bandage five times. The blood had soaked through the white fabric.

"Come with me." She'd walked him down the stairs, out onto the street, and two blocks to the emergency room of the local hospital. Beecher had gotten ten stitches. Later, they'd returned to the apartment, exhausted and spent, to find Esther nibbling goldfish crackers.

When Stewart Walker had returned home after his shift that night, he had sat Dom down, told her what a brave and responsible thing she had done. That she and Beecher had to stick together.

Late that night, she had snuck to Beecher's bed and hugged the little boy. "Me and you. Two in a pod." He had smiled and repeated it. It had stuck.

In the quiet, empty apartment on Elizabeth she said, "Get some sleep. I'll check in with you in the morning."

"Good luck, Dom. Goodnight."

Chapter Forty-Two

It was 1 A.M. and the darkness was thick over the glow of the city's lights. Just outside the empty apartment, a water tower loomed like an inky, eight-legged spider peering down for victims wandering the streets below.

All this talk about Esther and the ex had made Dom's mind uneasy, skipping across a hundred unsatisfying thoughts, like searching for a singular missing file in hundreds of folders on a crammed hard drive. What was Esther so determined to tell them? Was she destined to always live in the shadow of a shamed NYPD officer? Had everything she had known about Stewart Walker been a lie? His kindness, his devotion to her and Beecher, his moral strength – all a facade of a thief and criminal? How had she not seen a single bad trait? Who would she be if she had a different past? Would she have been light and carefree? Laughing easily?

She turned and walked for the fiftieth time back to the kitchen counter and the light of the laptop. No one had appeared on the video cameras for two hours, the last activity being a pizza delivery guy who had gotten off on the second floor.

All she had ever wanted to be was proud FBI. Never NYPD. There was too much water under that bridge.

Something moved in the darkness outside the lobby doors.

Dom lunged to the counter and squinted at the laptop screen.

A dark small figure slipped into the lobby. The figure wore a dark hoodie with the hood pulled over their face. White sneakers glowed in the darkness.

Just as she had predicted: a hoodie. But this guy didn't move like the gaunt man. Something was different.

Dom glanced to the Glock at the end of the counter.

The dark figure stepped to the elevator and pressed a button.

Was the hooded person a woman?

The elevator arrived, the doors opened, the figure stepped in, and the doors slid shut.

Dom held her breath. One. Two. Three. Four. Five. The view from the fifth-floor camera showed a dim stillness.

The elevator doors opened, spilling light onto the fifth-floor carpet.

Dom scooped up the laptop, took two long strides to the end of the counter by the door, set it down, and positioned it to face the door.

With her left hand, she swept up the Glock and transferred it to her right.

The dark small figure was moving swiftly down the hallway. Definitely a woman.

Dom pointed the gun to the ceiling. Ready.

The figure slowed as she approached the apartment.

Dom tensed, waiting for the knock.

Just on the other side of the door, the figure pulled something from the back of her pants. It was something white. An envelope.

Dom held her breath, her finger gently rubbing the trigger.

The figure knelt.

At Dom's feet, the envelope slid across the floor. It was addressed *Aristophanes*.

Dom glanced at the laptop screen. The figure was racing down the hallway.

Dom stepped over the envelope, yanked the door open, and cornered into the hallway.

The figure reached the open elevator and jumped inside.

Dom raced in pursuit. "Shit, shit."

The light on the carpet narrowed as the elevator doors closed.

"Shit! Shit!"

Dom skidded to a stop in front of the elevator doors, glancing overhead to the display panel. Below in the lobby, the elevator arrived.

She imagined the doors sliding open and the figure racing from the building. She lowered the Glock.

The figure wasn't their gaunt man. Or an assassin. It was a messenger.

Chapter Forty-Three

Thursday

They had hiked along the solitary desert road for hours, a slow line of four men, weary but with a mission. The moon had been bright and they had packed away the night vision goggles. The three had carried their M4s loosely but Slap had kept his rifle against his chest.

There was no one out there. Only once they saw headlights in the distance, four clicks out. They laid in the sand, thirty feet from the road as the beat-up sedan passed them unawares. They could have commandeered the car, but they had agreed the plan was to keep a low profile. Ghosts in the desert. Ghosts in Karbala. Ghosts in Kuwait.

It was just as the sun pinkened the sky that they stumbled across a solitary farm. Skinny goats bleated as the four men moved into formation around the central cinder block house.

O'Dore was once again the one who banged on the door.

A middle-aged man opened it with a wide grin of darkened teeth. He waved them in and sat them down on an ancient carpet. He clapped his hands and two teenage girls appeared with cheap glasses and three bottles of what appeared to be alcohol. The man poured them each a tall glass of brownish liquid, poured himself one, all the while chatting in Arabic and waving his hands around.

Slap was on alert. His eyes kept careful watch of the grinning man, his two girls, and the windows at the front. This all felt far too friendly.

O'Dore, John-John, and Morgenstein threw back the alcohol. The grinning man drank his shot in a big gulp and poured them another round.

Slap walked to the front window, peered outside. The sun was rising over the desert. The single road was empty. A chicken walked across the dusty farmyard.

The grinning man was watching him, carefully. The two girls were watching him.

Slap slipped out his Beretta 9 mm and shot the man between the eyes.

The two girls screamed.

O'Dore shrugged.

John-John laughed maniacally.

The girls kept screaming.

Morgenstein leaned over, grabbed the bottle, and poured four glasses.

This time, Slap drank with them.

O'Dore eyed the girls, said from the side of his mouth, "Slappy, maybe you don't want to stay inside for this. Maybe you keep watch. Outside."

Slap took up the bottle, slowly poured himself a second shot. O'Dore didn't know about trailers with violent fathers. He didn't know about beatings and starvation. He didn't know how easy it was to displace revenge on a younger sister.

The girls dropped to the floor, desperately hugging. Streams of snot bubbled across their lips as they wailed into each other's necks.

Slap felt the pulse in his balls, shook his head, and said, "I'll stay."

Chapter Forty-Four

Lea rushed to Dom's desk and delivered two coffees.

Dom said rapidly, "Thank God you're here."

"Are you shitting me? With this whopping big kahuna break, I wouldn't miss it!"

Dom tapped a slim plastic bag; inside was the manila folder with *Aristophanes* written in ballpoint. She handed Lea plastic gloves and they both snapped them on. "This came under the door about an hour ago at the bait apartment." She pulled out a pair of tweezers from the pen cup and turned to Lea, "You ready?"

"Fuck, yes."

Dom opened the plastic bag and with the tweezers slid out the envelope. She carefully sliced a tweezer arm along the edge of the flap, breaking the seal, pinched the papers inside, and slid out what looked like Excel spreadsheets.

"What the fuck?" Lea whispered.

Dom carefully flipped through twenty pages for them both to scan. All spreadsheets. Across the top in bold, capital letters it read, *HIGHLY CONFIDENTIAL.* She reached the last page where someone had written in blue pen, *BAM?*

Lea spoke first. "Is that some kind of code?"

They returned to the first page to start the scan again.

Dom said, "Ok, no logo. No identifying markings. We're not sure if there are prints."

Both women leaned in to read the 8-point font of words across the headings.

Last Name
First Name
Start Date
M/F
Identifier

Under each column, alphabetical by the last name, were the list of names with identifying information.

Lea said, "It's some kind of roster. Start date makes it sound like employment start date, so some kind of list of staff?"

Dom nodded. "What's this identifier column?"

In one of the columns, was a single letter identifier against each name.

C
B
A
H
NA

They flipped through the twenty pages. Fifty names had multiple letter identifiers.

C G
A B
B G

NA T

Dom caught it first. "Caucasian, Black, Asian, Hispanic, Native American."

Lea whispered, "And Gay, Bisexual. Nancy Pepper on page fourteen has a T. My bet is 'T' for 'Transgender.'"

"Why would someone deliver a Human Resources list from an unknown company to our baited journalist at 1 AM? Undercover? Wearing a hoodie?"

"That BAM note stands out."

"Agreed. Can you run this down to Becky in forensics? Let's see if she can pull prints. Remind her this is unofficial."

"Or as part of the case of the shibacle restaurant in Jersey City."

"Exactly. Whichever she's comfortable with." Trust your friend's judgment. Especially when they work for the FBI. "When you get back, I'll call my civilian who set the bait, the journo. Now I'll see what I can find on BAM."

Lea scooped up the document and took off at a trot.

Thirty minutes later, Lea leaned over Dom's shoulder and scrutinized the computer screen, "What have you got?"

"I'm just searching for BAM. Wikipedia thinks it may be the Bureau for Asset Management, part of the New York Comptroller's office."

Lea looked up across the floor and stiffened.

Whatever it is, not now. We're on to something.

Lea stood.

No, seriously, not now. This may be the BAM we're looking for. Dom's eyes continued to scan the Wikipedia page.

Lea whispered in a sexy voice, "What have we here?"

Damn it. Dom looked up.

"Hmm, hmm. That is a rare sight in this building."

Striding through the middle of the floor was a tall, very fit male agent in a blue suit. He had dark hair and broad shoulders. He held a manila folder.

"Oh shit, he's heading this way," Lea whispered.

He was indeed heading across the empty floor toward their far corner.

Dom sat back and crossed her arms over her chest. *What the fuck is this?*

Lea stood, taking a feline-smooth step from behind the desk. *How does she do that?*

As he approached, she held out her hand. "Staff Operations Specialist Lea Peck."

He shook her hand. "Owen Whyte."

"How can we help you, Agent Whyte?"

"You can call me Owen.'"

Lea grinned at him. "Owen."

Seriously, how does she do that so easily?

He turned to Dom. "Are you Walker?"

Whatever this is, we don't have time. Dom nodded.

He held out the manila folder. "Are you looking into the Ben Kirschner case?"

Scratch that. We have time.

Lea pulled over an empty chair. "Here, have a seat, Owen." She winked at Dom.

He placed the folder on the desk.

Dom said, "The Ben Kirschner case is not an official Bureau case."

Owen tapped the folder. "Not yet."

Lea nodded. "I'm liking the sound of this."

He sat. "I've got something that should be of interest." Owen Whyte told them a story of Ben Kirschner's tweet that listed a Suspicious Activity Report that led to the discovery of a ghosted mercenary named Moreno.

It sounded a lot like Ben's Twitter research that Viv had found. A lot.

Owen continued, "Someone accessed a SAR and leaked it to a reporter. That's a very big deal. In fact, it's a federal crime. I was able to do some tracking down of this Moreno. The only address in the city is a locked warehouse over in Hell's Kitchen."

This didn't sound like it had anything to do with Peter Wilson or Jason Lui. Had they focused on the wrong Ben Kirschner research topic? In the grand scheme of motives, money was most often at the heart of a crime. Maybe Ben had stumbled onto a big money scandal? Better to correct midcourse than chase the wrong lead. Dom straightened. "Keep going."

"I'm not exactly sure, but I think it may have something to do with a corporation. I think a corporation is paying this guy Moreno to hide stuff that could come out publicly and devalue or destroy a company."

Yup, he was talking big money. Dom leaned forward. "What do you know about the Bureau of Asset Management, aka BAM?"

His eyes widened. "Over at the City Comptroller?"

Dom held up her finger. "Hold on. I've got a civilian working with me on this case. She's an investigative journo. She was friends with Ben Kirschner."

Owen blinked.

Dom shrugged without further explanation.

Owen shrugged in response, as if to say, *no problem*.

Lea grinned as she glanced between them.

Dom dialed a number and Viv answered with a sleepy voice. "Dom?"

"Yeah, we got something."

Viv was instantly awake. "What? What did you get?"

"Hold on. I'm going to put you on speakerphone. I'm here with Special Operations Specialist Lea Peck and Special Agent Owen Whyte." She pressed the *speaker* button, set down the phone, and brought both Viv and Owen up to speed. "So, somebody in a hoodie two hours ago dropped off a list of employees from a big company. We don't know which company. We're calling it Company X for now. Rough count around 15,000 employees on the list. Last name, first name, work start date. Then it tags employees by gender, ethnicity, and sexual preference. We believe a mole in this Company X wanted us to have this list. Something about this list of employees is dangerous enough to threaten a company. There is a notation on one of the pages that reads *BAM*—"

Viv said, "Yes! I had that in my last article. Ben was asking around about Diversity and Inclusion. He'd also asked around about BAM! Both topics! Maybe his volunteer research army on Twitter found something!"

Owen nodded slowly. "Bureau for Asset Management. The Comptroller has fiscal responsibility for the city's five pension funds. Last I checked, the Comptroller was responsible for investing about $207.96 billion. They invest that money in order to make a return for the city's pensioners."

Big money. Scratch that. Huge money. Huge motivation.

All four went silent.

Lea spoke first. "Well, motherfucking shit. Some company is hiding good Goddamned employee demographic information from the good Goddamned New York City Comptroller."

Owen said, "Information that has big implications."

Viv whispered, "Big enough to have Ben followed and killed."

Lea pointed a finger at Dom. "We are no longer floundering, oh swami."

Chapter Forty-Five

Owen said, "What do you all know about corporate reporting?"

Lea shook her head, Viv remained silent, and Dom replied, "Not much."

"Every quarter, a company is required to publish its financial statements – income statements, balance sheets, statements of cash flow, etc. Companies hold quarterly earnings call to explain these results. The requirement keeps the system transparent for investors to gauge a company's health. Based on this data, share prices go up or down."

Lea asked, "What happens if a company misrepresents in their report?"

"Exactly. If they misrepresent what's happening to the company, that's fraud. After the 2008 financial crash, the government enacted stricter requirements."

Dom pointed to the spreadsheet. "Are these types of numbers, these staffing numbers, reported quarterly?"

Owen shook his head. "They are not required, unless they are material, which means unless they would impact the operating or value of the company. But…" He raised a finger. "There is growing interest in companies reporting on the diversity of their human resources."

Dom finished his thought. "Ben Kirschner may have uncovered that Company X was hiding this data. That may be fraud. If so, it would have big implications."

"Yes. And I think Moreno is some kind of thug hired by your Company X."

Dom stood. "Ok, I'm taking this up the line. Let's see if we can't make this an official FBI investigation."

"OK." Viv's voice was small and the intonation off.

Dom cocked her head. "Viv, what's wrong? Is everything ok?"

"Uh, something may have happened."

Dom reached for the handset to move the conversation off speaker, but both Owen and Lea raised hands in protest. The FBI was a team. When one was in trouble, they all were.

Dom sat down. "Viv, we're listening."

"When I went out last night, I saw somebody creepy. At the time, I didn't think anything about it. By the time I got home, I wasn't sure if I had imagined it. I mean this is New York City. There are crazies all over."

Dom's heart rate kicked up. "Keep talking."

"Now with this whole BAM connection and the higher stakes… Maybe… I dunno, maybe he was watching me. He wasn't there very long. But he had on sunglasses, which was weird."

A low hum of activity hung in the air.

Dom asked, "Your gut said he was watching you?"

"Well, at first no, but then I took photos of him and he skedaddled."

Dom said, "Send me those photos."

They could hear the rustle as Viv sent the photos from her phone.

"I don't like coincidences. Not in the middle of a investigation. You got somewhere to go for the next few days?"

"Yes, my friend Ellen Doberman's."

"Give me Ellen's number."

Viv read the number out loud.

Dom softened her voice. "Viv, it's ok to quit and leave this with me."

"Oh, hell no, I'm not quitting. Ben would one thousand percent do this for me if our roles were reversed."

"Ok, but we're putting you at even longer arm's length. You stay at your friend's for now. Don't go back to your apartment. And no more articles. We're gonna use your brain and your research capabilities. That's it."

"OK."

Dom ended the call

Owen stood. "I'm going to chase this lead. To Cayman Islands."

Lea reared back. "Seriously? Did you just say that? Cayman Islands?"

"That's where Moreno's been hiding his cash. Follow the money, as they say."

Lea eyed him up and down. "As they do, indeed."

"In Financial Forensics, Grand Cayman comes up a lot. I end up going a lot."

"Rough."

"There are some perks." He glanced at Dom. "This may be integral to your case. Maybe you should come?"

Color burned Dom's skin. *Why was she embarrassed? A colleague had asked her if she wanted in on his case, not on a date, for crying out loud.* "Uh, no. I'll chase this down here."

"Right." And he was gone.

The flush stayed on her face for another five minutes. Lea grinned through it all.

Behind Fontaine's chair, the sky over downtown Manhattan was turning red and pink as the sun rose over the East River. The city was best at sunrise and sunset when the sun cast a clean glow, hiding the years of underlying grit. A few windows caught the rays like flash bombs frozen in time.

Fontaine leaned back in his chair. He looked tired. "You're here early."

She leaned against the wall. "You too. How's your son?"

"He's home."

"Good. Good for you, sir."

He put his feet up on the desk and crossed his hands behind his head, a dramatic display of patience for what was to come next. His shoes were mahogany brogues, their leather soles scuffed. Expensive shoes that he wore the shit out of. It made her like him more: not cheap, but not wasteful. He watched her. "Talk to me."

"It's getting complicated."

"How could I have guessed that? Special Agent Domini Walker lands in another complicated investigation. It's almost as if you go looking for them."

"I don't."

"They just find you?"

She swallowed before laying out the steps in their investigation on Ben Kirschner, ending with the bait planted by Viv in BuzzFeed.

"You've involved a civilian?"

"She involved herself."

"That is not the answer I was looking for, Agent."

"Sir, I couldn't stop her. She would have done it without my protection."

"I strongly suspect there is more to this story, so you may continue. But be aware I am extremely displeased."

"Noted." She took a deep breath. "We are in possession of data that leads us to believe that the journalist uncovered corporate fraud somehow related to the New York City Comptroller."

Wait for it. Wait for it.

He pushed his feet off, dropped them on the floor with a loud bang, placed both hands, fingers wide, on the desk, and bellowed, "*The* New York City Comptroller's office?"

She nodded. In her mind, Stewart Walker whispered, *Stand tall, my Dom. You are smart.*

He pointed his finger at her nose. "And who the hell is we? Please, for the belabored love of all things having to do with proper authority, tell me you did not ignore my conditions? I am the ADIC and I explicitly told you no support."

Dom held up her hand. *Time to take the lumps.* "Lea Peck did a very small favor for me—"

He raised his voice. "I very deliberately—"

She moved toward him. "Sir, the twist in this case came from a forensic accountant in the Financial Crimes Section of CID. His investigation and mine are related. Intimately."

He squinted, and his breathing was heavy. "If anyone hears that you're looking into the Comptroller's office, I will never – as in N E V E R – hear the end of it. For years. Are you clear on the possible ramifications of being wrong? The impact that could have on my career?"

She nodded. *He was giving her slack on the leash!* She backed toward the door.

He held up a palm. "I want complete deniability."

"Yes, sir." She nodded solemnly.

He pointed at her. "Still unofficial. You have twenty-four hours to prove this should be official. That's it. Then I'm shutting this shit down. Dead journalist or no dead journalist. You do not play lightly in the sandbox that is the New York City Comptroller."

Chapter Forty-Six

Mila frowned outside the door of the Pearl Street address for the law firm of Myer and Bigg, located in Lower Manhattan a block from South Street Seaport. A wooden door stood tightly closed behind an iron gate covered in crisscrossing cobwebs. This wasn't good.

She turned a full circle and noticed the large marble facade of a three-story building next door. Overhead a carved emblem read, *New York Police Benevolent Association.*

Mila's skin tingled. It was only three months ago that Robert Gessen and Mike Turner of the Filthy Five had come after her, chased her through the dark, made her take refuge with Dom and Beecher. But what were the odds either of those two were inside that building at this exact time? Extraordinarily small odds. Like infinitesimally small.

She pushed through the imposing twin doors into the quiet of the front lobby. Swallowing against a dry throat, she let her eyes adjust to the weak light from a single bulb in a brass pendant. Wooden walls were covered with photos of uniformed police and the oriental rug was threadbare. The room smelled like dry grass and dust. A deep male laugh echoed off the stone walls from deep inside the building.

"Hello?" she called out, but not with any volume.

She moved slowly along the left wall, examining the photos. Many of them looked to be official police ceremonies—on stages, everyone in full uniform—from years ago. She was no history buff, but many of these looked like the era of Bugsy Malone and prohibition.

She moved to the photos on the right wall. One had a number of grim-looking officers above a tag that read, *"First ceremony with World Trade Center Breast Bar."*

An antique reception desk stood sentry by a closed door. She cracked open the door. "Hello?"

From behind, she heard shuffles.

"Well, hello, young lady. I'm Officer Doll. What can I do for you?" He must have been around ninety years old. His white Caesar haircut encircled a round, wizened face with smiling elf eyes and a mouthful of smiling dentures.

She pushed out her hand. "Hello. I'm Mila, Officer Doll. How are you?"

He leaned slightly forward, as if his balance were off. A doddering little elf. "Yes, yes, fine, fine. What can I do for you?"

Tell the truth or lie? She went with the truth. "Sir, I'm an NYU student studying criminology."

"Isn't that something." Officer Doll clasped knobby hands. "How can I help you today?"

"I'm taking this class on law enforcement procedures and I was doing some research on a law firm that appears to have been located just next door. A lawyer there, Simon Bigg, was involved in a case I'm researching."

"Yes, yes, Myer and Bigg."

"That's the one."

"You say you're looking for Simon Bigg?" He wasn't confused by the request. For an old, happy elf, he seemed quite quick.

"Yes, that's right."

"Well, yes, they did a lot of work for our members over the years. But they've been retired now for about a year. I'm afraid that office is all closed up."

"I saw that. I wonder if you have any forwarding information? I'd really like to interview Simon Bigg."

"Oh yes." Officer Elf's rheumy eyes scanned the room and landed on a photo along the left wall. He pointed a bent finger. "That's them."

It was a photo of two men standing with what appeared to be a chief or commissioner. All three men were smiling. It was dated 1997.

Officer Elf rubbed his thinning, gray hair. "Come and let's see what we can find." He shuffled to the desk with tiny steps that took forever and lowered himself into the old chair that creaked under his weight. "Hmm, let me see. Simon and Bigg. Yes, we started accepting their mail, you know, as a favor. The postmen don't know what to do with it." His gnarled fingers riffled through a folder stuffed with dog-eared documents and sealed envelopes and his head leaned close to see the writing. He mumbled, "Humph. Humph. There's a girl who takes care of the mail."

Girl? Surely, he meant woman. These old guys were something else.

"But she only comes now once a week. We don't need her every day. She just files her nails."

Yup, he definitely meant a woman. She found a reservoir of patience. "It's interesting that Myer and Bigg was right next door."

"Oh." He looked up, the file closing.

At this rate, this would take hours.

He nodded to himself. "They always supported us. Pro bono. They had other clients, mind you, but they got a lot of us through some tough times. Well, I shouldn't say a lot. That makes it sound like we were always getting ourselves into trouble. That's not what I'm saying at all. But they were there when we needed them."

She nodded to the folder. "Any luck there, Officer Doll?"

He blinked blankly, then lowered his head and his fingers started back at the beginning of the folder.

She sighed.

His mumbling continued. "That girl just never kept these files in any kind of order. You know they come in here, read those trashy magazines, and just don't do their jobs. None are really ever that good." His shoulders rose. "Oh, here." He struggled to slide out a sealed envelope.

She moved around the desk to help him.

It was an official envelope from *Horizons Home, New Jersey* addressed to Simon Bigg, care of New York Police Benevolent Association. It was dated last month.

"Well, I'm sorry, but I'm sure that's all we've got for Simon. Some mail that has to be returned."

Oh, it's a lot more than that, Officer Doll. It's a clue. And I'm on it. "No, no, this is fine. Thanks, Officer Doll!"

Chapter Forty-Seven

Chambers and Centre Streets intersected north of Brooklyn Bridge in the financial district. Dom stood outside 1 Centre Street and peered into the gloom of the barrel-vaulted passageway behind the three-floor-high Corinthian columns. "Shit, shit, shit," she whispered to herself.

The David N. Dinkins Municipal Building was one of the largest government office buildings in the world, housing the city's administrative offices. Over two thousand people worked here, and at 9 A.M. the immense plaza funneled streaming horde of incoming city employees like salmon swimming up a river. Staring up at the vast ceiling, she wondered again how this case had escalated so exponentially. Who knew that a simple spreadsheet with the details of employees at a big, as yet unnamed, corporation could arrive as a proverbial shitbomb.

Dom took a deep breath and stepped in line with the surging crowd.

Fifteen minutes later, the elevator doors opened on the fifth floor and she stepped out with six employees. White badges hung on dull lanyards. From a quick search, she had learned the Comptroller oversaw the city's 'fiscal health,' which included dealing with waste, fraud, and abuse, as well as reviewing contracts, claims, and wage policies. She glanced up and down the hallway as staffers stepped through doors. Of the eight hundred employees working for the Comptroller's office, at least one of them had to have been approached by Ben Kirschner. The goal was to find that person, the solitary needle in the haystack.

She pulled out her cell phone.

Lea had texted. *"Hottie Owen is heading to the bank in Cayman."*

Dom felt her face flush.

She typed out a text to Viv as comptroller employees strode past, full of purpose and vigor. *"Can you check Ben's Twitter for any mention of BAM staffers?"*

When in doubt, case the joint out. She put the phone to her ear and walked slowly down the hall while pretending to be on an important call. She eyed the titles engraved on the doors. *Budget. Personnel Management.* Who would Ben have approached?

The tide of commuting employees slowed and the hallway cleared as the morning routine settled in. The hum of phones, the clacking of keys, and the din of chatter could be heard through doors. She felt conspicuous, but no one asked who she was. Her eyes darted left and right. *Procurement. Storage. Communications.* She paused and blinked. *Communications.*

She lowered the phone. Yes, of course, as a reporter, Ben would have had reason to be in touch with anyone in an external relations role in the communications office.

She slipped the phone in her jeans pocket and stepped to the door, hand out.

Just then, the door pushed open and she jumped back. A 5'8" white man with salt-and-pepper hair and an expensive suit strode past.

Dom sucked in her lungs. The salt-and-pepper-haired man was the Comptroller. Ross Linden.

He was followed quickly by a woman in a slim red dress and perfect sleek hair carrying a clipboard and a young man in a shirt and tie holding two briefcases. The three turned toward the elevators and moved quickly down the hallway.

Dom fell in line behind.

Red Dress said to Linden, "Local affiliates ABC and NBC are here. CNN isn't covering it. Bloomberg should be here."

Linden nodded. "Got it."

The elevator pinged open and the three stepped inside. Dom followed, her face to the doors.

Red Dress continued. "The release is embargoed until 10:30. That gives them a window of twenty minutes. You know the toughest questions. I don't expect anything other than the ones we've covered for you. You want me to cut them off at 10:30?"

Linden replied, "No, I'll take questions as long as they want."

The elevator slid to the ground floor and the doors swept open.

Dom stepped to the side, let them exit, and followed at a good distance. The three took a right down a long passageway. Two minutes later, they stepped into a huge atrium where a podium on a small stage had been set up. A gaggle of thirty reporters circled the stage. Behind them, five cameras on tripods towered over the crowd. Stage lights clicked on around the atrium.

Oh shit.

Linden leaned over to Red Dress and whispered something.

She nodded.

He stepped up onto the stage and waved to the crowd. "Good morning. Glad you all could make it. We've got an important announcement to make today."

Oh shit was right. Coincidences in an investigation were almost never purely coincidental.

Chapter Forty-Eight

Linden waited for the crowd to settle like a man comfortable on a stage, then he grabbed both sides of the podium and straightened his shoulders. "Today we are announcing the launch of the Spotlight Initiative. For the last few years, we've been engaging on the issue of diversity with leaders across those companies in which we invest. They have been telling us about their efforts to create a more equal workplace."

Hit. Surely, this is what Ben discovered.

He continued, "In addition, we've been studying the lack of progress toward equality across all S&P 1000 companies. What we have seen is a further consolidation of white male supremacy in senior positions. It means minorities – that means women, people of color, people with disabilities, and LGBTQ – are being overlooked." He paused, leaning close to the mic. "They are being silenced. They are being shushed, shut up, shut down, pushed from the rooms of power."

This has to be it. Ben had to have someone give him a

heads up about Company X. Someone had leaked him Company X's terrible diversity numbers. She typed out a text to Viv – *You ok? Text me.* – and sent it.

Linden looked out over the crowd. "Further, we have correlated this across the performance of our market leaders. Our findings are extraordinary. When you shut out diverse thoughts and approaches, it limits performance." He paused, took a read on the crowd as they digested his topic. "We have seen the proof. Less diverse management means lower corporate performance. End of story."

He shook his head. "The New York Comptroller's Office has enormous wealth to invest. We know that with that wealth comes influence. With that influence comes responsibility. We do not take it lightly. We are responsible for the long-term financial wealth of our clients who entrust us with their pensions. As a result, we are putting our money where our mouth is.

"Today we are announcing the Spotlight Initiative. All publicly traded companies in which we invest must prove that they have been working to ensure there is diversity among their senior ranks. If not, we will pull our investments.

"We will be doing this, not only because it's the right thing for our country and our clients, but because it will make those companies outperform, and that is our fiscal responsibility."

Direct hit. Ben Kirschner had discovered that the Comptroller would require companies to have a proven track record on diversity. If the companies didn't, it would cost them millions. Scratch that. It would cost them billions.

Red Dress stepped up on stage, held up two printed pages, and spoke to the crowd. "The press release with full details has been published online on our site and many of you would have gotten a copy in your inboxes. Feel free to get in touch with me for future queries. Comptroller Linden will be conducting one-on-one interviews throughout the day."

Dom leaned into a nearby reporter. "Who is that woman?"

"Gabrielle Packer, the Comptroller's press secretary."

That sounded like someone Ben Kirschner would have been in touch with.

Later, after the crowd had thinned, Gabrielle Packer turned to head back to the elevators.

Dom stepped into her path. "Gabrielle Packer?"

Packer nodded.

Dom flashed her badge. "I'm Special Agent Domini Walker, FBI. Can I have a few minutes of your time?"

"Sure. Let's take this upstairs to my office."

Dom sat across from Packer in a cluttered office on the fifth floor. "Do you know Ben Kirschner?"

"The reporter for Business News? Sure."

"I'm afraid he's dead."

She petted her throat. "What?"

"Two days ago. In his apartment."

"Oh my God." Packer blinked and her mouth gaped. It was news to her.

"Did you know him well?"

"No, I wouldn't say well. No. I can't believe he's dead. I just saw him... what... last week?"

"Was Ben working a story on the Spotlight Initiative?"

"I'm sorry?" Shock took time to allow the brain to process.

"Was Ben working a story on the Spotlight Initiative?"

"You think this has something to do with his death?"

Dom nodded. "Possibly. We're chasing down all leads."

"Oh my God. Uhm. Yes, I believe he was. Although all information on the project was strictly confidential and embargoed. But yes, he was working it."

"Can you tell me about that?"

"Ben covers financial titans in New York. We know of him and, of course, he's interviewed me over the last few years. I've been here since the Comptroller was elected the previous term." She took a deep breath. "About a month ago, he started working his sources here—"

"What does that look like?"

She gave a cynical chuckle. "Journalists try to scoop a story before it goes official. That's what Ben was doing."

"Do you know who these sources would have been?"

"I try my best to incentivize our staff against leaks. Especially around important initiatives. We deal in very serious issues here. The returns for the city's retirees are on the line. We can't have our decisions bandied about in the public."

"Ok?"

"All our staff sign ironlad nondisclosure agreements. They also have regular training on how to handle confidential information. But some are not as reliable. Eight hundred is a lot to keep track of and our systems don't have the greatest security."

Dom asked, "So, there are leaks?"

"Yes. As with every office in the city."

"Did Ben get any insider or early information?"

"The truth is, I don't know."

"If he had, what would that have meant? What would he have done with it?"

She sighed. "I'm not sure. If he was a legit ethical reporter, he would have sniffed down the side stories."

"Explain that please."

She took a moment to think it through. "If I were Ben, I would have tried to identify certain companies that may be impacted negatively by the Spotlight Initiative. I would have tried to find those companies that didn't live up to their promises to the Comptroller to create diversity in senior management. Because if the Comptroller found out he had been lied to, he would pull the investment from that company immediately." She blew out her cheeks, the gravity of the situation coming into focus.

"That sounds like a big deal."

"If Ben had discovered that lying company, yes it would have been a big deal." She whispered, "Yes, a very big deal."

"I'll need to talk to anyone you think may have spoken with Ben. Anyone working on the Spotlight Initiative."

"That could be about twenty people."

"Let's start right away."

Chapter Forty-Nine

Bern pushed back from her desk and gathered up her purse. She had enough money this week to treat herself to a takeout lunch somewhere in Madison Square Park. The sun was out. It was the perfect day to splurge.

The elevator door opened to a thin man near the back. He nodded as she stepped in. The lobby button was already lit.

From behind her, the thin man said, "Bernadette Hax?"

She swallowed and turned.

He had dark eyes, a gaunt, lined face. "Are you Bernadette Hax?"

She blinked.

"Are you?"

She nodded.

"I need to speak with you."

She blinked as her mind spun. They'd discovered her actions. The spreadsheet. The apartment building on Houston. Slipping the envelope under the door. They'd found her. *Oh, God, what will they do to me?*

The elevator doors slid open to the ground floor lobby. He reached around her and hit the button for the 26th floor. The doors slid shut.

He continued to face the doors as the elevator swept upwards.

Her heart pounded.

He stared at a spot on the mirrored doors.

The door opened to an almost empty floor, lit brightly from the sun. There were no carpets, only gray cement. This must be the floor they were redoing.

He crooked his finger at her and they stepped from the elevator. He led her around to the right where up ahead a desk and a chair sat next to the far windows.

She followed numbly. *Is he going to fire me on the spot?*

As if reading her mind, he said, "I'll need you to sit here. This should take about thirty minutes." His voice sent an echo ricocheting through the emptiness.

Thirty minutes. Yes, he was going to fire me. She squinted against the sun as they walked to the table by the windows.

He pulled out a chair and waited for her.

She slowly sat down. The metal was cold through the cotton of her skirt and the view from the window of the park made her feel small and vulnerable.

He settled across from her.

"Bernadette Hax."

She swallowed and nodded.

"How old are you?"

"23."

"Back in the Iraq war, I got hurt. I took a bullet in the spine. My squad made a sled, pulled me through the desert for hours. I had to get surgery, fuse shit together. It's hurt ever since. Bad. Every day."

What was he talking about?

"It was a young woman who shot me. We were leaving a farm where we'd stayed. She ran after us. She should have left well enough alone." He rolled his shoulders. "It was a lucky shot for a stupid girl. It cost her." His eyes were dark and impenetrable. "I do security for the CEO."

Somehow that didn't make her feel better.

"Bernadette, as an HR professional you know full well what your boundaries are in personnel systems."

He's firing me. I was doing so well. My recovery was doing so well. Now I won't have a job. Dad is going to be so disappointed. Why was this man so scary? A haunted scent of talcum stung her nose.

"You've accessed a part of the system you are not allowed to. That was stupid."

She felt her eyes tearing up. *Oh God, please don't let me cry.*

"You then printed out a spreadsheet that was confidential."

I'm sorry, Dad.

"This means we have a serious problem."

He reached down, picked up a plastic bottle of water, set it near her elbow.

She didn't want water.

"Did you send that spreadsheet to anyone?"

The tears started. She shouldn't be crying. She should be thinking of a lie. But she was without words. Her throat was dry and thick and the tears rolled down her cheeks.

"Have some water."

She shook her head. There was no way she could drink from that bottle without her hands shaking and the water spilling down the front of her shirt.

"Did you send the spreadsheet to anyone?"

Crying now. Just full-on crying. Snot down her nose.

"Is that a yes?"

She nodded.

"Who? Who did you send it to?"

She sniffed hard. "A reporter."

His face was stern, angry. Those eyes were onyx. Evil.

He reached to his lower back and pulled a matte black gun.

Oh, God. What? What? Her mind stumbled. *What was happening? Is that a gun? Why had he just pulled out a gun? Oh, God.*

He placed the gun near his right hand. "I'm going to need you to drink that water. All of it."

His words hung in the air, as if time had stopped. The sun beat through the window. The chair was cold against her back. Her heart slowed its regular beating. Her mind froze on a single conclusion. *There's something in the water.*

"That water. I need you to drink it."

The water was poisoned. He wanted to poison her.

After all she'd survived, this was how it was going to end? With some evil man with a gun and poisoned water in an empty floor at her new job?

She shook him off.

He petted the gun. "Yes, you will, Bernadette Hax. You will drink that water."

She blinked. Numb.

"You will drink that water because I said so."

The sun streamed in through the window. If she ran, he would shoot her. If she stayed still, he would either shoot her or strangle her. She would not be strangled again.

She had agency now. She made her own choices.

This evil man would not hurt her.

There were no more tears.

There was no need to argue, to try to use words.

She grasped the small plastic bottle. It was room

temperature. She twisted the cap. It opened easily—the seal had been broken before. Her hand started shaking.

He caressed the gun. "Yes, that's right, Bernadette. I'm going to need you to drink that water. There are no other options." His eyes were black. Dark. Impenetrable. No sign of a human inside.

You do not get to win this time. This time it's my choice.

She picked up the bottle. She placed it to her lips.

I am a survivor.

She swallowed the first gulp. It tasted of salt.

I was a survivor.

Chapter Fifty

Mila had taken a ride-share that had cost eighty dollars and had dropped her off outside Horizons Home in Paramus, New Jersey. It was a low brick building with a white canopy over the entrance at the top of a curved drive. She ambled into the quiet lobby. The pale wood tiles were shiny and clean.

At the wide reception desk, she lied. "I'm here to see my great-uncle. Mr. Simon Bigg."

"Sure thing, honey," said a heavy blonde in a white medical top and blue pants. "You can wait in the lounge. I'll bring him in."

They should have had better security, shouldn't they? But then again, how many people were showing up at nursing homes lying about their identities?

She found a flowered maroon and yellow chair by a window and settled back against the thick pillows. The smell of meatloaf and peas wafted from a back door along with the sounds of a daytime game show.

It didn't take long for a large black orderly to roll in a wizened man in a wheelchair.

Suddenly, the plan seemed ludicrous and extremely dangerous. What if good ole Mr. Bigg didn't want a visitor?

The orderly smiled. "You visiting with Mr. Bigg today, my dear?"

The archaic guy in the wheelchair stared with a dead gaze. The fear receded.

"Yes. Yes, I am."

The orderly clicked the brakes on the wheelchair. "I'll just leave him here. Let the front desk know on your way out."

She wondered how quickly they would come get him once she left. Everybody knew about the horrible negligence that went on in these old places. But this one looked clean and tidy. And so far the staff couldn't have been nicer. Maybe Mr. Bigg's family had done their homework and gotten him a good rest home.

She focused on Mr. Bigg's wrinkled face. His pale blue eyes were rheumy under big bushy white wizard eyebrows. Come to think of it, he really looked like a wizard.

"Mr. Bigg?"

Nothing.

"Mr. Simon Bigg?"

Nothing. *Uh-oh.*

"My name is Mila Pascale. I'm in school at NYU. I'm studying to be an FBI agent. You know, chase down bad guys. I'm thinking of specializing in child kidnapping cases, but that's a while off before I get to make that decision. I've got some questions for you, Mr. Bigg, about your time as a lawyer. Do you mind if I ask those?"

Nothing. Just a wizened old wizard's face.

Huh. She had just wasted a hundred and sixty dollars for the round trip.

Well, might as well entertain this old guy before she left, in case inside that frozen mask his mind really was working.

Mila spoke to Mr. Simon Bigg for another thirty minutes. She explained what had happened to her brother, Jimmy, and how she had met Special Agent Domini Walker. She explained how she wanted to be like Dom. She talked about Beecher and the dog Tinks. She explained how she wasn't quite ready to move back out on her own, although she had really liked her last apartment. It was so clean and quiet. The Walkers' house was kinda busy and loud. Neither Beecher nor Dom were exactly quiet. But she liked the safety and the warmth at the Walkers. She told old Simon Bigg about school and the research and all the other kids who were fine. Normal kids. Just not any who were real close friends. She didn't have close friends. She didn't really want close friends. That wasn't her jam.

Eventually, she stood, gave him a hug, and told the receptionist on her way out that Simon Bigg was sitting alone in the common room.

The blonde lady had smiled sweetly.

Outside, she stood looking over the green lawn, thinking about what Simon Bigg had been. A lawyer in a small firm next to the New York Police Benevolent Association, taking cases to defend policemen accused of wrongdoing. Had he been assigned the Stewart Walker case by someone? Had Stewart sought him out? Maybe there was someone else who had worked in that small law firm.

A lightbulb went off. Maybe, like at the Benevolent Association, there had been a 'girl' who'd done her nails, read gossip magazines, and who'd worked at Myer and Bigg.

She pulled up her phone and did an internet search, found a dead link for www.simonbigg.com. She smiled and typed in *Wayback Machine*, then entered the same www.simonbigg.com. After a few minutes, the archived website blew up on her screen. A few clicks and she found the name of the former executive assistant. *Regina Maria D'Angela.*

The wind rustled the grass.

That was quite a name. Surely, there weren't too many women in the New York area who used that full name as their professional names. Odds were low. She typed it in and got her answer.

Only one Regina Maria D'Angela was now working in New York at a new law firm downtown.

Mila dialed the number.

A soft woman's voice answered, "Seymour Weiz's office."

"Is this Regina Maria D'Angela?"

"This is she."

"Hi, Ms. D'Angela. My name is Mila Pascale. Are you the same Regina Maria who worked with Simon Bigg?"

A mild hesitation. "Yes? Can I help you?"

Start with the truth, if it wasn't too bad. "Yes, thank you. I'm a criminology student over at NYU. I'm doing some research on the work your former firm did for the NYPD. I wanted to ask Mr. Bigg about a case he had a few years ago. So I went to see him. I'm afraid I didn't get much."

A pause, then, "I'm sorry. What was your name again, dear?"

"Mila Pascale."

"Mila, did you go out to Horizons Home?"

She looked up at the white canopy. "I'm actually here now."

"Yes, well, were you able to see him?"

"Yes."

"Then you know, dear."

"Yes, ma'am. That's why I'm calling. I had a question for him, a fairly simple question, but I'm stuck now. Perhaps I could ask you?"

"Go ahead," she said in a nice teacher voice.

"I was wondering about the Stewart Walker case."

A slight but audible gasp.

"You see, I'm helping his family. We just want to make sure we have gotten all the information that was available about the case and the indictment. You know, to ease the pain."

Regina Maria D'Angelo's voice was just above a whisper. "Perhaps you should come see me, Mila."

Chapter Fifty-One

The storage room was sterile and cold with filing cabinets along all four walls. Dom sat at the lone table across from a young staffer who looked about eighteen years old but was apparently twenty-five. Wesley Nott's blue bow tie and cold indifference both spoke of Ivy League entitlement and summer homes with ocean views. He was her eleventh interview and the first to recognize Ben Kirschner's photo on her phone.

"Yeah, he was here," Wesley said. "He was asking us about the buzz. Said he'd heard there were rumors of a new initiative. But I didn't get the impression he knew about the substance of Spotlight."

"You don't think he knew the details?"

"No. What we do down here is kept under extremely tight lock and key. I mean, the Comptroller can move markets. We don't mess around with leaks and we sure as shit don't talk to reporters. Even with Spotlight."

Even? What did that mean? "What do you think of the Spotlight Initiative?"

He shrugged. "It's not up to me to think about it."

"I'm asking."

"I do not necessarily believe in the underlying premise. I don't think diversity is an indicator of better management, better strategy, or better product. I don't think they can prove the premise and I don't think investment should follow it as a theory."

"You don't think women and minorities bring added value?"

"I don't think that's a worthy investment criteria."

Sexism and racism were no different in the finance sector. How ordinary and predictable. "Your boss seems to think it does."

He shrugged.

Entitled brat. "What did you think of Ben Kirschner?"

He couldn't help the pride and smugness of someone who was on the inside looking out. "I will give him this, he knew most of the big players down here in this building. He was pretty sussed that way. Linden. Stille."

"As in, he spoke their names?"

"Oh yeah, he asked me questions about our senior management."

"What specific questions?"

"Look, I told him to stop sniffing."

She paused, lowered her voice, and said slowly, "Wesley, that's not what I asked."

He narrowed his eyes. "He asked about Linden. What was he like to work with? How long had he been here? Lots of people ask about Linden. He's like the Wizard of Oz. His decisions have heft. Then he asked about Stille. Same stuff. Like how long he'd worked here, what they did before. He wanted to know about Stille leaving."

Ping. She flattened her hands. "Who's Stille?"

"Theodore Stille. He was my boss up until a month ago. He was the Chief Investment Officer."

"Tell me more."

"I mean, he ran our group, made sure our investments were sound, that we were getting the right portfolios, watching the trends and spreads, hedging properly. It's the CIO's job to make sure we don't lose money."

"And?"

"I guess it's just not often a CIO leaves."

Double ping. "What's Stille like?"

"As in, like as a person?"

"Yes, Wesley, as in, like as a person."

His chin jutted. "Good enough. Knew his business. Made solid returns for the retirement accounts of New Yorkers. Nice enough. Stayed in his office. Didn't yell at people or anything. I'd say, he wasn't oozing charm, but that's not why the Comptrollers hire any of us."

You can say that again. "And Ben Kirschner was asking about Theodore Stille?"

"Oh, yeah. For sure. I remember that."

"What did you tell him?"

"Nothing. Kirschner was trying to get gossip and I gave him none." He was proud of himself.

"Did Stille leave under good circumstances?"

"I dunno. He and Linden seemed to get along fine."

"Did Ben Kirschner ask about that?"

Wesley took a moment, trying to recall. Then he jutted out his lower lip. "You know, I think he did ask that. Like how Stille left."

She leaned a fraction of an inch closer. "Where's Stille now?"

"I dunno."

"Where do former Chief Investment Officers generally go?"

"To a hedge fund or private equity. He'll make big money in the private sector." Wesley Nott crossed his arms as if he too was going to follow Stille's path at some point in the future. "Stille is gonna make a shit ton."

Triple ping. Follow the money. Right to one recently retired CIO.

Chapter Fifty-Two

The plane taxied across the black tarmac and stopped beside the International Airport on Grand Cayman. The sun was blazing. The work the country had done to upgrade the building had been a long time coming but the white and glass arching roof looked modern.

A hot wave of air swept through the airplane as the door was opened. Owen wondered how many times in his career he had made this trip to this exact airport. Maybe fifty?

He sailed through the immigration hall using his personal blue passport. No reason to highlight to the authorities that an FBI special agent was on their territory. He moved through the exit hall with the backpack and got in line at the taxi queue. He knew exactly where he was going.

The National Cayman Bank Trust headquarters was on Elgin Street in Georgetown, not far from the airport. The traffic had gotten worse over the years Owen had been traveling here. If you didn't time it correctly, you could sit in a standstill for thirty minutes. This morning he was lucky, and the taxi sped through the nondescript streets of Georgetown. As one of the banking capitols of the world, as well as a cruise destination, Grand Cayman was an odd mix of locals, cheesy tourists, and the undercurrent of big amounts of quiet money. The buildings reflected this: nothing much to speak of from the outside — lots of square cement structures that felt like they were built in the 1970s.

It was the first time Owen has paused in three days. As the foreign world swept by, fresh and jarring in its difference from his New York life, his mind wandered to existential issues. He had gotten in the Bureau based on his skill set and his acumen in forensic accounting. He loved his job. He loved the Bureau. The politics in New York were over the top, but if you're a forensic accountant it was the epicenter of the universe. Owen had worked bloody hard to get the job and to stay there. He was good at what he did. Actually, he was excellent at what he did. But for the last few years the successes entailed sending greedy, rich white men to luxury prisons. It wasn't exactly the stuff the movies were made of.

This time Owen Whyte was part of a team on the hunt for a predator. And fucking yes that felt good.

Fifteen minutes later he arrived in front of a huge, blue and white building surrounded by green lawn and tall palm trees. In the heat, it had a sleepy feel: there were no pedestrians and a lazy security guy sat in an air-conditioned shed by the parking lot entrance.

Inside the frigid, air-conditioned lobby, he laid his badge down on the counter at reception and said, "I'm Special

Agent Owen Whyte with the US FBI. I'd like to speak with a manager please."

He didn't have to wait long.

A heavyset black woman in a blue uniform and the no-nonsense look of a patient but tough mother approached with an outstretched hand. "I'm Theresa Gillespie. I'm a manager here."

The soft Caymanian accent – a mix of English, American Southern drawl, Scottish, and Welsh – reminded him of Jamaica.

"Thank you, Ms. Gillespie. I'm Owen Whyte, Special Agent from the FBI in New York."

She led him to a private room and sat behind a clean desk with a single computer. "I'll need your ID again please, Special Agent." She inspected his badge and passport and handed them back. "What can I do for you today?"

The Caymanians he had worked with over the years were respectful and charming. Theresa Gillespie was no different. "I'm hoping this is a quick meeting. We've turned up a question about a Suspicious Activity Report that was entered into the system. I just wanted to follow it down. I'd like appropriate access to the transactions from the related account."

She smiled. "Of course. Can I see your warrant?"

He grinned pleasantly because he had arranged the paperwork before the flight. He reached into his breast pocket and slid the folded warrant across the desk.

She examined meticulously before setting it to the side and positioning herself in front of the computer. "I'll need the bank account details."

He relayed the bank account number. "Mr. M. Moreno."

Her long red nails tapped on the keyboard. "Yes, here we are. What can I help you with?"

"When did Mr. Moreno open the account?"

"Eighteen months ago."

"In person?"

"Yes."

What ID was this ghost using? "Did he use identification?"

She gave him a smug look, as if warning him not to condescend to her. "Of course."

"Do you have a copy of it in the file?"

"No. We confirm identity in person. We do not keep those on file."

"Does it say what ID he used to open the file?"

She peered at the screen. "No."

"What does one need?"

"A passport, a driver's license if US citizen, a birth certificate."

"How much did he use to open the account?"

"$30,000."

"The activity I'm interested in occurred over the last five months. Was there any activity prior to that period?"

She scanned the screen. "No. He opened the account and then nothing till the period about which you are inquiring."

"From what we know from our SAR, a US bank wired Mr. Moreno's account in tranches roughly $15,000 to $20,000 over the last few months."

"Yes, that's what I see as well." She nodded. "There were other deposits via wire."

Hair tingled on the back of his neck. "What others?"

"This account had three deposits over the last three months. Each of $100,000."

Holy shit. Someone had sent big money to Moreno. "From who?"

She blinked. "It says here a Willowgrass LLC. Based in Greenwich Connecticut."

They both knew it was a cut out. It would take time to find out who owned Willowgrass. He asked, "Did Moreno move out any of the funds that were deposited into that account at any time over the last five months?"

"Oh, indeed."

"How much?"

"He withdrew $200,000."

Moreno was moving that money to someone else.

"The rest is still in the account?"

"Yes."

But keeping some for himself. "How did he withdraw that $200?"

"In one lump sum. A cashier's check."

Hair tingled.

"Can a client order a cashier's check online?"

She gave him a grin. "No, Special Agent, a client has to present themselves in person to order a cashier's check from National Cayman Bank Trust."

"He was here?"

She nodded, giving him a small smile.

"When did he get the cashier's check?"

"Two months ago. Saturday the 5th."

Moreno had come to Cayman to move money in an untraceable cashier's check. He smiled at Ms. Gillespie. "Thank you. You've been extremely helpful."

"We are supportive of law enforcement, Agent."

Chapter Fifty-Three

"Well, get on with it. What have you got?" Fontaine was standing by the window, looking out over the city with a face that was simultaneously weary and wary.

Dom needed official approval. She needed the resources to pursue this. She straightened her shoulders and took a deep breath. In her mind, Stewart Walker whispered, *Don't worry, my Dom, you got this. It's a solid case and you're an excellent agent.* She relayed the story of the Spotlight Initiative and the focus on human resources diversity metrics in each of the Comptroller's investments.

As he watched her, his face displayed disbelief. "Are you seriously talking about the race and gender type shit? Those numbers?"

"Yes, sir."

"You have got to be kidding me."

"No, sir."

"As in human resources tracking the numbers of women and minorities and this has something to do with a murder?" Fontaine squinted. Diversity and inclusion were high priorities at the Bureau. They didn't have enough minorities or women in senior management. Fontaine himself was a rare minority. But that was an administration issue. Not operations.

"Yes, sir. I can't connect all the dots yet. But I believe there is motive. I have a working theory."

"Expound."

"One. This initiative was secret until today. Two. If a Comptroller-invested company has been lying about bad diversity numbers, advance intel about the initiative would be worth something. Three. The Comptroller's Chief Investment Officer resigned last month. My theory is that the Chief Investment Officer sold this info to a company and Ben Kirschner figured that out."

His eyes widened as the implications took form in his mind. "That's fraud. That's ongoing, blatant fraud. That's Security Exchange Commission level fraud."

"Yes, sir."

"By a very big company."

She nodded.

He cracked his neck and he scowled. "All right. Yes. You've got yourself an official investigation."

Stewart Walker whispered, *I told you, my Dom. You're enough.* She gave Fontaine a quick nod. "And, sir, good luck with your son."

Lea waggled her hands over her head. "We rocking and rolling?"

Dom grinned. "It's official."

"Lord Almighty, diligent hands will rule. This is some

crazy-ass white-man shit. You keep turning over the rocks with the wealthy underneath."

"I know, right?"

"Girl, that is not gonna help your career here in the city."

"I'm fine just where I am."

"True. And Fontaine has got your back. But don't let the other boys around here hear about the boss man moving so fast for you." She whistled. "What do you need from me, my pet?"

Dom sat, cracking her neck. Time for a regroup. "I'm gonna need a trap and trace on Ben Kirschner's cell and Theodore Stille's cell."

Lea made a note. "It will take a day. Maybe twenty hours."

"In the meantime, let's open up Stille, see what we find."

Lea grinned to herself. "Follow the money. Like hot baller Owen Whyte." Lea gave her a side-eye. "I Googled him."

"No, you didn't."

"Honestly, Walker. Sometimes I feel like you were *born* fifty years old. Everybody Googles everybody." She sat back. "Our boy does endurance events."

Why was this intriguing? It shouldn't have been intriguing. It should not have been intriguing in the slightest. What Owen Whyte did on his free time was his business. They had a case to focus on.

"He's done the Arctic Circle Ski Race in Greenland – they cross-country ski for three days and sleep in tents. In the Arctic." Lea pulled up a site on her screen with snow-covered mountains. "You know what that is? That's the motherfucking Annapurna Range." She pointed to the largest peak. "That's Annapurna I. It's the tenth largest mountain in the world. Our boy Owen has climbed that."

So not interesting.

"Two years ago, he did the Dakar Rally in South America." She glanced over her shoulder. "But that wouldn't interest you at all, given how you're totally *not* into racing or cars."

"Sounds like personality substitution if you ask me."

Lea snorted. "Says the FBI Special Agent who leads teams into crack houses to rescue kids. Isn't that the Coffee. Kettle. Black."

"If you're so into him, why don't *you* ask him out?" The pang in Dom's chest was real.

"Look, Miss Dom, you know I'm all about the United Colors of Benetton. If they're tall and handsome, I'm in. But I also know when a man's attentions are not on me."

Dom didn't say a word. Not one word.

"And when they're sighted on someone else."

"Shut it."

Lea chuckled. "Seriously, if he had cow eyes for me, I'd be all about it."

"Shut it."

"I'd be happy to have a glass of that deliciousness." She closed her eyes and leaned her head back. "Hmmmmm, I bet he's like a long sip of a succulent Cabernet Sauvignon... Full-bodied, intense, with some light notes."

"Shut it."

"Go. Eat your food with gladness, and drink your wine with a joyful heart, for God has already approved what you do."

"You made that up."

"Ecclesiastes 9:7. The sentiment is translated in any Bible version you read." She leaned forward and placed her fingertips on her keyboard. "I mean if God says drink some damn wine…"

"We're following the money. Let's dig into Stille."

"Mm-hmm. See me, I'm digging into Stille. I'm on it. But I'm thinking about God telling people to drink some damn wine…"

Chapter Fifty-Four

Alone at her desk an hour later, Lea cracked her knuckles. This was her kind of roll. "Ok, Mr. Stille-I'm-a-banker-with-a-nice-wife-two kids-and-Labradors, let's see what's under your hood."

First, she pulled his credit cards. He had an American Express and a Citibank Visa. Most months he bought groceries for roughly $500, paid his Amazon bills of a couple $100, and had regular monthly withdrawals to the Old Greenwich Country Club of $1,500. She whistled. Apparently public service at BAM wasn't too shabby. But there were no unusual expenditures on either card going back eight months. No clothes expenditures, not a lot of dining out. He looked clean. In fact, he looked boring. No casinos, no shows, no hotel sexy stays.

When Lea got married, she would insist on date nights.

She pulled the credit cards of Miranda Stille. A whole lot of Whole Foods spending. Jeez this woman could rack up some money on fine food. She also bought $1,000 a month in clothing items, mostly from online. She also got herself a facial and a massage about twice a month. But also, nothing unusual on Mrs. Stille's expenditures. Staying at home in Greenwich must be monotonous.

Maybe the Stilles used cash.

She searched online for social accounts of either Stille or his wife. Nothing.

She plugged in the son's name, Theodore Jr, and found a Facebook page. From his bio he was seventeen years old and a senior at Old Greenwich High, but otherwise the account privacy was locked down. He had no other social media accounts.

She typed in *Chanel Stille*. The daughter had no Facebook. These young kids were savvy about social media. But she did have an Instagram. Lea scrolled through the photos going backwards. Chanel was a pretty girl, long blonde hair, no makeup, around the age of fifteen. She had posted many athletic photos with friends on various soccer fields.

Lea's finger paused on the mouse. Two months ago, Chanel had posted a selfie. A huge smile on a beaming face in front of a marina in a tropical setting. "Oh, hello, tropics."

She leaned close to the screen.

In the background, under a clear sky, a single pier reached out into a blue ocean. Two sailboats were docked, their sterns facing the photograph. On the left, the boat was named *The Princess* and was registered in Bahamas. The second boat was named *Aurora*, registered in South Keys, Florida. Definitely Caribbean.

She cracked her knuckles and clicked on the next photo.

Chanel had taken a wide panoramic photo of the marina. Six palm trees lined the beach. To the right of the pier, a small inlet harbored more boats docked against five short piers. A white gazebo sat between the inlet and a small gravel parking lot. Two wheelbarrows were pitched upwards by the gazebo.

"Here we go." She cracked her neck.

Lea's fingers flied over the keyboards, searching marinas in the top four Caribbean countries with banking loopholes. The Cayman Islands had eleven, Panama had six, the Bahamas had nineteen, and the British Virgin Islands had twenty.

She printed out the list of the Cayman. Why not start where hottie Owen was? She moved quickly to the printer and picked up the list.

She searched the name of the first Cayman marina, pulled up the official website, and scanned the photo gallery. No gazebo. No inlet. She moved to the second marina and repeated the search. Twenty minutes later, she found the gazebo.

She jumped up and raced to Dom's desk. "I pulled Stille and his wife's credit cards. Nothing. I checked Facebook. Nothing. But his daughter has an Instagram." Lea pushed Dom's hands off her keyboard, and typed in a website, hit enter.

A marina on a tropical island filled the screen.

"Harbor Yacht Club along Governor's Creek, Cypress Pointe, Grand Cayman."

Dom opened her mouth to speak.

Lea held up her finger, "Please, Miss Dom. I ain't done." She pointed to the screen along the bottom of the Instagram photo. It was dated two months ago. "Then I pulled the son's credit card. And this here righteous researcher discovered four plane tickets to Grand Cayman two months ago."

Dom's eyes widened. "Stille was hiding the trip."

Lea raised both hands high above her head and slashed fingers downwards in peace signs. "Deuces."

Dom yanked up her phone.

Owen picked up on the second ring.

She blurted, "We've got Stille at Harbor Yacht Club on Governor's Creek. Two months ago. With his family. He went using his son's credit card."

"On it." He hung up.

Chapter Fifty-Five

The taxi pulled into the gravel parking of the Harbor Yacht Club on Governor's Creek. Owen paid the driver and stretched out. The golden rays of a setting sun cast pink over rolling waves that broke softly on a white sand beach. In a marina, past a gazebo, boats rode swells, their halyards clinking gently against masts.

A grizzled black man in a faded t-shirt and white captain's hat approached from the marina building at the back of the lot.

Owen met him on the grass. "My name is Owen Whyte. I'm an agent for the United States FBI."

The black man's eyes widened. "Arden Seymour. Proprietor and all-around dock master. How can I help you?"

"I'm trying to confirm some folks who visited here two months ago."

"Ok, well if they took a trip on one of our boats, I'd have those records."

"That would be great."

"Can I see some ID?"

Well done. Never bad to be cautious. Owen handed over his badge.

Arden chatted as they crossed the lot. "Sometimes visitors want to go a fishin'. Sometimes they want to go sailin'. I even run them out for snorkelin' up north. We do all kinds of boats out of here. I keep logs of everyone I take on a boat. You, know, to keep record."

"You confirm against an ID?"

"Oh yea. I ask for their passports. I wanna know who's on my boats."

Inside the building, Arden motioned him past a bar covered with flags and thick ropes. In the office, the AC was on high, diffusing the sweet smell of teak and oil. The windows were foggy with salt.

The old captain made his way around his desk. "What date you say?"

"August 5th."

Arden pulled out a black book and his wizened old finger flipped through pages of handwritten names and details. "Yeah, here it is. August 5th I took a family and their friend out."

"Was the friend a male?"

"Yeah, thin guy. Didn't talk much."

"What did they do?"

"Just sailin'. Up north and then return. We stopped for some swimmin' and a lunch. I pack chips and sandwiches and sodas." He slid the book around and pushed it across the desk, his finger pointing to the names written in a scrawling script.

Theodore Stille,
Miranda Stille,
Theodore Stille Jr
Chanel Stille

Chase Richter

Wait, what? Where was Moreno? Owen straightened. Who the fuck was Chase Richter? "Did he call himself Chase Richter?"

Arden nodded.

"Ok, thanks for that, my friend."

"Sure. Good luck, Agent."

Outside the sun had set and the cicada had kicked up a chorus. Owen pulled out his phone. "Marty, it's Owen."

"Hey, man. What's up?"

"You know that file your Army contact sent over on Moreno?"

"Sure. Yeah."

"I need you to pull that again."

"Yeah, sure. Hold on." He grunted as he reached across his desk. "Yup, got it."

"I remember you said something about his entire squad getting killed. All at the same time."

"Yeah." Flipping pages. "Yup. 2004. Fallujah. KIA. All five of them."

"Can you read me the names?"

"Marquicio Moreno, John O'Dore, Adam Morgenstein, John Martin, and their captain, Chase Richter"

Inside the inlet, the waves crashed gently on the rocks.

"You're a genius. Thanks, Marty."

Owen pulled out his burner phone.

The other side picked up. "Companies R Us."

"Reg. It's Owen."

"Look, man, I told you—"

"Listen, I get it. Just so you know, I'm on my burner phone. Not traceable. No records."

"Owen, I can't—"

"I get it. I do. I don't have time for a warrant. But trust me, I could get it." He leaned over, took a deep inhale of salty air. "Let's just do it this way. Hang up if what I'm about to say is correct."

Silence.

"Trusted Security Services has one owner. Chase Richter."

Reggie hung up.

Owen stood. In the distance the darkening sky met the blue ocean in a single, well defined line.

A highly trained top sniper who disappeared from the Army, spent ten years off the grid, and recently emerged with the assumed identity of his former dead commanding officer, was now an extremely well-paid security consultant shifting hundreds of thousands of dollars to off shore accounts and was wrapped up in a fraud worth millions of dollars. The whole saga was diabolically well planned. Which meant things had just gotten very dangerous.

Chapter Fifty-Six

As her mind awakened, the first thing Viv noticed was the tightness in her lungs. Even before opening her eyes, she exhaled and inhaled four times, noticing the shortness, the constriction, the heavy weight surrounding her chest. It confused her. Was someone sitting on her? But of course not. Was something pushing down on her? No, there was no pressure from the outside. It was inside, inside the cavity between her ribs. Yes, the lungs. It was the lungs.

She inhaled sharply through her nose, trying to jump start the lungs into filling up more.

Damnit, what's going on with my lungs? She opened her eyes.

It was pitch-black. She blinked. What was wrong with her eyes? Why couldn't she see anything? She kept blinking. The darkness didn't lighten. It was onyx.

She rolled her head to the left. Still dark.

Where was she? Her brain felt slow. Every thought had a fuzziness to it, lacking clarity, like being under water.

Wait. Where was she? Her nose and throat were scratchy.

Something tickled the back of her brain, a sense hiding in the recesses. She knew the tingling. It was something everyone knew, instinctively. The sensation moved through the sludge, moving forward, slowly but steadily.

It exploded across the front of her mind. It had a name. Terror.

Suddenly she was aware of everything happening to her body simultaneously. Her head was resting on something hard and the back of her skull was sore as if it had been in the same position for a very long time. Her knees were bent and twisted to the left. She pushed her legs straight, but her feet tapped against a wall. A hard wall.

Her wrists were mashed together. She stretched against them, but something kept them pressed, some kind of binding. A binding.

Terror thumped through her veins like hot ice.

She was on her back, bound at the wrists, in a pitch-black confined space, bigger than a coffin but not by a lot.

Oh God. What's happening? Jesus fucking christ, where am I? I'm in a pitch-black fucking coffin.

Thoughts ricocheted like ping-pong balls. But there were no recent memories. She had no idea how she had gotten here.

She rocked her head back and forth violently, pulled back against her shoulder blades, yanking against the wrist bindings. She was sweating.

Where the fuck am I?

Her chest constricted.

Oh God, I can't breathe.

She inhaled quickly against the adrenaline coursing in her veins. Air rushed in and out of a dry nose. The pressure bore down on her chest.

She was getting woozy. She hated darkness. She hated

being confined. Thoughts were colliding, morphing, merging.

Dizziness swept across her face like a warm wave, gentle against her skin.

Oh God, I'm going to pass out.

Chapter Fifty-Seven

Friday

It was 5 A.M. and the sun was only a pink hint in the sky over the sleepy Westchester suburb. An hour earlier, Becky from Forensics had called. "Dom. You're not going to believe this. We got a hit on a print from that spreadsheet document Lea dropped off. It was in the NYPD records. A Bernadette Hax. Twenty-three years old. She was the victim of a brutal assault and rape last year. She filed a report so she's in the system."

"Did they catch the guy?"

"No."

"Can you text me her home address?"

Becky had said, "Sure. It's up in Westchester."

Dom stood from the car, shut the door, strode to the front door of the Hax house, and gave the red door two strong knocks.

A fifty-year-old woman with tears running down her face opened the door. "Oh, thank God."

"FBI, ma'am." She held up her badge. "Special Agent Domini Walker."

"Police?"

"No, ma'am, I'm FBI."

The woman shook her head, confused. "I only called the police ten minutes ago." Her mouth gaped open and her brow crinkled.

"About what, ma'am?"

"Bern."

"Bernadette Hax?"

"Yes! My daughter."

"What about her?"

Mrs. Hax's voice came out as a high-pitched wail. "She's missing!"

"Can I come in?"

"She's been missing since yesterday. She didn't come home last night." The mother's brain was misfiring. She stood in the doorframe. "What am I supposed to do? What am I supposed to do?"

The sound of a parent's anguish never got normal. "Ma'am, can I come in?"

Dom guided Mrs. Hax into a small living room with chintz sofas and gently asked her to sit down.

Mrs. Hax wailed. "Oh God, where is Bern?"

Dom swallowed. "Who did Bernadette work for?"

"Smithson Health Insurance."

Oh Shit. One of the top ten insurance companies in the country. Enormous. "In their city headquarters?"

Mrs. Hax gaped at her. "You think this has something to do with Smithson?"

"What did she do there?"

"She's an executive assistant."

"In what department?"

"Human Resources."

Here we go.

"Two nights ago, she came home yesterday from work but then went back out really late, after we were in bed. That is *very* unusual for her." Mrs. Hax sniffed hard against the tears.

Two nights ago. That corresponded to the messenger pushing the spreadsheet under the door at the bait apartment.

"Then yesterday she went off to work like always. But she didn't come home." Mrs. Hax wailed.

"You called the police yesterday?"

"Yes, but they told me to wait. They needed twenty-four hours for someone to be missing."

The tears were flowing. Mrs. Hax blew her nose and the tissue fell apart in her hands.

Dom picked up the nearby tissue box, handed it to her. "Tell me about Bernadette. What's she like?"

"She's shy. Getting better. Always every day getting better. Working hard on her sadness."

Dom waited.

"There was an incident. Her last year in college. A man raped her." The words were difficult for her to say. "Violently. After, she… mentally, retreated."

"How long has she been working at Smithson?"

"She's only been there six months."

"Can I see her room?"

Dom closed the door behind her, muting the sound of the mother's crying. Bernadette Hax's room was soothing and soft. The young woman had an eye for pastels and they covered all available spaces. Pale pinks and yellows were offset by softly hued blue walls. A rose bedspread had been made over a queen-sized bed. Prints of florals in the vein of Georgia O'Keeffe had pride of place on all four walls. This woman, so brutally assaulted, had made a private safe place here with colors and flowers.

Tears stung Dom's eyes. Bern hadn't been safe. She had stumbled across something at her work that had gotten her in trouble. *Where are you, Bernadette?*

She touched the frames of photos with Bernadette and friends at college. Smiling, carefree, free. Safe.

She looked over books, mostly romance and thrillers.

In the top drawer of the desk, she found a key that led her to a locked box in the back of the closet's top shelf. Inside was a single folder with the NYPD incident report. It was similar to many Dom had seen, many she had helped write.

Bernadette's assailant had been vicious, demented.

Dom's anger grew.

She pushed the folder back into the lockbox and returned it to the closet.

In the living room, Mrs. Hax was gulping for air. "I can't. Where is she?"

"I'm going to try to retrace her steps from work yesterday. Would she have spoken to friends? Are there people that may have spoken with her throughout the day?"

"Maybe her therapist?"

"Yes. Let's call her."

The therapist, Rhonda, knew something was wrong

right away. Across the speaker phone she said, "Oh God. Bern called me yesterday."

Dom said, "Don't break patient-doctor confidentiality. I'm not interested in her therapy. But perhaps just tell us what Bernadette was doing yesterday when she called you? Where she was? I just need some locators."

"She was speaking very quickly, saying she had uncovered something on her work's systems. She was at work. She was not supposed to be allowed into that system, but there was a glitch. She saw numbers that didn't look right. We talked about her options." Rhonda sucked in air. "At the time, I thought she was being overly sensitive because…" She stopped herself. Patient confidentially was a fine line. "But she was definitely at work."

Dom asked, "What options did you discuss?"

"We talked about what someone could do if they had uncovered an ethical issue."

"Would that include making those findings public?"

"We didn't say that explicitly, but yes, that would have been an option for Bern. To take control of the situation and do something she felt was right."

Dom looked at Mrs. Hax. She was nodding.

Mrs. Hax said, "Bern has been working on finding strength, on finding herself, on being a survivor, not a victim."

Dom asked, "And that might have involved her doing something with this ethical dilemma she uncovered?"

Mrs. Hax tears were free-flowing and her hands were shaking. "Oh yes. Bern may have done something if she had discovered Smithson was doing something corrupt. Oh God."

On the speakerphone, Rhonda said quietly, "I agree with that."

Inside the sports car, Dom called Lea. "First. Our company committing fraud is Smithson."

"Holy mother of shitloads. Shitload mountain. Aren't they like a Fortune 500?"

"Second, I think they kidnapped our mole."

"Kidnapped? Jesus Christ."

Dom filled her in on the missing Bernadette Hax. "Get a ping on her cell ASAP. They could have stashed her anywhere."

"Copy that."

"I'm going to roll on their headquarters in Madison Square."

"Copy that."

"But, Lea..."

"Yes?"

"I'm not calling in backup. I gotta be nimble. We have no idea where they've hidden Bernadette."

"Copy that."

"If I need to squeeze someone..." They'd worked together long enough to know Dom would never do anything illegal, but sometimes you had to think outside the box.

"Understood."

"I need you to get trackers on Smithson's senior guys. Use cell phones."

"I'm on it. Will take a bit."

Dom looked at the clock on her phone. "We've got about an hour."

"Roger that."

Dom's phone vibrated and she switched over to a new call.

"Agent Walker?" The female's voice was tremulous.

"Yes?"

"This is Ellen Doberman. Vivienne Preston gave me your number."

Along her neckline, Dom's skin tingled. "Yes?"

"Viv didn't come home last night."

Chapter Fifty-Eight

The sports car surged down the highway as Dom pressed the pedal to the floor.

This is not happening. No, no, no. Those motherfuckers took Bernadette Hax and now Viv is missing. No, no, no. This is not happening on my watch.

She shot the car through gaps in the traffic, missing bumpers by inches.

No, no, no. Not on my fucking watch.

The earphone in her ear chimed with an incoming call. She pressed *answer* without taking her eyes off the road.

"It's Lea."

"Talk to me."

"Bernadette's last ping was inside the Smithson headquarters building in Madison Square Park. Last night."

No, no, no.

"I've got background on Smithson."

"Go."

"Over one hundred locations spread across North America. Headquarters, as you know, down on Madison

Square Park. That's where most of their senior folks are. Fifth largest health insurance company in the US. Fortune 500. Income at $2 billion. They sell health care, dental, pharmacy, and long-term care insurance. Most of their investors are institutional, the big ones—BlackRock, Vanguard. Of course, NY Comptroller is heavily invested."

"His name. Tell me his name."

"The CEO is a fifty-five-year-old white male by the name of Tyler Huntington."

Tyler Huntington.

Tyler Huntington.

I'm coming for you, Tyler Huntington, and your scum thug.

"His residence is in Old Greenwich, Connecticut. His office is on the fiftieth floor of their headquarters building. He's been at Smithson for five years. Before that, he was CEO of NatureLife Insurance. Prior to that, he was a senior VP at three other insurance companies. Last year, his total compensation was $18 million." Her voiced dropped. "Dom, you want me to call the headquarters, confirm he's on site?"

"No." She shifted into fourth and careened through two slower cars. "No. I want them blind."

"Copy that." Lea hung up.

The huge building dominated an entire city block. The gray stone walls loomed fifty floors up, capped with a giant gold pyramid like a cathedral. The main entrance on Madison Square Park was ensconced with a thirty-foot-high archway over huge iron-gated lobby doors. Ten security cameras were angled high on the walls, covering all possible approaches.

Dom parked on 26th on the side of the street of the park, slipped on mirrored sunglasses, and hurled from the car into the crisp morning. *Bern and Viv may be locked inside that building.*

From the trunk, she yanked the Glock 17 and strapped it in her pancake holster at the small of her back. She lifted a nondescript blue baseball hat and pulled it tight against her ponytail. She slipped into a navy FBI jacket, then pulled a jean jacket over it. Slamming the trunk closed, she strode at a brisk pace to the building's far corner. In the park, a breeze was ruffling the leaves.

Not on my watch, you don't, motherfuckers.

At Madison Avenue, she hooked a left, passing the corner coffee shop. The Smithson building rose on her left, heavy stone blocks resembling an ancient rampart. The glass of storefronts were fitted in the arches of the old citadel. Along Madison Avenue, the building appeared impervious.

At the next corner on 27th Street, she hooked a left along the rear of the building.

More storefronts presented an impenetrable defensive wall to the inner Smithson building.

Halfway down the block, a white panel truck was parked by a single-door service entrance. Two cameras were positioned over the service entrance. Twenty feet past the truck, a ramp emerged from an underground parking lot. An attendant sat in a booth, watching traffic with a dazed look.

She slowed, crossed the street, and pressed the phone against her ear, pretending to be on a call. She slowed her breathing. She needed to bring down the anger, replace it with steel.

From behind the mirrored sunglasses, she surveyed the building.

Focus, focus.

Three cars exited from the lot, slow and steady.

The service entrance opened and two workers, one bald with a goatee, the other dark-haired, maneuvered a dolly loaded with cardboard boxes toward the panel truck. Both were average height, average weight, and each wore bright orange vests.

She lowered the phone.

The workers began loading the boxes into the truck.

She stepped off the curb, crossed the street and flashed her badge. "FBI."

Both men paused.

"You making a delivery?"

Bald guy said, "We're taking out paper for disposal. Shredding. Offsite."

"You do that often?"

"Once a week."

"Same time every week?"

He nodded.

"Tell me about the building."

"Uh... Um, we only go to the mailroom." He pointed at the metal door. "It's just there. They have all the stuff delivered there."

"This the only service door back here?"

"I think they have a smaller service entrance up front."

The dark-haired guy glanced at the parking lot entrance.

"What?" Dom asked.

He shook his head.

"I asked about entrances and you looked at the lot," she prodded.

"They have a bigger service elevator at the bottom of

the parking lot. But it's being used for some kind of construction."

"What kind of construction?"

"I dunno. I just seen stuff going in and out."

She nodded and strode toward the parking lot.

The mid-twenties attendant in a small shed wore a yellow uniform over a big belly. She flashed him her badge. "I hear they're doing construction here."

He nodded. Not even remotely afraid of her.

"How long have you worked here?" she asked.

"A year."

"How long has the construction been going on?"

"Maybe three months? Trucks come in, head to the service entrance, move on out a few hours later."

"They down there now?"

"Nah, not yet."

"Any chance you know what floors they're working on?"

"Oh, yeah. 26 and 27. I hear 'em yelling all day long."

She pointed at his nose. "You did not see me."

He nodded.

She stepped around the shed and descended into the fortress and the smell of car exhaust and oil. Past rows of cars, fifty feet ahead, a service entrance was secured by a steel garage door. Next to it, an elevator lobby was brightly lit.

She paused. The red lights of surveillance cameras blinked from the walls on either side of the area.

She turned, heading back up the ramp.

Out on the street, her phone vibrated. "Walker."

"It's Whyte. I just landed."

She crossed the street, turned, and stood facing the fortress. "I can't talk."

"I know the story. I spoke with Lea. Your guy, my guy, is

Tyler Huntington's private security. Birth name Mauricio Moreno. Alias Chase Richter. He's our guy."

A sigh blew through her mind, clearing the clutter.

Tyler Huntington's thug was named Mauricio Moreno aka Chase Richter.

I'm coming for you, Moreno, and your boss.

Owen was in her ear. "You need to be careful, Moreno is slippery smart and a very solid sniper."

Bring it.

Owen asked, "Where are you?"

"You need to stand down. You're not field."

"Dom, I've been in the field before. Where are you?"

"I'm outside Smithson staring at their fucking parking garage."

"You think Viv and Bernadette are in that building?"

"We've got Bernadette's last ping from inside the building. If they haven't moved her yet, it's my best shot. I've got no intel on Viv."

"You going in?"

In that moment, she had very few people she could trust. She blew a breath between tight lips. "The whole building is wired with cameras. Every angle, every entrance. The lobby, the service entrance, the garage. If I go in official, Huntington and Moreno will be alerted and they'll move the women."

"What about frontal SWAT?"

Even with Fontaine's support, she didn't have enough to warrant it. "I don't have enough for an approval."

He waited, knowing that operations had to be led by the agent in the field.

Across the street, a red Volvo rolled up from the parking lot ramp. The driver, an older man, looked left and right, nice and calm, like he didn't have a care in the world. Like there weren't two kidnapped and bound women somewhere up in that fucking stronghold.

She sucked in against tight lips. "It's a fortress. No matter how I take it, they'll see me coming."

"Where are you exactly?"

"Around the back on 27th."

He dropped his voice. "Dom, I have a burner phone with me."

Owen's proposal was like a crowbar jamming into spinning gears. She blinked. Down 27th street, the red Volvo slowed to a stop at the corner. Slowly. Red taillights flickered against her pupils. They wouldn't notice her coming in if everyone was rushing out.

He spoke the thought. "I can call in a bomb threat."

She was already sprinting down the sidewalk toward the corner. "Give me five."

"Copy that."

Chapter Fifty-Nine

Viv's mind came back on. It was still dark. She was still in the big coffin. But this time, her brain was working normally. She blinked.

A voice inside her head said calmly, *Don't panic, the worst thing you could do was panic.*

Another voice replied, *"Yeah, fuck you, I'M BOUND INSIDE A FUCKING COFFIN!"*

From the soreness against her lower back and the back of her head, she could tell she'd been in here for hours. Where ever this was. She breathed deeply. The pressure against her lungs had loosened. A small reprieve against the terror.

Think, Viv. Think.

She tensed her wrists. They were still bound.

She moved her knees upwards. Her feet were not bound.

Rocking back and forth she gauged the soreness. Nothing was broken. She was just bound, surrounded by darkness.

But if you're gonna get out of here, you gotta get your wits about you and figure out an escape.

Her stomach growled. She must have been in here for hours.

Wait, who the fuck put me here?

She pushed that thought aside. Now was not the time.

Maybe if she started feeling around and found a way out her captor would not be outside the coffin. Something smelled like piss.

Oh God, have I pissed on myself?

No. Her pants felt dry. Her heart raced as adrenaline surged.

Jesus Christ, someone was in here before me.

Calm down. If you're gonna get out of here, you need to calm down.

Fuck you. Somebody knocked me out and put me in a fucking coffin.

I hear you. I do. I hear you. But now is not the time to panic.

She breathed. In and out. In and out. Her brain focused on the dilemma, pushed the thought of her captivity and any other captives aside. Hard aside.

She rolled on her side and with bound hands felt the walls. They were cold metal. She pushed her feet as far as they could go against the far wall. She was in some kind of container about five feet by three feet. Pushing down on her hands, she crouched upwards, spine first. Her spine tapped a ceiling about 4 feet high and it moved slightly, as if hinged on one side.

She took a deep breath, pushed back the claustrophobia and the terror.

She laid back down. *I'm in a container with a lid. I'm in a dumpster. I'm in a fucking dumpster.*

The last thing she remembered was talking to Dom and her team. About the guy at the ice cream shop.

He must have followed her. The stalker in the weird sunglasses must have followed her home.

She shoved the thought aside. Right now, it didn't matter who had put her here. Escape was all that mattered.

She brought her wrists to her face and mouthed the binding. It was smooth with sharp edges smelled of chemical, like mild adhesive. Duct tape.

She took the edge of the tape between her front teeth and started working it apart, thread by thread.

Chapter Sixty

Dom skidded around the corner on 26th Street as the building's alarms began to wail. Across the street, Madison Square Park was serene and quiet. She slipped off the jean jacket, threw it to the ground, and slowed to a swift stride.

The lobby entrance was fifty feet out, forty-five feet out, forty feet out.

She needed to time the approach with the rush of people from the building's lobby.

Thirty feet. Twenty feet.

The doors burst open and the first crush of people rushed out onto the sidewalk in orderly but frenetic lines. A security guard moved into the street, held up his hand to pause the traffic, and waved the lines of workers into the park.

Blocks away, police sirens bayed.

Dom jogged to the entrance and pushed inside against the tide of bodies. The building's alarm wailed in undulating waves.

A second security guard near the reception desk urged,

"Keep moving! Out to your assigned location." He looked like the kid too dumb to be a cop.

She stepped close to him, flashed her badge low by his waist, and whispered, "FBI. Remain calm. Take me to your security office. Now."

He glanced at the badge and gave a curt nod. He pulled a walkie-talkie from a belt clip at the back of his waist and clicked it on. "This is Brooks in the lobby. I'm coming to you. I've got law enforcement with me."

The walkie-talkie crackled. "Copy that."

He pushed gently through the oncoming crowd. "Keep moving, folks."

She fell in line behind him as they moved through the lobby.

Overhead the sirens screamed.

Using both hands, Brooks pushed through a swing door that read *PRIVATE, NO ENTRY.* into a long interior hall, red alarm lights flashing.

Dom followed tightly on his tail.

He pushed on a door that read *SECURITY* and stood to the side.

Inside, an older black man, late sixties, stood scanning a wall of security screens. He turned and held out his hand. "Prescott Graves, ma'am."

"FBI Agent Walker. I heard this is a bomb threat."

"Yeah, it was just called in from NYPD. They're on their way."

She nodded to the screens. "Your people getting out?"

"This is New York City. We have a fire drill every quarter. They're moving just as they should."

"Good. What are your protocols?"

"Fire wardens on each floor. They have yellow vests. They get everyone out through the staircases, do final checks, come out. Most of the meeting points are across the street in the park."

"How long does it take to clear a floor?"

"Usually ten minutes." He looked to the screens. "I haven't seen a warden come down through the lobby yet. We've got another five minutes."

"OK."

NYPD Counterintelligence and SWAT would be there in fifteen minutes. The city did not mess around with bomb threats. *"If I were a bomber, I'd need an empty space that was not frequently visited. I'd need to get in and drop off a bomb. Where in this building is a space like that?*

"The mailroom on this floor has a number of small rooms and closets. But the main room is pretty busy."

She nodded to the wall of screens. "Show me."

Graves pointed to a screen halfway up on the left. The camera angle covered a large, open room with aisles of filing cabinets and long workbenches. At the top of the screen, five photocopiers dominated the far corner. The room was empty. *Is there someplace to hide two women there?*

"How many people work in there?"

"Usually five."

"Busy all day?"

"Yeah," he whispered, "it would be tough to hide a bomb there."

"Where is less traffic?"

He pointed to a screen far to the right of the top row. "That darkened one. It's the auditorium on fifth."

It was a dimly lit cavernous space, easily forty rows, twenty seats across descending to a stage and screen backdrop. Two signs that read *"EXIT"* were lit above doors on either side by the stage.

"Often empty like this?"

"Most of the time. We only use it for big town-hall-type meetings."

"And what's backstage?"

"Nothing. A small room for tech. There's no prep space."

In a screen close to her line of sight, the camera covered the lobby. Lines of employees were making their way outside. "What's the protocol for getting your senior managers out of the building?"

"They take Elevator 3 down to Level 4 of the parking lot. It's the VIP parking level."

"Is your CEO on the move?"

He glanced across five screens and pointed to one. It was the wide-angle view of a dark parking floor. "Yes. There. There he is."

She leaned in close. Two men were talking by a long limousine. "Tell me who they are."

He pointed to the figure on the right. "Tyler Huntington, CEO."

There you are, motherfucker. My eyes are on you now.

She pressed her fingertip on the screen over the other man's face. "And this one?"

"That's Mr. Richter."

And you as well, Moreno.

"Mr. Huntington's private security."

Oh yes, she knew who Moreno was. "Private?"

"Yes. Mr. Richter is not a Smithson employee." He shrugged. "I guess when you're worth tens of millions, you hire your own."

She leaned in, watched Moreno usher Huntington into the limo, shut the door, and bang on the roof with two quick snaps. The limo took off, slow and steady.

Stick with Moreno. He's got the girls.

In the dimly lit garage, Moreno looked around, cocking his head as he listened to the wail of the siren.

Dom leaned in closer.

He turned, walked along the parked cars, and stepped to a black SUV.

She held her breath.

Moreno walked around to the back of the SUV and peered into the trunk area.

Were the girls in there?

Moreno strode toward the driver's door.

She slipped her hand into her jeans pocket, curling her fingers around the Lancia's key.

But Moreno stepped past the car and strode to the elevator.

Her grip loosened.

He moved to the elevator lobby.

Dom glanced to the next screen.

In the lighted elevator lobby, Moreno stepped to the elevator and pushed a button.

She held her breath.

The elevator door slid open and he stepped inside.

Dom snapped her fingers at the younger guard. "Brooks, come here."

Brooks stepped closer.

She pointed at the SUV. "I need you to go check that car."

Brooks gaped at her.

Graves said, "What? Wait—"

She pointed a finger at Graves to silence him, turned to Brooks. "Go. Go now. To the parking lot. Open the doors and check inside Mr. Moreno's car."

"I don't know how to jimmy a car door." He glanced up and to the left.

She leaned within an inch of his face, smelled his stale breath.

He blinked rapidly, looked away.

"Yes, you do." She plucked a walkie-talkie from the shelf and waggled it. "Go do it and let me know what you find."

From behind her, Graves barked, "Now, Brooks."

Brooks grabbed the walkie-talkie and raced from the room.

She turned to Graves. "I'll explain later."

He nodded with the wisdom of a man who'd seen all kinds of life's surprises.

"Are there any other spaces in this building where someone would have access – it would be mostly empty, and things could be hidden? Your guy in the parking lot told me there's construction happening."

He nodded, this time with fuller understanding. "Yes. We're redoing floor 26 and 27."

She pointed to the wall of screens. "Show me."

Graves pointed to two screens in the lowest row. They held long views of expansive empty floors. The first floor was stripped to cement, empty windows bright in the morning sun. In the second empty floor, along the left wall building materials, crates, wood, rolled rugs, and rolled electrical wires. A single desk and chair sat near the right wall.

She pointed to the floor with the desk. "What floor is that?"

"26."

"How often are the workers up there?"

"Not much. They'll move down there next month."

"Is there a foreman?"

"No, they don't have an onsite foreman. There are

different contractors for each piece. They come and go in teams."

She tapped the screen. "Who uses that desk?"

He blinked, avoiding her gaze.

She whispered, "Have you seen Huntington's private security guy up there? At that desk?"

Graves nodded.

"I want you to review the videos from that floor, starting this morning and working backward. I need to know who was on that floor and when. Understood?"

He nodded with a swallow.

She held up the walkie-talkie. "You find me if you see something."

He nodded.

"And find me as soon as SWAT shows up." She held out her hand. "I need a swipe card. All access."

Graves moved quickly to reach into a box, pull out a shiny blank white card, and pass it to her.

She sprinted into the hallway. Sirens screeched overhead. She skidded into the empty elevator lobby and raced to smash the *up* button. The doors slid open and she careened inside, swiping the access card and pressing the button for 26.

Chapter Sixty-One

The elevator door slid open on Floor 26. The wail of the building's sirens bounced off the cement walls and floors and across the expanse. Sun streamed through the walls around all four sides.

Dom slipped the walkie-talkie into her jacket pocket, drew her Glock, held it bent arm pointed to the ceiling and stepped from the safety of the elevator.

The left corner of the space near the wall of windows was arranged neatly with building materials. Six huge, plastic-wrapped crates sat on bowed pallets. A forked truck jack was parked by the last crate. Long, raw wooden planks were neatly stacked in ten three-foot piles. Five fifteen-foot-long tube of gray carpet were rolled in a three-foot diameter tube. A massive spool of computer wires lay on its side.

Below the wail of the sirens, the silence of the floor was thick. No computers hummed. No timers clicked. Nothing moved.

Above her left shoulder, the security camera's light blinked red. She held up her left hand, letting Graves know she was on the floor, then took a step into the expanse and turned right. A worktable stood by the window with two chairs placed across from each other. The tabletop was empty. Behind the desk, three green construction waste dumpsters stood on wheels.

She stepped gently onto the cement floor and moved around the right side of the elevator shaft. The expanse behind the elevator was empty. Nothing. Nobody. Just yards of gray cement floor and bright glass window.

If Moreno was on this floor, he was behind the building materials.

Staying close to the wall, she circled the shaft and returned to the elevator doors, her grip on the Glock loose but primed.

The walkie-talkie chimed softly in her jacket pocket. With her left hand, she lifted it to her mouth, pressed the button, and whispered, "Walker. Go ahead."

Graves' voice was tremulous and he matched her whisper. "It's Mr. Richter. He was up there yesterday with a young woman. She followed him to the desk. I can only see the back of her."

Dom glanced at the three closed dumpsters. "Describe her."

"Blonde. Petite. She looked scared."

"What did they do?"

"Uhm...Uhm... As soon as they sat down, the video went dark."

Her hand froze in midair. "Repeat?"

"He turned off the video."

She blinked against the sun.

Graves said, "I don't know how. But he must have turned it off."

Jesus. Hadn't Owen said this bastard was slippery smart?

Graves whispered, "Agent?"

"Yes?"

"Right now, the video feed from Floor 26 is dark. He must have turned it off again. I can't see you."

She released the button as a chill swept through her and she glanced over her left shoulder. The light on the security camera was dark. She slipped the walkie-talkie back in her pocket, double grasped the Glock, and took long, quick strides toward the desk.

Let's do this.

She circled the desk, stepped to the first dumpster, and slid the Glock in its holster. The slide bolt lock had been left open. She reached out, grasped the cold lid, and heaved upward. The hinges squealed as the lid opened.

Inside, the container was empty. She exhaled.

Then the stench of urine hit her nose.

Oh, God. No.

On the bottom of the dumpster, a white hairband lay in a pool of liquid. With double hands, she hoisted herself on the edge of the dumpster, threw her legs over, and landed in the bottom. Her fingers grasped the hairband and long, blonde hair wafted against her palm. *Bernadette Hax.*

She pocketed the hairband, pulled out her cell phone, switched on its flashlight, and shone bright light across the bottom of the dumpster. The puddle was yellow, not red.

She pocketed the cell phone and heaved herself out of the dumpster.

She raced to the second dumpster and threw open its lid with a grunt. Empty. She breathed in deeply from her nose. No urine. She flashed the light from her phone across the bottom. Something flickered. She heaved herself inside, landing on the metal with thud. Her fingers closed around a small pendant. Diamond. Viv's.

Mental images flooded through. Viv would have been bound, likely gagged. She would initially have been unconscious. She would have woken, terrified. She would have struggled against her bindings.

Dom shook her head to clear the images. *You're mine now, Moreno.* She pocketed the pendant and heaved herself from the dumpster.

She pulled the Glock, pointed it at the corner of the building material, and leaned into a full stride. She moved swiftly, bending deep in her knees as she raced across the floor.

The crates extended left and right against the wall, tightly together. There was no light between them. She would have to choose one side. He would be hiding behind, in the alley between the crates and the wall. Corning would be the kill zone for her, the most dangerous move.

Her feet landed on concrete, right, left, right, left. The Glock was solid in both hands. The sun glared in her eyes as she closed in on the crate near the window.

She skidded to a soft stop by the corner pallet, held her breath, and listened.

You there, Moreno?

Nothing. Only silence.

She took a deep breath, Glock leading, stepped gently around the corner, and aimed down the alley.

Nothing.

Shadows.

Where are you, Moreno?

The crates loomed above her head. She would have to run the length of the alley, a sitting duck target in an ambush.

The blood in her ears thumped as she leaned into the

run. Her legs moved fast, spinning, her thighs burning. Her feet slapped the cement.

She skidded to slow her speed at the last crate and cornered, Glock first.

Nothing.

Fuck you, Moreno. You chicken shit. Where are you?

She strode to the front of the pallet and peered around.

The crack of a gun and a huge blast reverberated through the room. One of the windows shook and a spiderweb of cracks shot outward. She ducked back behind the crate.

He was fucking shooting. He had to be along the front of the crates.

She heard the glass shatter and shards rain down on cement.

Use the distraction.

Glock out front, she sprinted from the last crate and spun left down the length of the crates.

The blow crashed into her nose. Stewart Walker whispered, "*Oh Fuck,*" and everything turned black.

Chapter Sixty-Two

Regina Maria D'Angela and Mila sat outside a coffee shop in a sliver of sun that cut between the skyrises of Wall Street. They each sipped cafe lattes.

Regina seemed like a good person. She had dyed black hair and mild makeup – just enough to get by in a professional setting. She wore a yellow sweater set over a calf-length slim skirt. She was average weight, not skinny, not heavy.

She had accepted Mila's explanation without proof, as if after all these years she was ready to unburden herself.

She had a grandmother's smile, sensible and slightly bemused. "I'm glad someone is looking into it. I don't know much about the case other than what was in the trial and in the papers. Simon was very tight-lipped about it. He almost never spoke of it. I filed the paperwork with the court, like I always did. He had meetings in the jail with Stewart Walker. But there were no notes to file, or any correspondence that I had to deal with. I really didn't know much about it." She looked off into the distance. "There just wasn't a lot of paperwork."

"How do those cases normally go?"

"Well, normally, we hire a private investigator. I do the billing on those. The PI would go out and find stuff about the case and Simon would use that information in the trial. He would take affidavits, you know, stuff like that. Evidence that was introduced at trial."

Mila waited her out.

"But in the Walker case, he didn't do anything like that. There were a few meetings in the jail, and then the trial. Simon didn't do a lot of work." She looked down, cupping the coffee cup in both hands.

Mila waited.

"It was after Mr. Walker killed himself that I knew something was wrong with the case," Regina said.

Mila set her coffee down.

"Simon didn't come to work for a week. Then when he did, he looked dazed. In my life, I've experienced grief and I've experienced guilt. What Simon was walking around with was a combination of both. He had never looked that like before the case." She gazed into Mila's eyes with remorse. "I never asked Simon about it. In fact, we never mentioned the case again."

Mila opened her mouth to say something but was at a loss.

"That's all I know. I'm sorry, Mila, but that's all I know."

"How did you get the case? The others in the Filthy Five went with different lawyers."

"You know, I don't know. But we got most of our cases by referral from the NYPD Internal Affairs unit."

Mila leaned back. What was the weird name of the guy

in the Filthy Five news who had headed up Internal Affairs? Damien or something? Some swashbuckling name. "Do you remember the name of the head of that unit? The Internal Affairs unit?"

"Well, let's see. While I worked there, there were three of them. Steve Rogelio. Maybe 1994 to 1998. Then there was Miguel Castro. He was the last one I knew there. In between, there was a guy for a short time, that would have been Dartanian Velk. 1999 to 2002 I think. Somewhere around that timing."

Dartanian Velk. As in the Four Musketeers. Except Dartanian Velk was the freaking Head of Internal Affairs during the Filthy Five period, their arrest, their indictments, and Stewart Walker's incarceration.

D'Angelo smiled sadly. "But that Dartanian Velk, he left for another bigger job. Right after Walker died, I think. Over to Los Angeles or something. West Coast somewhere."

That was enough. That was certainly enough for Mila Pascale to go on.

Chapter Sixty-Three

Dom's eyes blinked open. Wind rushed across her face. Wind from the broken window. Wind from across Madison Square Park. Wind into the Smithson building. She rolled her head toward the bright sun. Her nose and the front of her face were screaming in pain.

Moreno had hit her with something. She reached up and felt her nose. The bones weren't broken, but the skin scared under the touch.

She rolled on her side. The concrete floor was hard and cold.

How long had she been out?

She pushed up on her hands into a seated position, the grit digging into her skin.

She glanced around her. There was no Glock.

Her brain felt foggy and the wind blew her hair across her eyes.

Next to her was a wooden plank.

Moreno had hit her in the face with the plank.

She surveyed the floor. It was empty. Where was he now?

She pushed off her hands, straight-armed into a lean, then slowly rose to a stand. Vertigo hit her immediately and she leaned over on her knees, breathing deeply. From the street below, she heard the wail of NYPD sirens.

She shuffled over, peered over the edge to see five police cruisers parked along the park, their lights flashing. Three more cruisers were coming in fast by the southern section of the park. A SWAT truck was parked in front of the lobby.

She'd been out long enough for all that blue to arrive.

She was alone. Moreno was gone. And he'd taken the girls with him. She fished into her pocket for her cell phone, but the walkie-talkie starting chiming. She pressed the button.

A loud voice boomed through. "Agent Walker, this is NYPD SWAT. We're downstairs. You ok? We're coming in."

"I'm coming down."

"Copy that."

But she wasn't going down to the NYPD chaos outside. She was going to go find the girls.

She gently set the walkie-talkie on the cement near her and pulled out her phone.

She dialed Owen.

He answered on the first ring. "I'm just getting here."

She glanced to the street; a yellow cab was pulling up to the chaos. "They're not here. He moved her."

"Moreno?"

"Yes. I confirmed it's Moreno."

The cab shuddered to a stop. "Where are you?"

She ignored the question. "Moreno is driving a black SUV."

"Listen to me, Agent. Moreno is a bad dude. He's got special ops background and then did some mercenary gigs."

She breathed against the dizziness. "Doesn't matter. He's got the girls. We need to find him.

"I think I know where he's going. That warehouse in Hell's Kitchen."

"We can't have all this NYPD heat. We need to go in quiet. I don't know how long ago he left. I don't know how far he's made it."

"Roger that. Wait, why don't you know?"

She squinted against the sun and the pain in her face. "He knocked me out."

"What?" The back door of the yellow cab opened. "Where are you? I'm coming to you."

She barked, "No, you need to follow Moreno."

He stood silently by the cab, staring up at the blown-out window.

"How many guns do you have?"

"None. I'm just coming off the plane."

"I've lost mine."

"Roger that."

He was looking up into the sun.

She pushed the phone tightly to her ear.

He gave her the address.

Her eyes glanced to the Lancia. It was parked far enough away from the NYPD crowd. She would make it down the back, out the garage, and to it without discovery. "You go there now. We need to jump on this in case he's moving the girls inside. I'm five to ten minutes behind you."

"Roger that." He ducked into the cab.

The cab reversed, spun into a 180, and sped off down the street.

Dom cracked her neck. The dizziness was subsiding.

She marched to the elevator with growing strength and dialed Lea. "We've got an emergency."

"Go."

"Any updates on Viv or Bern's phones?"

"No nothing. Bern's is still there. Viv's is not responding." Lea whispered in a rush, "Did you call in a bomb at Smithson?"

"Yes." She pressed the elevator button for the garage.

"Fontaine was just here. I told him about Bernadette and Viv. He said get you whatever you need. That was an order. That's what he said. Get Dom whatever she needs."

The elevator sunk downward. "We're going after Moreno. Owen's meeting me." She relayed the address of the warehouse. "I need weapons. Two."

"I'm on it." There was a long pause. "Dom, you be careful."

The line went dead as the elevator doors opened to the dim parking lot.

Chapter Sixty-Four

On an empty 48th street, Owen stood two buildings north of Moreno's warehouse, talking on his cell phone as the Lancia rolled to a stop. He leaned into the sports car. "That Lea does not mess around. Hold on." At the far corner of the street, an NYPD cruiser slid its nose out. Owen took off at a jog.

He returned with two Glock 19s and handed her the one.

Dom stood from the car and a wave of vertigo washed over her. She steadied herself on the roof.

"You ok?"

"Fine." She gritted her teeth. "What have you got on the building?"

The building had three floors, five windows on each, a few of them cracked. The front had a large garage door.

"Moreno owns it outright. Just now, I saw shadows. Someone is inside. I cased the place earlier. The front is shut tight, hasn't been opened in years. There's a long alley down the side. There's an old flimsy door through the rear. I don't think we'll have an issue kicking through it. But—"

"The noise will alert him."

Owen grimaced.

"He's already moved the girls from the Smithson building. My guess is they're in there. If he gets a hint of cops or SWAT, he'll kill them, hide the bodies." She swallowed against a dry throat.

"Agreed."

"I think the only option we have is to go in quiet with an ambush."

Owen nodded grimly. "There are windows along the rear."

"OK." She weighed the Glock 19 in her hand, passed it between left and right. She preferred her own, lighter version, but this would have to do.

Owen touched her arm. "I'll take point. We're gonna need you to have a clear shot if it comes to that." It was a smart tactical move. By taking the more vulnerable position, they were setting up their better shooter. His field training was showing.

She nodded.

Owen jogged down the side of the alley at a fast clip and she had trouble keeping up. The adrenaline crash from the Smithson encounter and a possible concussion were not working in her favor. Sunlight slashed through fence slats, lighting up the old bricks of the warehouse in staccato. Above their heads, a rusted iron fire escape loomed.

Owen hit the rear of the building and cornered left into the rear alley, Glock held high.

She kept tight on his heels.

Halfway down the alley, he skidded to a stop. She moved

in tight to his left. The door was wooden, easily twenty years old, made of raw plywood. It would be an easy kick.

She tapped his shoulder, then guided him to a nearby window. It similarly was old and decaying. The frame was bent and the paint, what paint there had been, had peeled years ago.

He nodded, slipped his Glock in the back of his belt, and pushed upward on the window. It moved smoothly, quietly. He heaved himself up and into the darkened interior. She followed quickly.

They stayed crouched as their eyes became accustomed to the dim lighting.

The ground floor was a cavernous space – the full depth of the block front to back – with forty-foot-high ceilings. A smell of dust and dry cement permeated the inside. An iron staircase led upward to a darkened second floor. A few cardboard boxes had been left to rot along the walls, but otherwise, the space was empty and still.

She whispered, "We need to clear this floor."

He nodded and took off at a quiet jog around the perimeter, the Glock swaying left and right in an even tempo. Dom fell in line behind him. Cobwebs brushed skin.

Overhead, open beams ran along exposed wooden floorboards and rusty pipes crisscrossed the length of the room. The rusty door of a circuit breaker hung limply open on its hinges. Along the front wall, a sewer pipe led out to the street. They took the corners and circled back to the rear.

Near the staircase, they leaned against the brick.

He pointed to his eyes, asking if she saw anything.

She shook him off and leaned in close to his ear. "He's gotta be upstairs somewhere."

Owen nodded.

They moved quietly to the bottom of the stairs. A bright orange extension cord ran down the middle, as if someone had been working here at night.

The hair on her neck stood up.

Owen set his foot on the first stair and leaned forward. The stair held without noise.

She tapped his right shoulder and they began stepping upward.

From above, a woman screamed.

They paused in mid-motion.

At least one of them is alive. Moreno, you cock-sucking roach, you're mine.

Owen moved slowly up the remaining stairs.

She followed close on his heels. Her heart raced and her nostrils vented loudly.

Pausing just under the opening to the second floor, Owen motioned for her to remain behind.

She tapped his ankle in the affirmative.

Slowly, Owen raised his head above the floorboards.

Her grip was clammy and her fingers stiffened around the gun.

Two feet above her, Owen yelled, "Mauricio Moreno. It's FBI Special Agent Owen Whyte. I've got a gun. I'm coming in." Owen lowered his left hand by his hip and waved her back down the stairs. He stepped up onto the second floor.

Chapter Sixty-Five

The old floorboards of the warehouse's second floor creaked as Owen stepped up with his full weight. "Moreno. I think you and I should take a time-out. Let's you and I do some talking."

Holding her breath, Dom stretched her right foot down, found the stair, and slowly moved into a descending crawl, using hands and feet.

Above her, Owen continued in a pleasant voice. "Backup is on the way, so let's you and I have a nice, easy conversation before they arrive. Let's do this nice and calm and sort out our options. Because there are always options. Always options."

The floorboards creaked as Owen moved away from the landing, toward the corner of the room.

"I'm going to lower my gun so we can have a calm conversation. How 'bout you lower yours?"

Dom paused on the stair. God *damn it. Moreno had a gun.*

From the front of the second floor, a male chuckled. "I know how this works. You're here to negotiate. But ultimately, you're here to arrest me." His voice sounded ice-cold and in control. "Or you're gonna get off a round in my head."

"No, no. Just here to talk." Owen's voice was calm.

Dom crawled down the stairs, holding her breath.

Moreno said, "I'm not gonna let either of those happen. I know what I'm talking about. You probably know that I've seen action. You don't scare me. Pansy-ass white-bread guys like you get me excited. You think you're all something. Go to expensive schools. Get into law enforcement. Gonna deliver justice. Spare me your entitled bullshit. I ate guys like you for breakfast."

"Yeah, ok. I hear that. But I'm not here to prove anything. I'm here to help you out. I think you're in a jam, and I'm the guy that's going to find you an exit path."

"Try that bullshit on someone who don't know better." Moreno's voice was like ice.

"Listen. We got lots of time to chat. Backup is a long way away. There's traffic out there. Just you and me now. Let's work out a deal."

Owen's voice was getting fainter as Dom reached the bottom of the staircase. Her foot felt the cement. She holstered the Glock, pushed up off the stairs, and broke into a run.

She heaved up and over the window frame and dropped into the back alley. Tearing down the alley, she hit the corner at full speed, hurled down the side alley to the fire escape, and skidded to a stop ten feet below the rusty ladder. If she pulled it down, it might squeak. But it was the only entrance she had.

Spinning in a circle, she scanned for something to boost her up to reach the ladder. Nothing.

The fence.

If she could balance on the top of the fence, she could jump across and grab the bottom of the ladder.

She took a running jump at the fence, landed her palms on the top, and grasped the edge. The wood shuddered against her weight but held. She pulled herself up and leaned her stomach on the top of the fence. The thin edges dug into her jacket and pushed the air from her lungs. Vertigo swept across her eyes and she paused, let it pass.

She swung her right leg up and over, her foot finding the top of a post. She slid slowly back till she could position the flat of her right foot on the post and rose into a crouch. All her weight was balanced on the right leg. The thigh burned. She twisted toward the fire escape.

She had one shot. She would have to leap up off the post, with the power of one leg, and fly across the width of the alley and hope to God a hand reached the fire escape.

She took a deep breath pushed off her right foot with all her might.

Her body moved up and out over the alley. Her hands reached out. Her body flew through the air. Her right hand hit the fire escape and clamped down. She swung her left arm up and grasped the fire escape. Rust jammed under nails, sending shards of pain through her fingers. Her legs followed through and her feet struck the brick wall. The weight of her body yanked against her hands and swayed, but her grip held.

She hung for a moment and her body stilled.

She slowly squeezed her abs. The crunch leveraging her right leg up and she shot her right foot up and over the iron platform, hooking the heel. With the better leverage, she pulled down on her right arm, moving her body upwards and her head above the platform. Releasing her left hand, she shot it upward and grasped a smooth, cold handrail.

Her right hand shot up and grasped the handrail. In a smooth move she swung both legs up onto the platform.

She laid her full weight on the landing and took another breath. *Here I come, Moreno.*

She crouched and crab-crawled under the second-floor window.

Inside, she imagined Owen standing in the middle of the room, his Glock raised, his other hand up and palm open. She could almost imagine his calm voice trying to soothe Moreno. Staying low, she crawled the short distance to the third-floor ladder.

Foot-over-foot on the rusty iron, she gently made her way upward. Blood was seeping from beneath her fingernails.

On the third-floor landing, the window was closed but the old wood frame was crumbling. Using both hands against the top of the frame, she pushed up. The window creaked against its housing and moved upward.

She scrambled inside. The third floor was another empty expanse. No boxes, no shelving, no nothing.

From below, Owen's voice was faint. "Moreno, I need to know the girls are here." His voice was moving away from the stairs and toward the middle of the second floor. Smart, fucking brave Owen. "I need to know the girls are alive."

"You'd like me to tell you that, wouldn't you? That both girls are alive. You'd be their savior. Agent – what was it? – Whyte? Whyte the Savior. Deliverer of justice."

"No, that's not what I'm after. I'm here to work out a deal for both of us."

The floorboards looked old and untrustworthy. Dom imagined placing her weight on one and the traitorous board screeching in protest. The game would be up.

Shit shit shit.

Chapter Sixty-Six

Dom glanced frantically across the third floor of the warehouse. It was completely empty. There were no cardboard boxes to use to distribute her weight as she crossed the floorboards. There were no beams overhead to use a hand-over-hand shimmy. Just fifty feet of old squeaking floorboards between herself and the top of the staircase.

Shit. Shit.

From below, Owen said loudly, "Moreno, tell me what you want. I'll call it in. You just say the word." He had moved toward the front of the building. He must have been twenty feet in front of Moreno. "Tell me. Just tell me what you want."

How was Owen so fucking calm?

Dom had only one option. She dropped gently to her knees and lay down on the floor. She tucked her arms across her chest and in her armpits, tightening the navy jacket around her body. She stretched her legs out straight. Drawing up patience, she began a deliberate roll, lengthwise, across the rough, unvarnished boards. Her face touched the dusty wood, then back again toward the ceiling. Not a single squeak. She carried on. Over and over.

Owen insisted, "We have each other hostage. But listen to me, I'm telling you, I'll call it in. A helicopter. Free passage to an airport. Tell me. Tell me what your demands are. Personally, I like Cuba. They've got no extradition treaty. They've got very decent healthcare when you get older. White sand beaches. Not a lot of Americans. Cheap girls." His voice had reached the middle of the second floor. He had put himself between the stair landing and Moreno. "And cheap all-around living. You could get by there, if you had some money stashed in a bank, in say, the Cayman Islands."

Dom paused.

"Yes, Moreno. Listen. This is why you want to make a deal with *me*, not some trigger-hot meathead with Kevlar. You want to deal with me. Because I know about your plan, Moreno."

Dom pushed into the roll. The landing was twenty feet away.

Owen spoke smoothly. "First, I know about Captain Chase Richter. I know your entire squad went MIA. In Iraq. I got that figured out."

Richter barked. "You don't know nothing, lawman."

She was moving in a smooth motion, onto her chest, onto her side, onto her back. The scruffy, dusty boards, the bare brick wall, the beams across the ceiling.

"This is what I think happened. You and your buddies killed your captain, Chase Richter. And I bet you saved his dog tag. Because if you're gonna impersonate someone ten years later, you better know for good-goddamned-sure that they're dead." Owen paused. "Did you take his tag while you hid is his body? Did you do that. Moreno?"

"Fuck you."

The landing to the stairs was getting closer and closer. Fifteen feet. Ten feet.

"So, I'm close. Ok. Then I suspect you and your Army buddies took off, went mercenary. I don't know how many of your squad there were left standing, maybe all four of you? Did you guys take off, hide out in Africa? Your buddies still there? How are my guesses, Moreno? Am I getting close?"

"I said shut the fuck up."

The landing was five feet out. Floor. Brick wall. Ceiling. Brick wall. Floor. Ceiling.

"Ten years later, you emerge, alive and well, long after the Army has forgotten you. You use your dead captain to get a new life. Set up an off-the-shelf company out of Delaware. Oh yeah, I figured that out. Trusted Security Services. The irony is clever. Real clever."

"I said fuck you, man. Shut the fuck up."

Dom reached the landing, face down, breathing into the dusty floor.

"Now here's the part that's a little messy in my mind. You sell yourself to Tyler Huntington, some millionaire CEO. Not sure how you met him, but that's not the point. You sold yourself as this Chase Richter with solid military credentials, West Point, officer and all. You convince ole Tyler Huntington that you can take care of any of his problems. How am I doing on the guesswork here, Moreno?"

Dom moved gently into a crouch, raised the Glock, and edged her feet out over the descending stairs.

"Ole Tyler has a plan. And he needs someone just like you. He wants you to buy off Stille. Pay Stille for what he knows. But the payoff has to be offshore. The money has to be cleaned and kept away from Huntington. Ole Tyler needs his hands clean." Owen paused. "Easy for you, right? You know how to hide money. You've been off-grid for ten years. Tyler pays Trusted Security Services as his private security. Trusted pays Moreno. Moreno shifts money to Cayman. Easy. Washed."

Dom placed one foot on the top step, moved her weight onto her toes. The step held in silence.

Owen continued, "I was just down there. I talked to the manager at the National Cayman Bank Trust. She's nice, that manager. I saw your account, Moreno. You've been skimming off the payouts to Stille. You have a very, very nice stash waiting for you down there. You were ready to pull the plug, get away from all this Tyler shit a few months ago, weren't you? You've been ready to call it quits for a while, haven't you? But then that fucking journo died."

Dom brought her left foot to the second step, placed it gently on the wood, slowly leaned into it. The second step held silently.

"And things got messy fast. People were sniffing around." He lowered his voice. "That girl Bernadette Hax. She's sniffing. And Vivienne Preston, she's sniffing. And you need to clean it all up. Clean up Tyler. Clean up the Ben Kirschner shit. And get out. How am I doing, Moreno?"

Fuck you, Moreno, I'm coming. Dom moved swiftly now, silently down the stairs, one foot in front of the other.

Owen slowed his voice. "I can make you a deal. With that stash, you have something we can work with. I'll want a cut, of course, but we can work that out. Before SWAT gets here."

Smart, smart Owen. Dom reached the top of the second-floor ceiling. If Owen had positioned himself correctly, Moreno was facing away from the stairs. It was a chance she had to take. She craned her neck, looked below the ceiling.

Owen had moved to the far side and middle of the floor, facing the staircase. He held his Glock against his hip, pointing to the floor. By the front window, Moreno was angled with his side and back to the stairs. Sweat ran down his face. He held an M24 against his chest, barrel by his shoulder.

Sweet Jesus. Owen had been having that entire conversation with a guy with a fucking M24.

Owen kept his stare on Moreno.

Moreno said, "Talk to me about a deal."

Owen said, "I take half."

She pushed against the wall and moved down the final three stairs. She took in deep breaths through her nostrils and noticed two dumpsters lined up against the rear wall. Just like the ones in the Smithson building. *Shit. Shit.*

Stewart Walker whispered, *"You were the best shot in your Quantico class, my Dom. You got this."*

Owen kept his tone smooth. "You give me fifty percent. I walk you out the back before SWAT gets here."

Go time. Dom raised the Glock to the ceiling in both hands and took one large stride out into the second floor. She steadied into a deep knee stance, lowered the Glock, and sighted on Moreno's head.

A scream emanated from one of the dumpsters.

Moreno startled.

Owen raised a hand. "Moreno, wait—"

Moreno, in a single move, raised the M24 and sighted on Owen.

Dom took the shot.

Moreno's head exploded and his body dropped like a sack.

Owen glanced at Dom with eyes wide and mouth open as his body sagged to the floor.

Chapter Sixty-Seven

Dom flew to Owen, set down the Glock, and searched for the bullet hole. His eyes fluttered and his lips quivered. By his right shoulder, a hole in his jacket began leaking thick blood.

She ripped open his white shirt. A bullet had penetrated the right shoulder. She smashed her hand hard on the hole. The skin was hot and blood oozed through her fingers. With her left hand, she grabbed his belt buckle and worked it open. She yanked the belt from around his waist.

He mumbled incoherently.

She rolled him on his side and worked the belt under his armpit, looping it back around to his chest. She threaded the leather through the buckle. She laid Owen on his back, yanked off her jacket, pulled off her T-shirt, and balled it up. She shoved the t-shirt under the belt and yanked the belt tight.

She yanked her phone and rang Lea. "Officer down. Whyte's down. I'm at the warehouse."

"I'm sending Emergency now."

She hung up, stood, and moved swiftly toward the rear of the floor and the two dumpsters.

From inside the left dumpster, a woman screamed and a foot pounded the metal wall.

Dom slid back the bolt and yanked open the lid. The smell of feces and urine hit her nose like a sledgehammer. Viv Preston looked up from the bottom of the dumpster, wide eyes blinking at the light. Her wrists were bound in silver duct tape.

Dom jumped onto the ledge and heaved herself inside. She landed beside Viv. "It's OK. It's OK."

Viv wailed. "Dom. Dom." She started crying and writhing against the duct tape.

Dom pulled out her Swiss army knife and sliced Viv's wrists free.

From the front windows, faint sirens pealed.

Viv gasped. "Oh God. Oh God."

Dom pulled her face to her. "You hurt anywhere?"

Viv's pupils were dilated, but she shook her head. "No, no. No, I'm not hurt."

Dom lifted her up and rested her against the front dumpster wall. She heaved herself over the edge and landed on the floorboards.

Viv was clawing at the ledge.

Dom reached over, angled her arms under Viv's armpits. "On three. One. Two. Three."

Viv jumped and Dom heaved. Viv's body moved out over the ledge and Dom caught her as they slid to the floor.

Viv noticed Moreno's body. "Is he dead?"

Dom stood, "Yeah, he's dead."

Viv spat.

Dom ran to the second dumpster, slid open the bolt, and

lifted the lid. Inside was Bernadette. Her eyes were closed, her skin was white, and she was still.

Dom leaped up and into the dumpster, landing with a crash. Bending down, she gently placed her fingertips on Bernadette's carotid artery. There was a faint pulse.

She pulled her phone, called Lea. "Three EMTS. I need three."

"Copy that." Lea was gone.

Dom slipped her right arm under Bernadette's back and knees and stood. The young woman was light, too light.

Viv had crawled over under the dumpster. "Is there someone?"

Dom looked over the edge, "Yes."

Viv's hands moved upward, grasping the air. "Give her to me. Give her to me."

Dom leaned her own weight against the front wall of the dumpster and swung Bernadette's limp body over. She lowered Bernadette into Viv's arms. Viv held her against her chest, cradling the limp head.

Dom heaved herself out and sat down next to them.

Viv rocked Bernadette's limp body as tears streamed down her face.

Outside, sirens blared as they turned down the street.

Chapter Sixty-Eight

Saturday

A shadow fell across the floor of the hospital room as Fontaine stepped into the doorframe. He glanced at Owen in the hospital bed. "How's he doing?"

Dom rubbed her eyes. "They say he's going to be all right. The doctor said the bullet missed his arteries."

"How about the women?"

"Vivienne Preston is OK. They've got her down the hall. Dehydrated. But that's the only thing wrong with her physically." The psychological trauma was another issue. Who knew how long it would take Viv to get over her ordeal?

Fontaine watched her.

"Bernadette Hax is in ICU in a coma. Apparently, she had a lot of bruising and bleeding on the brain. Either self-inflicted inside the dumpster. Or Moreno beat her."

He shook his head. "I saw her parents in the waiting room." You see a lot of distraught people in their line of work. Nothing to be said about it. Nothing to make it better. They both knew that. He looked back at Owen. "What about *his* family? They been notified?"

"The doc said they've called the parents. Somewhere in the Midwest. They're on their way."

Fontaine nodded. "Nobody in NY?" He meant a lover or a partner or a spouse.

Her heart skipped. The sensation annoyed her because she couldn't control it. "Not that we know of."

"Sounds like you did the right thing with the bandage and the belt."

They taught a lot of things at Quantico that civilians didn't know. It wasn't always stuff you wanted to think about. She nodded.

"I spoke to Lea Peck. The Bureau has eyes on Huntington. He's not going anywhere."

She glanced at him. "Where is he?"

"At home in Connecticut. He went straight there after the bomb threat."

Nice way to look out for your staff.

"Speaking of a bomb threat, you know anything about that?"

She raised eyebrows and gave him a blank look. "Nope."

"Yeah, the fire department tracked the number. It was unregistered. Like a burner phone." He watched her with a slightly amused look. "Interesting that. No way to trace it. Just dumb luck, I guess." He smiled gently.

She nodded.

"When Whyte wakes up, you guys bring me the case against Huntington."

"Yes, sir." She fought through the headache in her temples and the pain in her fingers. "It's solid. We've got

Theodore Stille from the Comptrollers connected to Moreno. There's money exchanging. Bank records. All that. Whyte tracked it down to Cayman Islands."

"Good."

"We'll subpoena phone and emails, connect Moreno to Huntington. Moreno was definitely a known quantity over at Smithson." It all weighed so heavily. Ben's death, Viv and Bernadette's kidnappings, Owen's wound. "Huntington's got a lot to answer for."

"His time will come. We'll build it right. We'll nail him."

She looked into his dark eyes. "You promise?"

He nodded. "Oh yeah." He pointed at her. "Now, you were supposed to have been taking some time off."

She glanced at Owen.

"Listen to me, Walker. Job well done. You'll get a commendation for this. You and Whyte and Peck. Five days, that's really something."

"That's not necessary, sir."

"I know, Agent Walker. But if you're going to get promoted at some point, you're going to need that in your file."

She shook him off. "I'll take some of those days off, sir. That's enough."

He looked around the dimly lit room. "You gonna stay here?"

"Guess this is as good a place as any."

He gave her a small grin. "Good for you, Agent."

She was quick to correct him. "No, sir. No, it's nothing like that—"

"Uh-huh. Sure." He broke into a big grin as he walked out.

Chapter Sixty-Nine

Viv's hair was brushed against the white pillow, by either her mother or a nice nurse. Dom reached out and took her hand. It was warm, the heartbeat strong in the wrist.

Viv's eyes fluttered open and she turned to Dom. "Hey."

Dom nodded.

A tear escaped down Viv's cheek.

"How you doing?"

Viv's voice was scratchy, "Good. I guess. I can't remember much—"

"We think he used chloroform on you. Don't worry that you can't remember. It'll come back. Or it won't. Either way, you're alive and healthy and you're going to totally recover."

Viv nodded, but the tears kept falling. "How's Bernadette?"

"Nothing new." Moreno had made her drink chloroform.

"I heard about the brain hemorrhaging. Did he hit her?"

"It's not clear."

"Did he do that to her?"

"She may have done it to herself."

More tears. Viv whispered with personal knowledge. "Her head against the dumpster. She would have hit her head against the dumpster. I would have done that. If I had been in there too long, I would have tried to kill myself… If you hadn't come…"

Dom squeezed her hand. "Don't worry about that. Let's focus on you feeling better."

Viv's tears were huge and heavy.

"Tell you what. Let's leave all the big bad thoughts somewhere else for a bit. You think about what you're gonna do when you get out of here. What you're gonna eat. What ice cream you're gonna get. What stories you're gonna write. Because the bad guy is dead. He'll never hurt anyone again. And I'm gonna nail his boss to the wall. So you and Bernadette can get on with your lives. Normal lives, good lives, long lives. Ok?"

Viv nodded.

"But I get it, if you don't feel right. You're totally normal if you feel crazy. We'll find you someone to talk to. What you've been through was a brutal situation. It's totally okay for you to have crazy thoughts. It's not weakness, it's strength. We'll find you someone. Ok?"

Viv gave her a sad smile. "I had a visitor about an hour ago. It was one of the journalists at Business News that I interviewed. His name is Trevor Witherspoon."

"Ok?"

"He did a lot of collaborations with Ben."

Dom gave her a sad look.

"I explained to him what we found out at Longwood Manor. About the sex in the back. The rape that goes on there. I explained to him that we have a lead. That creep Aristophanes."

Spark plug was back. Thank God. "Oh yeah?"

"Yeah. He said he would like to take that on. As an investigatory story. He said it would help him find closure about Ben's death, if he uncovered a weird sex thing that Ben had initially discovered."

"That's cool. Cause I was gonna go there too."

"Yeah, I thought so. I told him when I get out of here, I'll give him all the research I have, all the stuff we discovered. And he and I are gonna dig in."

"And bring it to me. What you find, you bring it to me."

Viv's tears had stopped. She jutted out her chin. "Exactly. They don't get to just do that."

"Agreed."

Viv was watching her.

"What?"

"Beecher was here too. He was checking in."

"Yeah?"

"He said something about your mom. That she's coming up?"

A cold crept into her chest. Her father whispered, *It's ok, Dom. She can't abandon you a second time.* "Yeah, she wants to talk to us. Something about our father."

"Good for you, Dom."

She swallowed. "You know, it's one meeting. Good for some information. A different perspective. Maybe."

"Good for you. Takes courage. I'm proud of you."

"Yeah, I guess."

In the ICU bed, Bernadette looked tiny and fragile. The screen on the machine by the bed displayed a steady heartbeat, but Bernadette's face was sunken and sallow. Small hands were laid primly by her sides. Out in the hallway, two female nurses chatted in subdued voices.

Dom sat in a bedside chair and listened to the woman's soft breathing.

Bernadette had gone through more than anyone should have had to. Too much for someone so young and vulnerable.

The doctor had said the swelling was going down, that it was responding to the meds, but that Bernadette was still in deep trouble. They had no idea if she'd ever wake up.

What a terrible thing that had happened to a woman who had been so brave. To take on Tyler and Smithson. Tough girl. Strong girl.

Dom whispered, "You're one crazy brave woman, you know that? We need you back here with us. Come on back, 'cause we really need more tough chicks like you around. Ok? You hear me?"

Bern's eyelids fluttered in REM.

Dom stood, leaned into her ear. "Come on back, sweetheart."

Chapter Seventy

Three days later

Sitting next to Dom at her desk in Javits, Lea's head popped up from her computer screen and fixed on the door.

Ignoring her, Dom's fingers clacked on the keyboard. She was drafting the description of the warehouse for the Ben Kirschner file. The District Attorney had asked for it to be handed over within a week.

Lea whistled.

Dom clanged on the keyboard.

Lea said, "Well, well, well, Holy Mother of Recuperation, look who got released from the hospital."

Inside her chest, Dom's heart banged. *Damnit.* She slowly raised her head.

Special Agent Owen Whyte was progressing across the large floor. He looked out of breath, but otherwise in good shape. You wouldn't know he'd taken a bullet four days earlier.

Lea whispered, "Shit, even after a bullet, he still looks hot."

Did she read minds now? "You need to stop that."

"I'm not doin' nothin' but stating the obvious. I mean we are FBI. Aren't we about uncovering the truth?"

Owen reached their desk.

Lea said, "Good lord, you are a sight to behold. How you feeling?"

He smiled at both of them. "Doc says I need to go on bed rest for a week. But I'm walking and talking and breathing. So that's good."

"Amen."

He sat.

Dom felt her cheeks heat and flush red. *Goddamnit.*

He eyed her screen. "You getting it all down?"

"It's getting there. A couple missing pieces, but we're really close. They're debating how to break this up into two cases – the one on the fraud, the other on Huntington's conspiracy to murder Ben Kirschner. It's solid."

Lea rushed in. "Get this. We've got Huntington on calls after Ben Kirschner's death to the main number over at Precinct 7. They were the precinct working the case."

Owen said, "Wow."

Lea cocked her head toward Dom, "Yeah, those guys tried to slow our dream girl down."

Did she seriously just call her dream girl?

Owen nodded to Dom. "Wow."

It wasn't going to be pretty for Captain Wheeler or Detective Traister if the District Attorney uncovered any connection. "It's going to be a complicated case. I heard from the DA they're gonna ask you to lead on the financials."

"I am more than ready and able."

Lea whispered in a sexy voice, "Indeed."

How does she get away with that? Dom looked him in the eye. *Fucking ocean blue eyes.* "We're gonna nail Huntington, right?"

"Absolutely."

Lea snorted. "Good. Fucking preppy bastard needs to be behind bars."

Owen was watching Dom.

Lea paused to watch them.

Was that a twinkle in his eye? Dom glanced away.

He was staring at her.

Lea smiled.

Dom asked him, "What?"

He said, "Just thank you."

"You don't need to say that."

"I know. But I am. Thank you."

Blue eyes had turned sad and serious. Her heart flipped. "You're welcome."

"I could have died."

"You didn't. You're here."

Lea whispered, "And looking good."

No seriously, how does she get away with that gravelly voice?

Owen said gently to Dom, "You saved my life."

"Ok. Yeah, yeah. You'd have done the exact same thing. Now let's move on from that."

"Can I make it up to you?"

Lea chuckled. "Oh, hell yes, you can."

Dom broke out in a cold sweat. She grumbled, "No. Seriously. We're good. Let's move on."

Owen insisted, "Let me take you to dinner and drinks."

Lea hooted and clapped. "Oh yes, you did. Just. Like. That. Nice work, Agent Whyte."

Owen grinned at Dom.

Dom groused, "No need for all that."

"I think it's the least I can do."

"No need. We're good. We're solid."

He said softly, "I asked around about you. I know you're single."

Lea nodded vigorously. "Oh, hell yes! Here we go."

Dom stammered. "Way too many people in this building seem to care that I'm single."

He said, "What I'm trying to figure out is *why*."

Lea said, "Right?"

Dom glared at him. "Stop."

He grinned. "Stop what?"

"Trying to figure it out."

He leaned back. "But, that's the thing. I don't want to stop. I'm very curious. Very."

Those fucking blue eyes.

Lea laughed. "Oh hell-to-the-balls yes. I like you, Agent Owen Whyte. I like you a lot!"

Dom pointed at his nose. "No, you don't. Don't go mixing work and pleasure."

Lea nodded. "Go, go, go. Mix away."

He asked Dom, "So, you won't go out with me so I can repay you for saving my life?"

"You need to rest."

"Is that a no?"

Dom clamped her lips shut.

He winked at Lea.

He fucking winked. She squeezed her lips together.

Lea waggled her head.

He returned his gaze to Dom. "I'm going to leave this conversation where it is for now. But. You should know that you can run, Domini Walker, but you can't hide."

Lea raised both hands over her head, slashed peace signs. "Boom."

He stood, gave them a nod, and turned. Over his shoulder, he said, "See you in a week."

Dom exhaled.

Lea chuckled. "Oh hell yes, he just did. And, oh hell yes, Miss Dom is gonna hit that. Hit that riiiight."

Dom hissed, "Traitor."

"Uhm, hmmm." It rolled smoothly from Lea's lips, like melted butter.

How does she do that?

Chapter Seventy-One

They met in the back room of a local Italian restaurant. Mila had called ahead, reserved the private room, explaining to Beecher, "This kind of encounter would be better in private. Clearly."

Esther Walker was sitting at the far end at a table facing the door, her shoulders spooned inward and the bright, blonde hair of Dom's memory, now puddle gray.

Dom was empty. Any feelings for this woman were long gone, like the meat from an animal carcass having disintegrated under a hot sun, only parched white bones left. No affection, no sympathy, no anger.

Beecher brushed past Dom with a slight touch of reassurance on her back and walked to the table. "Esther, we're glad you came."

Through her apprehension, Esther gave him an unsure smile. "Beecher?"

"Yes, Esther, it's me."

She rose and shook his hand. "You've grown up to be so handsome. How tall you are."

Mila shuffled in, quiet as a mouse, and sat down with her laptop at a seat near the door.

Dom pulled out a chair near Mila and sat.

Esther's wrinkled skin had slipped downward. But the dazed eyes were the same.

Beecher motioned Esther to sit and he sat across from her.

Slowly, Esther turned to Dom. "Domini, how are you?"

I'm numb. I've got nothing for you. In response, she simply shrugged.

Beecher said, "That's our friend, Mila."

Esther nodded to her.

Beecher took over the meeting. "How was the trip, Esther?"

She gazed into the distance as if something other than this meeting were more important. Some other story, some other set of people.

Dom's teeth ached from the familiarity of that look.

Esther's voice was tender. "It was fine. The airplane ride was long."

"Did you come alone?" he asked.

"Oh no. Can you imagine me flying alone? Oh no. Ed is upstairs. He came with me. He thought it was important that I come."

Ed was the dentist. The man who'd taken her in. As Dom watched this broken, untethered woman, she realized Ed was less sinister and more sympathetic than she had believed all these years. He must have seen Esther as a lost soul.

Beecher asked, "How is Florida?"

Dom didn't care about Florida. She didn't want any answers to any normal questions. *Why did you leave us? What made you think I could take care of a ten-year-old boy? Did you ever regret leaving us? Did you ever come check on us without us knowing? All those years, did you ever care?* Esther had left her in charge of Beecher at the age of fifteen. That fact was never going away.

Dom straightened her back and waited for Beecher to walk through the pleasantries.

Esther's voice was faint. "Well, it's hot at the moment. We reached a hundred degrees earlier in the week. And it's been raining. The mosquitos come out when it gets wet. We stay inside mostly."

I don't care about your life or your mosquitos.

Beecher nodded. "How is the hotel room?"

"What do you mean?"

"Is it nice?"

"Yes, I suppose it is. Yes." Her voice was watery, as if she still hadn't realized the gravity of sitting with her two grown children after twenty years.

A waiter emerged and they ordered coffee and waters.

Once they were served, Beecher broached the topic. "You said you wanted to come visit with us. That you had something to tell us?"

Mila straightened.

Dom clasped her hands on her lap.

Esther said, "I got a note a few months ago. A letter. It came on nice fine paper and had very proper handwriting. It read, *Miss Esther Walker*." She looked off in the distance. "I haven't been called that in a long time."

Twenty years, in fact, Dom thought.

"I read it. I've brought it with me. I thought you and Domini should know about it." She leaned down from the table and rummaged in a purse by her side. She gingerly lifted out the envelope and handed it to Beecher.

He read the letter out loud. *"My husband was caught up in*

the Filthy Five story in New York all those years ago. He was one of the lucky ones. He didn't serve any time. One night a few months ago, he got very drunk at a wedding. On our way home, he mumbled something about the Filthy Five. I pressed him. He said, and I remember it very clearly, 'They nailed the wrong one. Stewart was one of the good ones.' " Beecher looked up, gaped at Dom.

Was there the remotest possibility Stewart Walker was innocent? Had their lifetime of shame been a mistake? Dom's heart ached. Could it be true that Stewart Walker was innocent? It felt as if the walls of the restaurant were expanding outwards, possibilities emerging. Her brain buzzed.

Mila leaned forward.

Beecher finished the letter. *"I'm not sure if that helps you or your family now. But it has been weighing very heavily on me. Truth always comes out, they say, one way or another. At least I hope this can be part of your healing."* He looked over at Dom, a mix of sadness and hope in his eyes.

Mila asked, "Is the letter signed?"

Beecher's mouth dropped open as he read the signature. "Mrs. Robert Gessen."

Mila yelped, "The wife of Robert Gessen?"

Silence.

Robert Gessen. The NYPD officer that had terrorized Mila in the middle of the night for researching the Filthy Five. The thug that Dom had warned off, just over two weeks ago. Dom gave Mila a gentle look. "Don't you worry. He won't get to you."

Mila nodded, then whispered. "Ask her about Velk."

Beecher said, "Mila, what did you just say?"

Mila raised her voice. "I was wondering if Miss Esther knows anyone by the name of Velk. Does that ring a bell?"

Esther wrinkled her brow, her brain turning on it.

Mila sat up straight. "Dartanian Velk?"

Esther's eyes lit up. "Yes. There was a Dartanian. Yes, I think his last name was Velk."

Beecher asked, "Mila, what did you find?"

"Dartanian Velk was Head of Internal Affairs. During the Filthy Five trial."

Both Beecher and Dom eyed her.

Esther rubbed her forehead. "Yes, yes. He came to our house. He and Stewart had beer out on the back porch."

Ping. "When?"

Esther's eyes glazed. These were details she couldn't retrieve. "Well, I don't know now."

"How old was I?" Dom asked.

"You would have been a teenager. I remember because you brought them beers out back. You had your hair in a ponytail, like you do now, and you were wearing those red running shorts, those track-and-field shorts."

She had worn those shorts the last time she had played organized sports. After that year, she'd been home for Beecher after school. Esther was talking about the year their father had gone to jail.

Dartanian Velk, the Head of NYPD's Internal Affairs, had been having beers with Stewart Walker the year he had gone to jail. How was that connected to the new possibility of his innocence?

Beecher looked across the room at Dom and Mila. "If Dad was so corrupt, why was the Head of NYPD Internal Affairs coming over for beers? Why are cops still talking about his innocence?"

Stewart Walker whispered, *That's my boy, Beech. Exactly.*

Mila nodded. "Yes! That! Why?"

In her mind, Stewart Walker whispered, *See, my Dom. Your instincts about me were right all along.*

Mila said, "We can re-open the case! Prove your dad was innocent!"

Dom exhaled. "Exactly."

Esther blinked in confusion, as if the mention of the past was too real, too tangible, too vivid for her foggy brain. She put up a skinny finger. "There's something else."

All eyes turned.

"I went to see your father in jail. He didn't want me coming. That time I went, we cried."

The image of her father and Esther crying in a huddle crashed across Dom's brain. Her throat constricted.

"He said something to me. He said, 'When the whole story comes out, I will be vindicated.' " Esther sat back, lowered her finger. "I always knew he was a good man."

The chair banged back as Dom bolted up. Esther was not allowed to hijack their father's memory.

Dom shook her head at Beecher. The memories of her father were not going to be tainted by this woman.

Beecher nodded.

Dom turned and strode out the door. Esther was not allowed to be the one to exonerate him. Not Esther.

If anyone was going to clear Stewart Walker's name, it was going to be FBI Special Agent Domini Walker.

Outside on the street, she dialed Viv's cell phone.

Viv's voice was weak but steady. "Hi, Dom. How're you doing?"

"More importantly, how are you?"

"I'm good. I'm in bed. Mom and Dad are here. They're making chicken soup. Dad bought me a soundbar for my TV."

Dom imagined her parents fussing about in the kitchen of Viv's apartment. "You sleeping ok?"

"Yeah. OK."

"Pain?"

"No, not really."

"Trevor come by?"

"Nah, but we've been chatting by phone. We have a plan for the Longwood Manor research."

"Good."

"Dom, what's up?"

Dom glanced at the restaurant. "I have a question for you about that case, the Die Hard crew."

"Yeah?"

"You mentioned the wives thought the Los Angeles Head of Internal Affairs was maybe dirty. You said he was the same guy that was here at NYPD during the Filthy Five case."

"Yeah, exactly."

"What was his name?"

"Dartanian Velk."

Ping.

Viv said, "Does that mean something to you?"

"It does. It does indeed." She blinked in the sun. "Get better soon. I need you for my next investigation. We've got some new clues on the Filthy Five. It's time to re-open up a cold case."

Viv paused, understood. "Good on you, Dom. Good on you. We'll dig in. We've got a good team now. We'll sort it out. We'll clear your dad's name." Another long pause. "Any news on Bernadette?"

Dom exhaled. "No. No news."

Chapter Seventy-Two

Time to wake up, Bern-honey. You've been asleep for far too long. A funny, underwater sleep. Far too long. But we were healing. All kinds of scars. Weren't we, sweetheart? We survived this latest test, didn't we? Life threw some more shit and we made it through. That makes us a double survivor, a superwoman survivor, an Olympic survivor. I'm pretty sure, darling, that makes us invincible. I mean, it's crazy what we've survived. Now, listen to me, angel, it's time to wake up. One foot in front of the other. Tiny steps. Time to wake up. Cause you're a survivor. You're a superwoman survivor.

In the brightly lit ICU room, next to the beating of the heart monitor, Bernadette Hax opened her eyes.

Next in the FBI Agent Domini Walker Series

vinci-books.com/ofangels

He died a hero—or so they said. She's about to prove otherwise.

When Domini Walker finds new evidence suggesting her father's "suicide" was anything but, she reopens a case the LAPD would rather forget. But some secrets are buried for a reason—and digging too deep could cost her everything.

Turn the page for a free preview

Secrets of the Angels: Prologue

The telephone shrilled twice.

On socked feet, Dom Walker rushed into the kitchen and grabbed the shiny, yellow handset. "Walkers."

An older man with a raspy voice asked, "Esther Walker?"

It was the gravity of his tone that made her glance into the living room. Sitting in a bright sun patch on the red velvet couch, her mother, Esther, held a cup of tea and stared at the wall above the television. She wasn't watching the show on the television. She almost never watched the actual programs.

Dom lied, "Yes."

"This is Precinct 9."

Her heart thumped. "Yes?"

"There's been an arrest."

That must be what had kept their father, NYPD Officer Stewart Walker, late. He must be processing a criminal. Relieved, she breathed deeply. "Ah, ok."

The hoarse voice said, "Uh, no, ma'am. It's not like that."

From the back room, her young brother, Beecher, hollered, "Is it Dad?"

"Ma'am, I'm afraid to tell you that your husband has been arrested. Officer Walker has been booked into jail."

Dom blinked.

"I'm sorry to be the messenger, but this is just a courtesy call. I expect he'll be calling you soon. I advise you to stay by the phone."

"Yes."

"Goodbye." The phone line went dead.

In her ear, the dial tone buzzed. The large handset felt cold as she gently set it back on the hook. The long-curled cord swung against the kitchen wall.

Goodbye is a funny word. What is good about ending the conversation?

Just last night, her father had kissed her forehead as he had done for fifteen years. "I'll bring home donuts. Tell Beecher we can watch cartoons in the morning." And off he'd gone.

Dom turned toward the sun patch.

Esther took a sip of tea.

Beecher hollered, "Is that Dad? Is he coming?"

The phone warbled again.

She snatched the handset.

Her father, Stewart, said, "Dom?"

Her voice cracked. "Dad?"

"Hi, honey. Yes. It's me." He sounded calm.

Her heart raced. "Are you in jail?"

"It's a big mistake. It's going to be fine."

"Dad?"

"It's going to be fine. I am fairly sure I know what happened. There's been a mistake and I'm going to fix it."

"Dad—"

"My Dom, listen to me very carefully. This may take a few days to sort out. There is going to be stuff in the newspapers and on television. There may even be reporters that come to the apartment. I need you to look out for Beecher. You two have to stick together."

"Dad—"

"Don't talk to anyone. Just ignore it all. I'm going to sort it out. I promise. If they need your mother, you get Aunt Lucille to accompany her. Don't let your mother do anything on her own."

She understood. Her mother wasn't capable of handling the grocery store, let alone her husband in jail.

"You stay away from all this. You just focus on taking care of Beecher and staying away from all this mess."

Her voice squeaked. "Dad?"

"You are going to be fine, sweetheart." His voice was gentle. His voice was always gentle. "You are smart. And strong. You've always been strong."

That was the last thing he ever said to her.

Secrets of the Angels: Chapter Two

Dom Walker had been awake for twenty minutes watching the sunrise chase the shadows from the room. During their teen years, she and Beecher hadn't known to buy curtains. When Beecher went to college, she had gotten him cheap white curtains similar to the ones in the other dorm rooms. Later, he had taken those silly curtains into the city. When he moved back into her house, they had gotten nicer ones. But she noticed that, like her, he never drew them closed. She suspected he also preferred to see the sky. Childhood habits were hard to shake.

The guest room had new curtains. Sensitive to the new living situation, Dom had wanted Mila Pascale to feel as welcome and safe as possible, so she'd gone to a high-end store and purchased an expensive set. They must have worked, because Mila had been with them for six months.

She stretched her legs into the cold region of the sheets and pointed her toes. A mild shock rippled through her right foot. The physical therapist cautioned that toes, always in use, rarely healed smoothly or quickly. Dom would have a few more weeks of mild pain.

Next to her, Tinks the Tongue stretched into full-body extension. Tiny paws dug into her arm.

From the kitchen, water ran in the sink.

Beecher was up.

The full house had settled into a harmonious morning routine. Beecher woke at six a.m. and would put on the coffee. Tinks was second to the kitchen to ensure her breakfast. Mila followed a few minutes later and would walk Tinks around the block as Beecher got breakfast ready. Dom was last. They sipped their coffee silently at the kitchen table while reading their chosen news outlets. On the days that Beecher taught at City College, he would head out before eight. Mila always left the house twelve minutes before ten for the train to NYU. You could set your clock by that girl's movements.

Dom was the only one without a morning routine. Investigations made that impossible.

The refrigerator door opened and Tinks poked her head out from under the sheet.

Dom whispered, "Go ahead."

The Chihuahua scurried over the pillow and jumped off the bed. Toenails tapped down the hall.

The twang of coffee tickled Dom's nose. She rolled on her side and gazed out the window. Beyond, the sky was a cheerful blue as if to welcome a nice easy day between cases.

The back door banged open.

Dom held her breath.

A woman's deep voice boomed, "Beecher Walker, it borders on sinful for you to look so heavenly this early in the morning. You are a divine sight for tired eyes."

Beecher laughed. "Lea Peck."

"The smell of that caffeine is an absolute aphrodisiac."

Beecher said, "It'll be ready in two minutes."

FBI Staff Operations Specialist Lea Peck was here on a Saturday morning. Unannounced.

Dom sat up, rolled off the bed, and grabbed a sweatshirt.

Sitting at the table, Lea Peck rolled her eyes upwards and savored another sip of coffee. "Amen."

Lea had worked with Dom over the last three years. She was the sharp, sassy product of a Baptist pastor father, an English teacher mother, and a small southern town. Her verbal embellishments were equal parts Biblical references and bold swear words. Her mind was as quick as a computer. She was the ideal research support.

Dom sat opposite Lea as Beecher settled at the head of the table.

Lea set her mug down. "How is everything this fine morning?"

From the hallway, Mila shuffled into the room. Her big black eyes took in the scene as she poured herself a cup of coffee, sat in the remaining chair, and waved Tinks into her lap.

Lea looked to Dom. "I'm here for a reason."

Dom said, "We gathered that."

"Well, I've got something to tell y'all."

This was unusual. "You don't want to do this in the office?"

"It's actually for all of y'all." Lea raised her palms. "It's not going to be life changing, but small can be powerful."

Three sets of eyes watched her.

"It's about Dartanian Velk."

All three leaned back.

Dom and Beecher's father, Stewart Walker, had been an NYPD officer until he had been caught with four others in a department sting. The Filthy Five had stood trial. Three of the five had been acquitted. Stewart was sentenced to two years. A month into his prison sentence, he committed suicide. Not long after, their mother Esther had abandoned them. The family guilt was never far from Beecher and Dom, like the storm on the horizon of a perfect summer day.

Last month, in a stunning series of events, Esther arrived in New York and announced that she had received a drunken confession letter from the wife of one of the Filthy Five. Stewart had been set up.

Earlier, Mila had taken it upon herself to research the Filthy Five and had uncovered a tenuous reference to Dartanian Velk, the NYPD Head of Internal Affairs at the time of the Filthy Five. In the shocking meeting last month, Esther had recognized the name.

Lea said, "We acknowledge that the Velk thread is super interesting, right?"

Beecher shrugged. "Esther isn't exactly a reliable source. Just because she remembers Velk, doesn't mean he had anything to do with it. And a drunken confession isn't exactly state's evidence."

"Yes, but as NYPD Head of Internal Affairs, Velk surely would have known about the sting."

Dom's jaw tightened. Stewart's death, coupled with Esther's mental illness, had precipitated their childhood abandonment. She wasn't prepared to open the Stewart Walker wounds, despite the possibilities of the new revelations.

Lea turned to her. "Dom, I know you said we'd wait. That you wanted to sit on this new intel. But I was finishing up a shift last night at around 2 a.m. and as I was sitting at the screen, I thought, why not sniff around. When I get going, I get going. And boy, is Velk interesting. So, he was here in New York as Head of Internal Affairs for six years. From 1997 to 2003. He's the top IA guy in the greatest city in the world. Crazy authority. Insane career. In short, he's at his peak. But then he moves to Philly to head up their IA. Who moves from New York to Philly? By any measure that's a demotion." Lea held up a finger. "I haven't actually answered that first question. But regardless, he then puts in five years in Philly."

Everyone took a sip of coffee.

Lea continued. "Now, this is where it gets really interesting. After five years, in 2008 he heads out to LA. Head of Internal Affairs LAPD. Nice move. West coast. Sunshine. Beaches. I'd take it, too, if New York weren't the fucking crown jewel. Which it is. But why all the moving? Seems weird, no? Maybe he's trying to run from something?"

She was met with blank faces.

"Ok, don't go there with me. That's fine. I spent enough time trying to figure it out and didn't find anything. I get your hesitancy." She waffled her hand in the air. "So, I changed tact. And get this: Velk moved to LA and gets himself a house in Brentwood."

More blank stares.

Lea held two hands out wide. "*Brentwood.*"

Beecher said, "I'm not following."

"O.J. Simpson, Nicole Brown? That Brentwood?"

Silence.

"Jennifer Garner and Ben Affleck? Tom Brady and Giselle?"

More silence.

Lea placed her hands on the table like a teacher finding

patience with a slow class. "Have none of you ever had aspirations to be a celebrity sports star, making bank, in the mags, walking the red carpet with a hot model? You know, with all the accoutrements that come with wealth? The mountain view infinity pool, the tinted Range Rover, the automatic gate, the live-in cook that makes Oprah's low-carb fried chicken?"

All three shook their heads.

Lea threw her hands up in defeat. "Ok, I can't with you people. Just know that Brentwood is some of the most valuable real estate in all of the United States and our man Velk is currently living much larger than law enforcement salary should allow."

Mila stroked Tinks head. "You were up all night on this?"

Lea pointed at Mila. "Listen, little miss, you never can tell where a lead will take you."

Beecher cleared his throat softly. "I mean, it *may* be something."

Lea snorted. "Hello, hot stuff. Not all investigations start with a smoking gun. They often start with a lil ole theory that you look to prove or disprove." She turned to Dom. "Am I right?"

Dom pushed back from the table, stood and took off at a slow pace around the kitchen. Esther's lead to Velk was worth exploring. But were they going to open that research now? Was it time to dig in?

She leaned on the edge of the sink. The possibility of her father's innocence was breathtaking. What if their research led to a dead end? Or even worse, what if they discovered Stewart Walker had been guilty as charged? Were they prepared to accept that finding? Would Beecher be ok? Would she?

She stared into the drain. Wasn't it better to know one way or the other? Sooner or later, they would have to get to the bottom of his guilt or innocence.

She gripped the edge of the sink. Their research would be unsanctioned. Further, it would be based on the personal vendetta of an FBI Special Agent over her dead father. And it potentially involved one of the most senior law enforcement officers in the country. This was dangerous, dangerous territory. This was job risking territory.

She glanced out the window. Not a single cloud was in the sky.

She turned.

All eyes were on her.

She nodded her head. "Yes. It's time. Let's do this."

Grab your copy…
vinci-books.com/ofangels

About the Author

H.N. Wake spent two decades across Africa, Asia, and Europe, working first with the U.S. State Department and then with a global bank. Her expertise in human rights, democracy, and sustainability gave her a front-row seat to some of the world's most significant complexities.

In the early 2000s, Wake returned to the States to further her career. It was during those early mornings before the sun rose that she first attempted to write and, over time, discovered a powerful release for her demons.

Her books are marked by snappy dialogue, relatable characters, and razor-sharp research. Critics rave that her savvy, fast-paced thrillers resonate with a healthy dose of zeitgeist and feel as if they have been ripped straight from the headlines.

When she's not crafting edge-of-your-seat narratives, H.N. Wake is off traveling, sailing, or scuba diving—with many of her adventures sneaking into her plots. She currently calls the East Coast home, sharing life with her husband and their Tasmanian devil dog.

You can find her on a select few social media platforms.

www.ingramcontent.com/pod-product-compliance
Ingram Content Group UK Ltd.
Pitfield, Milton Keynes, MK11 3LW, UK
UKHW040628161125
465103UK00004B/144